Sri
Lanka

FOR
ELLEN, THANKS
FOR SITTING THROUGH
MY TALK,

Sri Lanka

a novel

Stephen Holgate

Blank Slate Press | Saint Louis, MO 63116

Blank Slate Press
Saint Louis, MO 63116
Copyright © 2020 Stephen Holgate
All rights reserved.
Blank Slate Press is an imprint of Amphorae Publishing Group, LLC
www.amphoraepublishing.com

For information, contact:
Blank Slate Press
 4168 Hartford Street, Saint Louis, MO 63116
www.amphoraepublishing.com
Manufactured in the United States of America
Cover Design by Kristina Blank Makansi & Elena Makansi
Cover art: Shutterstock
Set in Adobe Caslon Pro and Adobe Song
Library of Congress Control Number: 2020933923
ISBN: 9781943075676

To my brothers, Richard and Jeff

1

No one writes songs about Paris in the winter. There's little romance in the chill and the rain, and it's hard to find poetry in gray. When night falls, the upper floors of the city's dark buildings dissolve into the leaden sky, leaving only the yellow glow of lighted rooms.

I turn up the collar of my raincoat and jam my fists deep into my pockets. The two-mile walk from my place on the Place du Pantheon to Frank Schaeffer's apartment near the Ecole Militaire varies with the season. December's rain and gusting winds have robbed the city of autumn's agreeable melancholy, and the normally pleasant stroll along the boulevard becomes a head-down trudge between the lighted café windows and the bare, rain-dripping trees.

I could have taken the Metro, but after riding it into the embassy that morning and back again that night I've breathed enough dead air for one day. Besides, I know the city well enough now that its ancient curving streets don't throw me off as they did during my first posting to Paris more than twenty years ago.

It's funny. Memory gets in the way of any memoir. I don't mean the memory of what happened. Even now, what happened to me back then remains more vivid, more real than most of what happens to me now, perhaps because life itself seems sharper, clearer, more worthy of our full attention when we are young.

Memory, however, is a faithless guide. Many of my sharpest memories are of things that never happened. My life is larded with such beloved false friends. Perhaps what I've often retained is how it should have happened—which carries its own truth.

Everything had been new back then. Though we'd lived together on and off since college, Jean and I had been married less than two years, and when I got home in the evening to the small apartment near Montparnasse, she would hurry around the kitchen making dinner while I leaned in the door frame and recounted the highlights of my day, making fun of the old bulls who headed up the embassy's various sections. I laughed and told her how they'd become the Official Version of themselves—told her of everything but my yearning to become one of them.

The depth of my longing took me by surprise and showed me in some inexplicable way who I was, the son of a truck driver from the San Joaquin Valley of California. I wondered where I found the nerve to aspire to the heights populated by these august figures, the fathers of the foreign service.

My immediate reflex was to hide this craving to become one of the anointed, like a fighter protects his chin or a gambler to hold his cards close. That I felt an almost erotic desire to keep from Jean this secret ambition, to withhold from her an important part of my life, proved my second surprise and, though I didn't know it then, the far more dangerous.

For fear of revealing too much, and for the perverse pleasure of holding something back, I gradually told Jean less and less of my life at work. I saw in her face the pain and confusion it caused her. But I kept hidden, like a secret lover, my newly discovered lust for advancement.

Maybe things would have been better if we'd had kids. A marriage is stronger when there are children. Or maybe I'm kidding myself. Maybe we never should have married. For Jean, too, held something back, something so different from my own obsession that I couldn't see it—any more than she saw mine. She said she missed Stockton, her family, her friends. I wrote it off as nostalgia, easily indulged, easily dismissed. I mean, who in the world misses Stockton, California?

Once, lying in bed, I tried to tell Jean of this shadow inside me. Pushed by a desire to hold onto the intimacy that was bleeding out of us, I wanted to make love, grasping at sex as at a lifeline. Jean wanted to sleep. Grunting irritably, she rolled over, putting her back to me. With a fervor that surprised us both, I embraced her and blurted it out, "You know, babe, I've found that I'm really ambitious." If I thought that the confession of passion for advancement would serve as an erotic come-on, I deserved to be disappointed. She laughed.

I pretended to laugh with her at this presumption. I lay beside her for a long time, searching for the words to make her understand. But the moment passed and I too rolled over and we slept back to back—as loving, as distant, as brother and sister.

If she was confused, I was even more so. And if it slowly broke her heart, it did the same to me. I make it sound as if I'd gone crazy. And maybe I had. Perhaps a ravenous desire for advancement is a form of pathology encouraged by the very organization that instills it. Neither of us recognized the truth, that I had embraced this new life, which offered me an escape from my old one, while Jean, in her heart, had stayed in Stockton.

Jean is one of those people everyone likes. My folks loved her like a daughter. She knew how to make my mom laugh. And she learned not to talk to me about my father.

※

A sprinkle of rain brings me back to the present. I hunch my shoulders and walk past the kids playing soccer in the rain on the Champ de Mars, the pitch lit up like daylight and the Eiffel Tower rising like a dream at its far end. I look at my watch. I don't want to show up promptly for dinner—a singularly American trait in a city where American traits are not counted among the signal virtues.

More than twenty years after that first tour, I've realized one of my fondest ambitions, coming back to the embassy in Paris as Public Affairs Officer, head of both the press and cultural sections. But I find I'm not half so impressed with myself at forty-seven as I was with those old bulls when I was twenty-six. And in the intervening years Paris has become the haunt of ghosts—myself not least among them.

I'm still married, or, rather, married again—at least for the moment. When I finally got my posting to Paris, my wife and daughter announced they were staying in Washington. It didn't entail a big financial sacrifice. The Department pays an allowance to help family members compelled to stay in the United States, usually because of illness, though my wife has made clear that, after years of continued exposure, the only thing she's sick of is me.

I feel less sorrow at the break-up of my second marriage than I did at the first. This lack of regret makes me confront the creeping fatalism that has for years chipped away at my soul, has already devoured the part of me that wants to look at the many mistakes I've made in my life and try to set things right. In truth, one might as well try to retrieve a breath sighed out long ago as to make good the past. I know, because there was a time when I'd tried, and it nearly killed me.

Things were bad between us. Jean complained about living in a foreign country, complained about leaving home, at her lowest ebb saying she should have married Terry LaBianca, a guy she'd gone out with once or twice before we were together. Should have married him and stayed home and had babies, she said. After a moment of stunned silence, we both laughed.

Does it make it better or worse that I still loved her? The loss, though, is irretrievable

Jean's sister got married the spring of our second year in Paris. Jean took a flight back home to Stockton for the wedding. A week later I got a letter from her telling me she wasn't coming back.

※

A gust of wind blows me toward the steps of the upscale apartment house where Frank Schaeffer lives. I press the buzzer and the door clicks open.

Schaeffer is head of the embassy's political section, which allows him a large apartment, suitable for entertaining his many contacts. It's a spacious, modern sort of place with chrome in the kitchen and too many white walls. Frank insists it exudes a sense of modernity and scale fitting for a Senior American Diplomat, a title which I always imagine embroidered across the back of his bathrobe. Me? I think the place has all the charm of an operating room.

Drink in hand, Schaeffer comes to the door and smiles. "Philip Reid! Hey, buddy!" He has this patronizing way of calling me "buddy" that irritates an ancient nerve. I'm certain he sees it, though he can't know why, and I'm equally sure that's why he does it.

Frank looks around, frowning. "Where the hell's the boy I hired to answer the door?"

I throw my raincoat over a chair and Frank leads me into the living room, an over-bright salon with a row of windows giving on the Seine.

The dinner guests include a couple of think-tank mavens, a woman from the British Embassy, and the usual mix of politicos and Foreign Ministry types. A dozen all together. As always, the French appear elegant and burned out, and have the sort of impeccable manners that I once imagined movie stars had until I met a couple of them. The Englishwoman is earnest and dowdy, wearing a dress that looks as if it's done time as a sofa covering. Before I can manage to shake hands around the room, a voice calls us to dinner.

The "boy" Frank mentioned he's hired for the night is a South Asian. He stands straight as a soldier in the archway leading to the dining room, a touch of gray at his temples, dressed in a waiter's shapeless white coat and a pair of black slacks that no longer hold a crease. "*Á table*," he tells us again, his voice oddly expressionless, as if some essential part of him no longer lives in his body.

Schaeffer looks at me and laughs "What's the matter? You look like you've seen a ghost."

I lean against a chair and manage to wave him off. "No, I'm just ... I didn't have any lunch today, and I'm suddenly...."

Frank smiles and nods reassuringly at a couple of guests who are looking at me.

"I'm fine," I tell him, and look again at the figure in the doorway. Time can devastate a man, yet leave the features and form of his youth recognizable under the debris. I knew him instantly. For a short time, no more than a few months, he had been like a brother to me. But that was a lifetime ago and on the other side of the world—a time and place I have struggled, and failed, to lose from memory.

Bandula.

Like the evocation of a neglected djinn, the name calls up memories of tropical heat and the heavy, oppressive air of Sri Lanka. It recalls the memory of a woman I loved, and an unbearable remorse that for years threatened my sanity. On countless nights, when sleep will not come and the past rises up from where I buried it in the shallow grave of memory, I think of Sri Lanka, of what happened to me and to those I cared for, and how I learned the toll that secrets could demand. Not once, as I recalled those times, did I ever think I would see Bandula again.

While the other guests file into the dining room to find their places around the dining table, I waver between the impulse to run back out into the street and an urge to reach out a hand and touch him, if only to test the reality of what my eyes tell me.

Bandula stares, unmoving, into the empty living room. He does not so much as glance at me.

Frank places me between the Englishwoman and a mid-level officer from the Foreign Ministry. I pretend to listen as the Frenchman talks of his government's policy toward some region I don't quite catch. But I never take my eyes off the figure who circles the table, mutely offering carrots and beef and potatoes to the guests, his waiter's garb rendering him invisible to the others.

I sense he has become invisible even to himself. His expression dead, he says nothing, makes eye contact with no one. Every pass around the table must tear at him like a turn on the rack—he who, with a raised eyebrow or the flick of a hand, once commanded servants, field workers and machine-gun-toting guards on his family's estate among the coconut groves outside of Colombo. A young man of wealth and position, he had hoped one day to end the civil war tearing his people apart and break the chains that kept them prisoners to their past.

Though I have for years indulged in—and cringed from—what I saw as my vaulting ambition, it was a pale and underfed thing next to Bandula's wish to remake the world into which he had been born.

Irrationally, I wait for the moment when he will, like the pitiful wretch in a folk tale, throw off these beggar's weeds and reveal himself as the prince passing in disguise. But, no, his kingdom has been long ago lost beyond recall. And I played my role in its overthrow.

The dinner seems to last forever. I sit like a rock, letting the stream of conversation flow around me. At one point I hear the English diplomat say, "But you only live once," to which I reply, "Most people don't even manage that," an observation that comes off as so cynical that even the Frenchman blinks.

After an endless couple of hours, dessert comes, followed by coffee. At last, the guests begin to move toward the door, retrieving their coats from Bandula as he brings them out from a back bedroom. Everyone makes their goodbyes to Frank, waving over their shoulders, telling him what a fine evening it has been. Frank wanders off to pay the cook, not noticing that one guest has not yet left. Me.

Bandula stands in the entryway, my raincoat over his arm, his eyes fixed on the uninhabited distance.

"Bandula." I speak the word quietly, as if invoking a charm that might waken him from a spell. "It's me."

After a timeless wait, he makes the barest nod. "I know who you are."

His voice is flat as death.

I grope for something to say, but can find only, "It's good to see you," the lie biting deep into our mutual dread.

For an instant, the thought of Bandula's family flickers across my mind. Somehow, he senses it as clearly as if I have written it on the air before us. The stone-like face slowly turns toward me and for a moment the mask slips. His chin tilts up and his eyes regain the hauteur he once carried as his birthright. "All of those people can go to hell."

Unable to escape the memory of my own share of the guilt in Bandula's break with his family, my role in the tragedy that he and I share—a tragedy that drove Bandula into lifelong exile even as it propelled me to professional success—his words pierce me like a shiv to the heart.

Before either of us can say more, Frank comes back into the room and frowns at me. "You still here?" He senses the tension between his "boy" and me, and a puzzled squint crosses his face as he looks first at me then at Bandula.

Yet, the possibility that some tie might exist between me, an American diplomat, and this servant hired by the night lies beyond his imagination.

Frank gives me a clap on the back that propels me toward the door. "Great to see you, buddy."

He looks to Bandula to open the door for me and blows out a little puff of exasperation when he is forced to do it himself. "Thanks for coming," he mutters.

Despite the weight of Frank's hand pushing me toward the elevator, I stand in the doorway a moment and try once more to catch Bandula's eye. Frank's puzzlement turns to irritation.

It doesn't matter. The moment has passed. Bandula has once again turned into a statue, beyond my reach.

※

Out on the street the rain has stopped and the wind picked up, swirling through the tops of the trees like an unbottled genie.

Where do these winds start, I ask myself, how far have they traveled to buffet me as I step into the street? I imagine them forming in tropical waters, from where they are drawn northward, sighing over faraway deserts and great forests, curling up into cold, ancient Europe, where, after losing their life-giving warmth, they turn once more toward their distant source. For a moment I picture these winds picking me up, whirling me into the air, carrying me back once again to the sun and the heat of the Indian Ocean, back to Sri Lanka, where I was a younger and better man, back to a time of war, long before I learned that every secret becomes an act of betrayal.

2

My first sight of Sri Lanka through the window of the airplane recalled to me every youthful notion I'd ever held of a tropical paradise. Below, a sparkling lagoon edged by palms disappeared beneath the wing, giving way to groves of coconut trees sheltering tile-roofed houses. Distant blue hills held a promise of waterfalls spilling into jungle pools.

Weighed down by a long, sleepless night and the psychic dislocation of too many miles covered too quickly, I felt my new life rushing up at me with unwelcome speed.

Throughout the long flight I had felt the presence of the empty seat beside me, the one that would have been Jean's. Though she hadn't yet filed for divorce, I felt her loss as irretrievable and its onus greatly my own.

The engines whined as we began our final approach. The view changed with kaleidoscope speed—a flash of palm trees, a narrow bridge over a sluggish river, a glimpse of chain-link fence. Very quickly now, a small stream, a machine gun emplacement and a hangar with two military planes—reminders of the smoldering civil war that was slowly destroying the country's soul. The tarmac appeared under the wing, then the bump and whoosh of the landing.

Gamini, the embassy's airport expediter, waited for me at the gate. Taking my carry-on bag—"No, sir, I insist," he told me—he trotted me quickly through the bureaucratic steeplechase. A few moments at immigration, a wave at customs, then through the doors and outside, the heat and humidity like a blow to the chest. An embassy van at curbside. The driver jumped out to open the door for me. Gamini bowed and said, "Welcome to Sri Lanka, Mr. Reid."

Before I could reply, he slammed the door shut, gave the roof a tap and the van slipped past the heavily armed airport guards and onto the highway,

"A nice flight, sir?"

Startled out of my funk, I looked at the driver. What had Gamini said his name was?

"Yes. A nice flight." I tried to think of something more but couldn't kick my tired mind into life.

Our drive into Colombo was wild as a video game, taking us along a two-lane highway crowded with stake-bed trucks, through clouds of tiny three-wheeled tuk-tuks and overloaded buses bulging with passengers hanging out of doors and windows like jam squeezed from a sandwich.

For all my driver's dodging of other vehicles, the sick-making lurches to right and left as he searches for some sliver of advantage, it took almost an hour to cover the twenty miles to the edge of town, driving past rows of cinder block shops and decaying colonial estates, half-hidden behind a fringe of dusty palms.

A crossroads shrine with a large seated Buddha encased in glass stood at the foot of a long bridge stretching over a muddy river. Downtown Colombo lay on the far bank. And here the swarming traffic snarled to a halt. We would be a long time getting across. The driver—Gita, that was his name—took the van out of gear, leaned back in his seat and closed his eyes, apparently ignoring the squawk of chatter from the two-way embassy radio.

I sighed and told myself to be patient. I gazed out the window at the palms edging the river. Beyond its sluggish waters rose the alien skyline of the city, shimmering in the heat.

I asked Gita what was holding us up.

He nodded at the radio. "An incident, sir."

"An incident?"

He waggled his head as if wondering why I wanted him to spell out the obvious. "A bomb, sir."

"A bomb." My tired mind seemed incapable of doing more than repeating what I heard.

"Yes sir, another suicide bomber."

As he said this, I noticed a crowd gathered at the foot of the bridge, perhaps fifty yards away. I opened the car door to get out.

Gita turned around in his seat. "Sir, please stay in the car. One never knows."

"Don't worry," I told him, "I won't get in anyone's way."

He frowned but said nothing. However foolish my behavior might seem to him, he didn't believe it his place to tell an American officer what to do.

And I didn't want to confess that I saw in the bombing an opportunity for a reporting cable, an eye-witness account of a terrorist attack, or at least its immediate aftermath. My first day in-country. The embassy and Washington would have to be impressed.

Lightheaded with fatigue and the oppressive heat, I walked through the mass of stalled vehicles. The other drivers sat in their cars, their engines off, waiting it out. Motor scooters and tuk-tuks sneaked through the gaps, climbing onto the sidewalks along the bridge, bulling their way through the swarms of pedestrians.

A shirt-sleeved crowd formed a circle around a point at the foot of the bridge. A burst of laughter, like a misplayed note, rose above the buzzing voices.

As I came nearer, a gap opened in the milling crowd. I caught a glimpse of shattered glass and bits of metal strewn on the road. A tuk-tuk, tipped on its side, lay amid its load of coconuts, spilled onto the pavement. Blood spread slowly among the scattered coconuts. I caught a glimpse of a body, perhaps more than one, partially screened by the crowd.

Suddenly I knew I wasn't ready for this. The gap in the crowd closed again and I didn't want to go any closer, didn't want to see the mangled flesh, the pooling blood. My legs trembling, I turned and walked back toward the embassy van. The decision saved my life.

As I stepped around a blue sedan, a flash of light reflected in its windshield and a powerful wave of heat hit me from behind, followed by a muffled *boom*. The force of the concussion hurled me against the fender of the blue sedan and onto the pavement. Gasping with shock, I reacted without thinking, wanting only to get away. I crawled on my hands and knees into the shadow of an idling truck. Screams filled the air, followed by the pounding of running feet. Terrified men and women, many of them spattered with blood, ran past me as I lay on the pavement.

Unable to think clearly, I fought opposing impulses to stay where I was and to dash back to the van or into the trees, to be anywhere but where I was.

"One never knows," Gita had said. Now I understood. He'd been trying to warn me that there might be a second bomb, timed to go off just long enough after the first one to ensure that a crowd had gathered.

I gagged on the smoke drifting among the cars as I struggled to my feet. My mind muddled by shock, I staggered not toward the safety of the embassy van, but toward the site of the blast.

Dazed, I couldn't fully register the chaos around me, saw only jagged images, like the pieces of a puzzle that I had no capacity to put together. Before me I saw the dead—six, eight, ten of them—lying amid the shattered vehicles and the gawking crowd, which, inconceivably, had re-formed after the second blast. I couldn't help but think how unhumanly relaxed the dead looked, relieved of all burdens.

The shattered hulk of the tuk-tuk, blown to pieces by the blast, lay scatted among the dead. Near it, a car lay overturned on the approach to the bridge. Three men in shirt sleeves stared at the car with strange intensity.

Then I saw her, the woman lying on the road, moaning in rapid, frightening gasps, her legs trapped under the overturned car, her eyes unseeing but filled with terror.

I stepped over the body of a man in shirtsleeves lying face down on the pavement and put my shoulder to one of the car's upturned fenders. Hardly knowing what I was doing, I began to push. The car didn't budge. I pushed harder, desperately, as if trying to free not her but myself. My sweating hands slipped off the hot metal. Others in the crowd stood and watched me.

"Help me!" I cried. No one moved. I pushed vainly against the car. The woman's moans began to fade and I feared she would die.

"Help me!" I felt as if I were pleading with the woman pinned under the car.

Suddenly, there were three men with me, probably the ones I'd first seen staring at the damage from the blast. Now they leaned with me, trying to push it over. At first slowly, then very quickly, the car tipped and fell back onto its wheels.

The woman screamed, then screamed again before falling into a continuous wailing that completely unnerved me until I forced myself to block it out.

I caught a glimpse of her mangled legs, covered in blood, and turned away.

Two men with a stretcher appeared through the snarled traffic. Shocked into paralysis, they could only gape at the scene.

Later, I could not remember jerking the stretcher from their hands or picking up the injured woman and laying her on it or ordering the men to take her to their ambulance. It certainly wasn't heroism. I only wanted to stop looking at her, stop hearing her screams. Nevertheless, the account in the following day's papers, backed up by a photograph, made me out to be a gallant and cool-headed savior.

All I could clearly recall later was Gita, the driver, standing beside me, taking me gently by the arm and leading me back toward the embassy car.

"Come sir, this is no place for you."

In the distance I heard the wail of an ambulance caught in the petrified traffic, like the protest of a fly trapped in amber.

3

"You okay, Reid?" Tony Spezza asked.

"Yeah, I'm fine. Let's get through this."

The embassy security officer, sat behind his desk, looking at me like a doctor who has heard a patient unwittingly describe the symptoms of a grave illness. An athletic, balding man, maybe forty years-old, he favored short-sleeve white shirts and thin black ties that made him look like a holdover from the Kennedy administration.

"We can do this tomorrow. Maybe you should take the day off."

I had slept poorly the night before, my first night in-country, waking with a start each time I drifted off, seeing before me not the car or the woman under it, but the man lying dead in the road, the one I had stepped over. In these brief and fractured dreams I wanted to turn him over, see his face. His image vanished each time I woke, waiting for me to fall back to sleep so he could reappear.

"No," I told Tony. "I want to get to work."

So I described the bomb and its aftermath, trying to sound offhand, unaffected by the whole thing. The look Tony gave me told me I wasn't fooling anyone. After I'd finished telling my story, he asked me a couple more questions then gave me his routine briefing on personal security in Sri Lanka.

Gazing at a pencil poised between his forefingers, he spent the next fifteen minutes describing the hazards of living in a country at war with itself, the need to remain alert and avoid crowds, to stay away from certain neighborhoods and a couple of notorious bars—in a nutshell, telling me to stay out of trouble. All of it delivered in a tone that told me I'd already failed in this basic task.

"Most importantly ..." Tony let the implied question hang in the air.

"If a bomb explodes, don't rush to the spot where it went off."

He grunted in affirmation.

The page one photo in the morning papers of me lifting the injured woman onto the stretcher, accompanied in a couple of papers by an exaggerated sidebar, had given me the dubious status of an instant celebrity. As I made the rounds of the embassy that morning, introducing myself to the other officers, their praise seemed tinged with resentment and a hint of unspoken judgment that making a hero of myself my first hour in-country was somehow in bad taste. No one suggested I write a cable. Bombs were a common occurrence. This one wasn't special just because I happened to be there when it went off.

Tony Spezza leaned his elbows on his desk, still looking at the pencil rather than at me. "I guess I don't need to tell you that you could've been killed."

"And if I had, you'd really be giving me hell now."

He didn't laugh.

"Look, Philip, it's not that I—" Something about the briefing, or my replies, or maybe simply the burden at that moment of being the security officer, a professional scold, tipped a switch in him and he abruptly pushed away from his desk and stood up.

"Come on. Let's get out of here."

※

We walked out past the Marine at Post One and onto the crowded sidewalk along Galle Road, the muggy heat already heavy as a steaming blanket, the air smelling of diesel fumes and tropical flowers and uncollected refuse. We passed the fading colonial swim club and the rows of ramshackle gem shops, stepped around the red stains left by the spitting of betel chewers, and avoided the rifle muzzles of the careless young soldiers standing guard at the intersections.

Between the gaps in the low, single story buildings, the Indian Ocean shone blue as the sky, its lazy breakers rolling listlessly up to shore, as if the heat and humidity had sapped even the sea of its strength. Offshore, a half dozen ships lay at anchor, waiting their turn to offload in the port.

The short walk in the tropical heat already had me sweating.

"So, what did you do before you joined the foreign service?" Tony asked.

"High school teacher."

"Stockton, California, right?"

Of course, he would have read the file. "Yes."

"Nice place?"

"Flat, dusty, hot and dull."

"And you gave up all that to come out here?"

I couldn't help smiling. "Yeah. How about you?"

He gave me the look of someone in the habit of asking questions, not answering them. "A cop. Boston. Eighty percent of Diplomatic Security are Catholic ex-cops. We understand sin."

"And absolution?"

Tony cocked his head in a negative way. "Someone else's department." We walked a little while in silence. "Look, Philip, I meant what I said about being careful. Try not to be in the wrong place at the wrong time."

"How am I supposed to—?"

"Use good sense. Get lucky." He made a fleeting smile at this absurdity. "You're the Public Affairs Officer. Your job is to get things out in the open. Mine is to deal with what's hidden. This place is made for my work, not yours. Everything that's important stays under cover here. So don't get fooled by surfaces. People—the people you'll be dealing with—stand in the daylight but live in the shadows. Until you learn how to see into those shadows, you'll never understand anything."

"You make it sound like I'm working at the wrong job here."

"You are." Again, that fleeting smile. "Figure out what you want from your time here. Some officers come to dance and drink, chase skirts. Some want to see the country, try to get to know the people. Some come for the Buddhist thing. Seekers." He grunted indifferently.

"How about the ones who come here trying to get promoted?"

"They're the ones who get into trouble." I felt the ex-cop's sidelong glance. "You got family?"

"A wife. But …" I couldn't finish the thought.

"Yeah, I guess I saw her name on your transfer orders."

"How about you?"

"A wife. Ex. A daughter. But." He made a little shrug of—what? Regret? Resignation?

I would learn that Tony was the sort to elicit confessions, not make them. He gave out few details about himself. I'd find out later that only a couple of people in the embassy knew Tony had been married, and I would ask myself why he had confided in me. I never really found an answer, but understood it at the time as an offer of friendship.

"How far away were you when the bomb went off?" he asked.

"Forty, fifty feet."

He let out a low whistle.

"Do you know what happened to the woman I put on the stretcher?" I asked.

Tony shook his head. "The war's a sometimes thing here in Colombo. Tamil versus Sinhala. Minority versus majority. The British favored the Tamils—the minority. Eventually, after independence, the Sinhala took power and decided to get even. And, boom, you've got yourself a civil war. Generally, it stays up north, where folks figure it belongs. They like to believe it hasn't got much to do with them. Things like yesterday's bomb remind them they're wrong."

We had reached the end of the promenade, both of us sweating in the heat and humidity. Tony took a handkerchief from his pocket, wiped his brow, and looked across a narrow channel toward the government buildings rising behind the walls of the old colonial fort. "You thinking of heading back out to the spot today?" he asked.

"No."

"Some people keep going back, y'know. Others avoid it like the gates of hell. In a funny way, it's the same thing, really. Can't get it out of their minds. If you go back, you'll see that one of the local peace groups has painted a dove on the roadway where the bomb went off, made a little rainbow, painted a few words pleading for an end to the war. In the meantime the tension ratchets up another notch. Everyone goes a little crazier." A long sigh ended in a humorless chuckle. "Like I say, the main thing is to stay out of trouble. It's going to be a lot harder than you think."

4

The blackout started near the Cinnamon Gardens and spread along the broad avenues toward the Maradana Road, throwing into darkness the dense stands of rain trees and coconut palms. Like the final ingredient in an exotic perfume, the darkness enhanced the scent of hibiscus and jasmine on the air and brought out the heavy aroma of the tropics, the odor of life in the process of both decomposition and rebirth.

I settled deeper into the back seat of the embassy car, unconsciously making room beside me for Jean—just as amputees accommodate a phantom limb—while the sedan crept forward against the ever-present chaos of cars, trucks, and buses that choked the streets at every hour.

Two months in country had accustomed me to these interruptions in electrical power, this loss of the very juice of modernity. The following day the newspapers would carry an official announcement stating that the blackout had resulted from long-planned maintenance of the electrical grid or the mischance of an automobile accident that had knocked down some distant but crucial pylon. Rumors that rebel sabotage lay behind the power failure did not merit denial, the articles insisted, and were circulated by those wishing to undermine the government's peace efforts.

Along the sidewalks, the owners of the wooden stalls displaying rice and spices and cigarettes lighted their oil lamps, the flames flickering like votive candles in the darkness, making the figures on the crowded sidewalks waver like phantoms. Men in sarongs and women in brightly colored saris loomed out of the darkness, caught for an instant against the beams of our headlights, like snapshots, before merging back into the darkness.

We're no longer allowed to consider anything—any place, any people—as exotic. The academics tell us Exoticism—you can hear the capital E as they speak—is a mindset that betrays the limitations of our occidental worldview, smacks of provincial, neo-colonialist attitudes, and denies the humanity of people of color. But, my god, this place, these people, cast a spell over me, like a waking dream in which I lived and worked.

Captivated by their otherworldliness, I forced myself to remember that they were not foreigners. I was the foreigner.

After perhaps half an hour in which we barely moved, the embassy driver, Jayasinghe, finally lost his Buddhic patience and demonstrated his fabled genius for getting out of traffic. With the aplomb of Houdini escaping a set of handcuffs, he eased past an overcrowded bus, turned up one deserted street then down another then a third, all of them lined with trees that formed a canopy over us, vines twisting from their limbs, overhanging the road like the tresses of a sorceress.

And, suddenly, we had left the city behind and were driving down a dark road edged with rice paddies and palm trees. Twenty minutes later we turned up a narrow drive, obscured by a grove of trees, that ended at an iron gate, where a military policeman shone a flashlight onto the car's diplomatic plate. He motioned to two soldiers to open the gate. Submachine guns slung negligently over their shoulders, they ambled over and pushed against the gate until it opened just enough to allow us in.

We stopped at the end of the long, winding drive. A servant opened the car door with an unctuous "Good evening, sir," and directed me down a dark walkway that led to an enormous tropical-colonial house, half hidden behind bougainvillea and banana palms. Inside, coconut oil lamps were scattered around the room to make up for the loss of power. They cast their orange glow, adding a dreamlike quality to the buzz of polite chatter in the crowded room. Stilled by the blackout, the ceiling fans in the large salon hung motionless and the tropical air barely stirred despite the open windows and the yawning French doors that opened onto the moonlit veranda.

I looked around the dimly-lighted salon for familiar faces. Nearly half the embassy's officers had changed over during the summer, and some of us were still barely more than strangers to each other. The new ambassador, Richard Donavan, had only arrived a couple of weeks earlier. He'd presented his credentials to the President of the Republic, Susan Guneratne, in a little ceremony at her official residence. A brief clip on state-run television showed the tall Midwesterner towering over the Sri Lankan, the two of them backed by their countries' flags. But everyone knew this formality served only as a preliminary to his true acceptance by the Sri Lankan establishment, which would come tonight when he presented himself to Chiran Jayatilaka, matriarch of the island's preeminent political family and its economic overlords.

Aunt of the current president, sister of the previous one, daughter of still a third, Chiran Jayatilaka, it was said, had once been offered the candidacy of the family's dominant National Reconciliation Party, the NRP, but dismissed the idea with a wave of her hand, saying, "Let Susan have it." Queens don't run for president.

Circulating around the room, I introduced myself to a few of the Sri Lankan guests, a collection of bankers, company chairmen and party officials, all associated in one way or another with the Jayatilaka family. I shook hands with a few journalists and a couple of dips from other embassies, all of us figuratively pissing on the corners and sniffing each other's behinds.

Eventually, I gravitated toward Robert McWhirter, head of the embassy's political section, and Burt Steadman, the Deputy Chief of Mission—DCM, in embassy parlance—the ambassador's right hand. A large, florid man, he had arrived at post only a couple of weeks before me.

"Hey, look who showed up," Steadman said, feigning surprise.

I faked a good-humored laugh. His comment was meant to sting. I had been notably absent from many of the unending social events that comprised so much of our work.

The DCM loosened his tie against the heat and undid the top button of his shirt. "Jesus, Reid, what can you do to get some air in this place?" he asked in the Oklahoma twang he turned on and off at will. "Why doesn't our hostess fire up some generators and get the AC pumping?"

"I'm told she hates the noise," McWhirter said, happy to show off his knowledge of the minutiae of life among the political class.

"So, where is she?" Steadman looked around the shadowed room.

McWhirter smiled. "Hostess or not, she won't show until the Ambassador arrives."

"What about her husband?" I asked. "Isn't he around here somewhere?"

McWhirter rolled his eyes at the DCM and replied without quite looking at me. "I forget, you're new here. No, he's not. He's lived abroad for years. No one ever speaks of him. Ever. So don't ask." He shot his cuffs as punctuation.

A stir near the front entrance caught the collective attention. A moment later, Ambassador Donovan strode into the room, absently brushing the hair off his damp forehead.

Tall, lanky and just past sixty, Richard Donovan was self-effacing, experienced and utterly American—Jimmy Stewart as diplomat. Behind his shoulder walked Chandrika Dias, the embassy's Sri Lankan protocol secretary, whispering to him the names of the people who came up to greet him. Donovan nodded and addressed them each with practiced ease as he made a slow progress around the room. He ended at the little knot of American officers.

Donovan gave his DCM a faint smile. "Well, Burt, you look radiant tonight."

Steadman ran a hand across his dripping face. "Sweatin' like a horse. This place is as bad as Jakarta."

The Ambassador shook my hand. "Philip, good to see you."

"Good evening, sir."

He turned to his political officer. "Ah, Robert, I was looking over your cable on Tissa Sandanayake before leaving the office tonight." I recognized the name of the charismatic young opposition leader. "I thought you needed to make clearer how much the present government sees him as a real threat in the spring elections. We want to let Washington know—"

Before Donovan could finish his thought, a new presence pulsed across the salon.

Like a fresh breeze chasing away the stale air, Chiran Jayatilaka swept into the room through a pair of tall doors that opened before her as if by magic. Wearing a glittering, self-assured smile, she came among us with her arms outstretched in matriarchal affection and proprietary right, as if enfolding everyone into her embrace.

Steadman leaned toward me and muttered, "Bette fucking Davis couldn't make a better entrance."

Like wayward comets the Sri Lankans in the room instantly fell into her gravity, smiling deferentially as they jockeyed to take her hand, make a witty remark, remind her of their presence. A short, plump woman, with jet black hair, she laughed like an opera star, batted her eyes like a coquette and spoke with the authority of a pope. Such behavior might have appeared excessive in someone else, but Chiran Jayatilaka's out-sized persona seemed exactly right as she glided through the ranks of courtiers around her and received the new ambassador to what was, almost literally, her country.

"Your Excellency," she proclaimed, "Welcome to Sri Lanka."

The assembled diplomats and dignitaries smiled and swarmed around her like worker bees tending their queen.

Or, all but one.

Leaning against the wall at the far side of the room, barely visible in the lamplight, slouched a young man, his open-necked shirt and white slacks contrasting sharply with the formal dress of other guests. Even more remarkable was the glowering regard he directed at Chiran Jayatilaka, evidently unable to bear either her presence or the words she spoke.

He must have sensed my eyes on him because he suddenly looked at me and frowned. For a moment he tried to stare me into turning away, but gave up the challenge and, his chin raised in defiance—the gesture hopelessly adolescent—he walked out of the room through the French doors. No one appeared to have noticed, yet I felt sure everyone had registered his hostility as well as his abrupt departure.

After our hostess finished her welcoming remarks and Ambassador Donovan had delivered a few deliberately innocuous words of thanks, the party recommenced at a slightly lower level of energy. Steadman and McWhirter each took a fresh drink from a passing waiter and started talking with a Norwegian diplomat about the spring elections, speaking, as the Ambassador had, of Tissa Sandanayake, the young opposition leader.

In my yearning to be regarded as a player, I stepped into the circle of their conversation.

The Norwegian looked at me as if he recognized me but couldn't think why. After a moment of narrow-eyed puzzlement, he exclaimed, "Ah! You're the fellow who saved that woman's life after the bombing."

There was no longer any point in protesting that the newspaper accounts had exaggerated my supposed heroism. By now people had fallen into two camps: either admiring the way I deflected praise or dismissing it as false modesty.

"I don't know if I saved her or not," I replied.

"Still. . ." the Norwegian said, his voice trailing off.

Reduced to a curiosity, I could only look on, envious, as the three men returned to their previous discussion with the ease of guys back home talking about football, all first names and shorthand allusions to things about which I knew little.

Suddenly, the stale air, the forced conversations, the burden of my desire to impress others rose up like a hand to my throat. I felt an overwhelming urge to breathe some unused air. I pulled away from the others and made my way across the crowded room toward the veranda.

Wanting to give the appearance of a man content to simply stroll in the moonlight, I walked past the other guests and along a grove of small palms. Within a few strides I lost the party around a curve in the hedge and felt a weight lift from my chest. The air outside felt lighter, cooler. The last buzz of distant conversation faded behind me, and I walked into a shadow of silence. Or so it seemed until I heard the familiar percussion of a basketball bouncing on a concrete court.

In the glare of several large gas lanterns, some young Sri Lankans were playing an enthusiastic but ragged game of three-on-three, complete with behind-the-back passes that too often disappeared into the darkness, and reverse lay-ups that mostly clanked off the rim.

It took a moment for me to recognize the young man who had walked out on Chiran Jayatilaka's remarks. Still dressed in his open-necked shirt and light slacks, he had put on a pair of expensive athletic shoes and was playing in a manner that somehow made clear that this was his court and the others his guests. With a start, I realized he had to be Chiran Jayatilaka's son.

I watched as they played and noticed a curious thing. While the others wore name-brand athletic shoes, bearing

iconic swooshes and whorls and stripes, one of the young
Sri Lankans, taller than the others, played barefoot, his
feet apparently as tough as any pair of shoes. In contrast
to the top-of-the-line shirts and shorts worn by the others,
he sported a ragged T-shirt only a couple of washes short
of disintegration and wore ill-fitting trunks that flapped
around his pencil-thin legs. Whatever his get-up, he played
with a clumsy aggressiveness that differed sharply with the
unproductive smoothness of the other players, and scored
repeatedly with a clunky jump shot and awkward lay-ups.
He fouled repeatedly and without remorse, acknowledging
his misdemeanors with nothing but a curt nod before
immediately returning to the attack.

I stood outside the circle of gaslight and watched from
the shadows, at first unnoticed, then—I felt the subtle shift
in atmosphere—noticed but unacknowledged.

The gangly kid in the faded T-shirt charged to the basket,
knocking over a pudgy defender, who came up limping and
angry. Oddly, the injured player did not turn on the lanky
dynamo who had run him down, but instead looked at the
others and then said something to the young man in the
open-necked shirt, as if this skinny kid were somehow their
host's responsibility.

Meanwhile, the barefoot player apparently claimed that
his victim had in fact fouled him. Without a glance at the
others, he walked to the free-throw line. His pudgy victim
took a few halting steps to demonstrate his injury, then
stood unhappily in the middle of the court, hands on his
hips and muttered something I didn't catch.

But the young man in the open necked shirt had heard it.
"You said something?" he asked in English, his voice tight
with warning.

The pudgy young man hesitated, then made a show of pulling himself up to all his modest height. "Ah, Bandula, I said you're all talk, talk, talk." He dismissively threw his hands in the air. "You talk about how you'll grow up and do great things, but"—and here he nodded toward the skinny kid at the free-throw line—"you can't even make your sweetheart—"

Before he could finish, the young man struck him in the face with his open hand. The pudgy player tried to back away, but his host grabbed him by his shirt and slapped him again. The player shrieked with a terror so comical that the others all laughed. Unmanned by his loss of face, he broke away from the young man's grip and scampered off court, where he sat on the ground next to an attractive young woman I hadn't noticed until then.

In the center of the court the young host glanced at the other players, gauging not so much their reaction to his assault as the effect on them of the injured player's taunts— words he had tried to erase by his attack, but had only managed to underline.

"Take his place," he said. It took me a moment to realize he was looking at me. "Take his place," he repeated, less an invitation than a command.

I looked over my shoulder toward the house and reminded myself that I was here on business. The demands of official duty required me to return to the party.

I walked onto the court.

I took off my tie and shirt, my shoes and socks. Looking at the others, I was suddenly conscious of how incredibly white I was, practically glowing in the gaslight. I suddenly understood why some people thought white folks looked unhealthy.

Once I began to play, I realized that the others were a little better than they looked from the sidelines. They were quick and handled the ball well, their game betrayed only by a wish to play better than their talents allowed.

The outsider in the faded t-shirt, though, let nothing betray him. He drove to the basket like a bulldozer and scored. I took the ball out for our side, made the inbound pass, pulled in a return pass and made my first bucket. The sweat and the hard play felt good. I realized how long it had been since I'd really worked out. I scored again and began to feel confident, ready to show them who could really play this game.

The kid in the faded shirt took a pass and drove toward the basket. Playing defense now, I set myself on the balls of my feet. The impact of the collision knocked me onto my back. As I lay sprawled on the court, the ball swished through the hoop and bounced off my chest.

A couple of the players laughed. The barefoot kid stood over me, looking down without expression.

I picked myself up. "Charging," I said, calling the foul.

He said something that clearly meant, "No way."

"Charging," I said again, motioning for the ball.

The other guy squared up, looked at me coldly. "No," he said in English.

I could feel the danger, knew we were an eye blink from a fight. Fleetingly, I wondered how our host ever persuaded anyone to play if every game was like this.

Before anyone could throw a punch our host, the one called Bandula, deftly stepped between me and his barefoot friend.

"Game over," he said, giving everyone around him a look that made clear this was his court, his house, his game, and he could stop it when he wanted.

Bandula caught the barefoot kid's eye and nodded toward me. For a moment he did nothing, his eyes locked on Bandula's in wordless protest. After a long, tense few seconds he blinked and, clearly against his will, reluctantly put out his hand to shake.

Despite the hostility in his eyes, the young man's grip felt tentative, even apologetic. His face stirred by crosscurrents of emotion, he nodded in acknowledgment of something I didn't quite grasp. With a last glance at Bandula, a glance that for an instant connected the two young men with a depth that startled me, he turned and walked off the court.

"Game over," our host repeated with finality.

On the sidelines I picked up a towel and ran it over my chest, combed back my sweaty hair and got dressed.

Slapping each other on the back and reliving the game they imagined they had played, the others retreated into the shadows. All except our host, who stood in the middle of the court, regarding me with an oddly speculative expression.

Increasingly unhappy with myself for getting roped into the game, I finished putting on my shoes and tried to ignore him.

"You're an American."

"Yeah."

"What's your name?"

"Philip Reid."

"Philip Reid. Yes, of course." He had it now, who I was. "We must talk sometime, Philip Reid."

"What about?"

The young man frowned momentarily, then looked at me with increased interest. "We will talk," he said, then walked off the court.

As he disappeared into the shadows beyond the lamplight, I caught a glimpse of the young woman sitting on the sidelines. Bandula eased himself onto the grass next to her in a familiar way. She inclined her head to catch something he said. As she did, I thought I caught her glancing at me in something more than a casual way. Or so I flattered myself.

I put on my coat and headed back to the main house, wondering why Bandula Jayatilaka insisted he wanted to talk with me. At the same time, I savored my modest secret, that while my embassy colleagues sweated in a dark room and chatted with the usual suspects about the usual topics, I had been playing basketball with the son of Chiran Jayatilaka.

※

A little breathless from the game, I headed back to the house, walking a little unevenly from a blister forming on my foot. I rejoined the party to find the Ambassador making his goodbyes. Feeling compelled to hide the fact I'd taken a little vacation, I went over to wish him goodnight.

"There you are," Richard Donovan said, "I've been looking for you. But excuse me for a moment …"

With a shock of embarrassment, I realized I'd managed to thrust myself between the Ambassador of the United States and the most powerful woman in the country as they were about to bid each other goodnight.

I stammered, "Of course, I—"

Our hostess smiled and cut me off. "I see you have been playing basketball with my son."

Sweaty as I was, my face flushed, it didn't take any great insight to figure out what I'd been up to.

The Ambassador raised his eyebrows in surprise.

Chandrika Jayatilaka regarded me for a moment, as if weighing something about me, then turned on her brightest smile. "I'm pleased you have met Bandula."

Ambassador Donovan looked at me curiously but said nothing before saying goodnight. As she followed him to the door, I enjoyed my sudden prominence, standing with the Ambassador and the uncrowned queen of Sri Lanka. It didn't last long. Chandrika, the protocol assistant, jealous of her position, deftly elbowed me aside and smiled at our hostess. With that, the evening was over.

5

Two days after the reception at the Jayatilakas, I asked the motor pool for a car and driver and went to the Ministry of Information to pay my first call on J. R. Thilakaratne, the Sri Lankan government's Official Censor. Despite its brutally candid title, his was an odd and shadowy position, the least public of public posts. My staff had warned me that Thilakaratne seldom granted meetings to anyone, so I'd been surprised when his secretary called and told me to come to his office at ten.

The accumulation of contacts is the juice a foreign service officer brings to every conversation he holds, to each cable he writes. It's the only answer to the question implied by every transaction: "What the hell do *you* know about it?" The greater the number of contacts an officer boasts, the higher their rank, the more mojo that officer brings to the table.

Among those interlocutors—to use a favored foreign service word—the range of personalities reflected the estates to which they belonged. Among the journalists, I'd found a wide gamut of sages, sycophants, hacks and pros. If on some issues even the best of them insisted on taking what seemed an eccentric viewpoint, I reminded myself that every country puts itself in the middle of the world map.

By contrast, the unfailingly gracious Sri Lankan university officials carried themselves with the dignity of those who have resolved to meet a fatal illness with quiet courage. Their world, founded on a bygone British model, was crumbling under the weight of overcrowded classes, deteriorating buildings, and the chaos wrought by gangs of radicalized students who played out the country's favorite blood sport—politics—on the nation's campuses

Government officials presented a different aspect. They were generally quiet, close-hold, giving away nothing, trying to make sure that nothing took place outside their control. And J. R. Thilakaratne stood as the avatar of such civil servants.

Word had it that Thilakaratne owed his position through some connection with the Jayatilaka family, though that could be said of half the government. And all understood that the variety of services he carried out for them had little to do with his official position. A slow-talking man of formal manners, he had dark, liquid eyes and a drooping mustache that hung over the corners of his mouth like an expression of deep melancholy.

His office, which lay far from the main corridors of the Information Ministry was plain as a monk's cell, with little furniture and no pictures or decorations, as if he had censored the room itself lest it reveal something about its occupant.

After we exchanged a few courtesies, Thilakaratne nodded toward a large sofa while he settled into an armchair, propped his elbows on its arms and gazed at me with the quiet absorption of a mind-reader. On the coffee table between us lay a copy of one of the morning newspapers, folded open to a brief account of Chiran Jayatilaka's reception for the Ambassador.

A pretty young woman came in, set a tea tray on the coffee table and backed out smiling. The Official Censor, as befitted his station, said nothing. With a vague sense that I had conceded some important point by speaking first, I ventured that the Sri Lankan press appeared quite lively—a clumsy opening bid, like telling the local undertaker how healthy everyone looks.

J. R. Thilakaratne pulled at his drooping mustache. "Yes. We are very proud of our journalistic community. The foundation of a vibrant democracy." He sounded like a man reading from a brochure.

"Then you probably don't have much to do during the course of—"

He spoke over my words, as if to spare me from expressing an unacceptable thought. "I like to think of my office as a service. Its presence reminds our journalists to be mindful of what they write, to think first of the democratic and socialist development of our country."

"Do you ..." I paused, searching for the right way to put it. "Do you need to remind them often of this obligation?"

Curling his short frame into something like a large question mark, he said, "They learn to repress inappropriate thoughts. As you imply, I end up with little to do." A slow smile raised the ends of his sad mustache.

"I had hoped to meet you at the reception the other night."

With a wave of his hand he indicated the newspaper on the coffee table. "I am seldom required at these events." He narrowed his eyes at me. "I trust you had a pleasant evening. You had a chance to meet Mrs. Jayatilaka?"

"Yes. Briefly." On an impulse, I added, "And her son."

The Official Censor blinked, the smallest of involuntary reflexes, like the twitch of a branch when a bird takes flight.

"Ah, yes. Young Bandula."

"You know him?" I had no clear idea where this was going, but I wanted to pursue the small opening I had made. "Did I detect a little tension between mother and son?"

With a frown of annoyance, Thilakaratne picked some imaginary lint from his coat, then smiled broadly, clearly not an expression that came to him naturally. "I have known Bandula since he was a young boy. His father and I—" He rethought his words, started over. "In Sri Lanka the relationship between a mother and a son is ever a loving one," he said, quietly shutting the door on that topic.

Yet there had been a rustling behind the curtain of the Sri Lankan's self-possession. Something to do with the son—and the father.

I decided to ignore McWhirter's advice to ask no questions about Chiran Jayatilaka's husband. "You must know his father. I suppose his absence from the country reflects—"

"Yes, of course," Thilakaratne interrupted again, his drooping mustache hiding whatever clues might be written in the set of his mouth. "But we are not here to gossip, are we, Mr. Reid?" The Official Censor leaned back in his chair, his eyes glinting oddly, as if, throughout our conversation, he had been looking for something in me and now had found it. "Tell me, Mr. Reid, whom do you serve?"

"Sorry?"

"Whom do you serve?" The Sri Lankan raised his chin a fraction, sure of himself now. "We public servants say that we are here to serve our respective democracies, to further mutual understanding, enhance our precious freedoms. Yes?" He flicked his hand in a small dismissive gesture. "All abstractions. No, Mr. Reid, we wish to serve not something, but someone. Someone who embodies these virtues, who represents the very essence of their people and country, someone in whom we can place trust."

"I'm not sure what you—"

"Tell me something." Though his expression remained bland as pudding, something in his tone told me we had arrived at his purpose in granting this meeting. Finally, the obvious occurred to me. It was no coincidence that Thilakaratne had asked me to visit two days after I had met Chiran Jayatilaka and her son. I couldn't yet see what he wanted of me, but I suddenly felt exactly what I was, a novice dealing with a subtle and capable veteran, one who understood far better than I the waters in which we were both swimming.

"Tell me, Mr. Reid, why did you attempt to save that woman at the bridge on the day you first arrived in our country?" Thilakaratne looked at me over the top of his steepled his fingers. Did I show annoyance? Or simply the uneasiness of a chess player who senses that his opponent is thinking at least one move ahead of him?

"I saw she might die if she didn't get attention right away," I replied. "And I was in a position to do something about it. That's all there was to it."

Thilakaratne spread his hands. "Yes, exactly. You are a man who wishes to take meaningful action. An American of the best sort—naive perhaps, but you want to do something that will make a difference. I greatly admire this quality." He smiled and let out a sigh. "Mr. Reid, you must wonder why I called you here—"

I jumped at the jangling of the telephone. Thilakaratne frowned at this interruption of his pitch at its most delicate moment.

Rising from his chair, Thilakaratne crossed to his desk and answered the telephone. "Yes?" He made an impatient click of his tongue. "I see. Of course." He set the receiver back in its cradle. "I am sorry, Mr. Reid. but we will have to resume this conversation another time. The Official Censor shook my hand. "May I give you a piece of advice. Mr. Reid? You would be wise not to speak too much about the Jayatilakas. And pay little attention to what you hear. You will soon find that everything becomes exaggerated here. Even reality." A sad little smile played across his face. "We will speak again."

It struck me that these were almost the same words Bandula Jayatilaka had spoken to me. A peculiar shiver coursed down my back as I said my goodbyes and left.

6

My lecture at the university had gone well. I'd spoken on the state of journalism in the United States, a topic of which I knew little, but my audience even less. The students smiled at me shyly as they filed out of the classroom. I nodded graciously and made a business of fiddling with my lecture notes to preclude the obligatory words of thanks or admiration or agreement, or, worse, disagreement, leading to those "tedious arguments of insidious intent."

"Well, Mr. Reid. What a pleasure to see you again."

Thinking myself trapped despite my efforts, I looked up and was surprised to find Bandula Jayatilaka granting me his most regal smile. Beside him stood the tall gangly fellow from the basketball game, appearing even more out of place in a lecture hall than on the court, like a feral dog in a show hall full of poodles. Shadowed behind them stood the girl I'd seen sitting on the grass outside the light of the gas lamps. That night, in the darkness, I'd imagined her as exotic and darkly attractive. In the light of day, I saw that my imagination had not done her justice—she was a tall and slender beauty with a delicate nose, full lips, and dark eyes that surprised me with their melancholy.

She ran a hand through her black hair and let it fall around her shoulders. Only when she looked away did I realize I'd been staring.

"I wanted to tell you how much I enjoyed your presentation." Bandula held himself like the aristocrat he was, chin up, posture perfect, yet somehow at ease. He seemed a different man from the angry and insecure youth I had seen on the basketball court. "Someday I must travel to your country and see if you are correct," he said, adding a faint smile that I could take as I wished. He looked at me narrow-eyed for a moment, as if waiting for some reaction to what he had said, then abruptly took my arm and, with the tone of a man who had never in his life been refused, said, "Come, you must join us for a cup of tea. I will pay."

Amused and flattered by his attention—maybe a touch annoyed by his presumption, or by the fact that he presumed correctly— I said yes.

※

We sat on wooden benches under a jacaranda tree, drinking strong tea from chipped cups. Bandula sat opposite me, the girl to his left. The tall outsider—I heard Bandula call him Kumar—stood a few feet off, as if he had drawn a circle around the rest of us and was determined to stay outside its arc.

Like a train stopping and starting, our conversation advanced with fitful beginnings and clanking halts. One moment, the young Jayatilaka appeared preoccupied, silent and brooding, the next moment he jabbered almost maniacally, dominating every exchange, spouting a torrent of opinions, facts and arguments—on the weather, the shortcomings of the university, the strengths of obscure authors—before falling silent once again.

After a harsh critique of the national cricket team, he took a long, slow breath and said, more quietly, "Americans are informal, so I shall call you Phil." He drew himself up, as if starting our conversation over. "So, Phil, what are your impressions of our country?"

People who ask that kind of question are generally looking for a particular answer, but I didn't want to make the effort to figure out what it was. "A beautiful island. A gracious people," I said.

A dark cloud crossed the young Jayatilaka's face. He leaned forward on his bench, his face inches from mine. "You're not taking me seriously." For a moment I thought he might take a swing at me, as he had at the pudgy young man on the basketball court that night.

While I tried to decide whether I should hit him back if he punched me, the young woman beside him quietly set her hand on his leg, like a mother cautioning an overwrought child. The effect was remarkable. At her touch, Bandula closed his eyes and let his head drop. For the span of two deep breaths he neither moved nor spoke. Then, as softly as she had laid her hand on him, she took it back and he again raised his face to mine, but now with a little waggle of the head that I might take as a tacit apology if I chose.

Behind the smokescreen of a forced laugh, he said, "I should have known better than to ask such a question of a diplomat."

The one called Kumar smiled.

"But how can I make small talk and expect revelations? And, besides, you're right, Phil. It is indeed a beautiful island, a gracious people! So how have we managed to make such a shambles of it?" Once more relaxed, his laugh took on a more genuine tone as he enjoyed his own brashness, no longer trying to provoke me. "And here I am asking questions when I should be giving answers. Forgive me." He held out his hand—an odd bit of grandstanding, the king's proud show of humility. Yet there was something attractive and honest in the gesture. I shook his hand, and in that moment felt I had made a friend.

Bandula cocked his head to one side and squinted at me, a knowing young man sharing a finely calculated confidence. "So, I will tell you what kind of place this is. It is a country of sheep who want to be fed and protected. Yet they are ruled by wolves who have no ambition beyond getting fat by eating them."

His blunt assessment of his fellow countrymen surprised me. "But aren't you the she-wolf's cub?"

For a moment I thought he had been struck ill. His lips compressed to a thin line, and his eyes closed as if in pain. I wondered what tempests raged within him, their force so violent and close to the surface that they might at any moment overwhelm him. I remembered his agonized appearance on the basketball court the moment before he had struck the other player. Then, too, he had been provoked by a remark about his family, and about Kumar.

The moment passed as quickly as it had come, though the young man's struggle to control some deep emotion was harrowing to watch.

After a moment he opened his eyes, his face lighted with a sudden and unconvincing smile. "So I am. The she-wolf's cub. And this poor country would be better off if we wolves were all taken out and shot."

The girl scoffed, "Why do you insist on celebrating the

fact that you don't like yourself, Bandula? Don't bore us with all that."

What bond did the young man share with this young woman? Were they lovers? Simply friends? Neither possibility seemed quite right.

Stung by her words, Bandula screwed his face into a mock pain I was sure hid a real one. "Yes, Lilani," he said with a theatrical lilt. "I am caught in a conflict of interests. Oh, whatever am I to do?"

I wanted to ask him to stop. I had liked him very much for a moment. Instead, I asked, "Wouldn't it be better for the Jayatilakas to trust in their countrymen and let them grow up on their own?"

Bandula's smile disappeared. His eyes fixed on mine, I saw an unexpressed thought swim through the young man's eyes like the shadow of a great shark, and then disappear into deeper waters.

He assumed again his blithe air, and made a show of again leaning back, his arms spread along the back of the bench, a man at his ease. "As I was in the classroom listening to your learned talk this morning do you know what I was thinking?"

I shook my head.

"I was thinking, 'This fellow certainly speaks better than he plays basketball.'" With this, Bandula laughed and jumped up from the bench. "Come, Phil. You must come with us to my house and have lunch."

Again, he grabbed my arm as if from proprietary right. "You can go back later and tell all your spies that you have penetrated the inner sanctum of the dreaded Jayatilakas and lived to tell the tale. You'll be king of the American Embassy."

I feared that following this mercurial young man and

his companions on an impromptu lark into the country would likely offer little more than a continuation of these tiresome, even disturbing, antics. Yet Bandula had known which button to push. King of the embassy? No. But an invitation to visit the home of the Jayatilakas would bring my standing up a notch or two, show that I could do something more than put people on stretchers. It didn't even occur to me to resist the temptation.

7

We followed Bandula across the parking lot to his BMW convertible. He waved at my driver to follow us, then jumped behind the wheel.

"Phil, come sit up front with me," he said. "You diplomats always sit in the back seat, like millionaires. Come up here and see the country for a change."

Kumar glowered at me as he crawled into the back seat while I appropriated his usual place next to Bandula. If Bandula noticed the tension, he made no sign. Grinning, he gunned the motor to life and glanced in the mirror

And there he stopped.

His hand still poised over the gearshift, his eyes in the mirror, his smile blinked out. Without a word, he turned off the engine and got out of the car.

The rest of us turned to watch as he walked toward the far edge of the parking lot.

There, in the shade of a jacaranda tree, stood J. R. Thilakaratne. The small, compact man, dressed in a dark suit, wore his habitual expression of deep sorrow. As Bandula approached, Thilakaratne lowered his head deferentially, as if he couldn't presume to look directly into the face of the young Jayatilaka.

How much of it was pose, how much honest self-effacement I couldn't tell, but as they spoke their postures of dominance and submission changed like a tide turning. Gradually, Thilakaratne turned to face Bandula and the young man's head sank as the Official Censor took control of the conversation. Bandula nodded a couple of times as the older man spoke. Finally, with an abrupt lift of his chin, he turned back toward the car, his face dark with agitation.

I wondered why Thilakaratne would come the several miles out to the university to speak to Bandula. Whatever he needed to say, it apparently could not be discussed over the phone. Yet I had understood that the Official Censor was the servant of the mother, not the son. Surely, if she had something she wished to say to Bandula, she would do it herself. It hit me. This was something his mother didn't know about.

Like anxious children pretending we hadn't seen our parents arguing, we came quickly around in our seats as Bandula approached. Without a glance at any of us, he got behind the wheel and slammed the door.

It took Lilani to ask what Kumar and I could not. "What did that old ghoul want?" Lilani asked. "I'd like to—"

Without looking at her, Bandula held up a warning hand. Lilani fell silent. Whatever he had been discussing with Thilakaratne, he was not about to share it with us. Instead, he spoke through his car. Racing the motor, Bandula slammed the convertible into gear and sped away from the campus. My driver, Jayasinghe, in the embassy car, quickly disappeared from the rearview mirror. I put on my seat belt.

His face a mask, Bandula drove as if he couldn't imagine anyone else daring to appear on the road. The BMW's tires squealed on the rough pavement as he let the car drift toward the outside of a long curve, missing by inches a man on a bicycle. Bandula floored the accelerator as we topped a rise at high speed. I felt my stomach float.

I thought of telling him to slow down, but whatever Thilakaratne had said back at the campus had put him in a murderous mood, and the young Sri Lankan had no interest in caution. Riding a wave of deep agitation, he drove instinctually, his actions unmediated by conscious thought, his hand light on the wheel, his feet by turns standing on the accelerator or caressing the brakes as his powerful car ate up the road.

A tight corner led to a long straightaway. With a powerful whine, the BMW's engine wound out toward the red line. Rice paddies passed in a blur of green. Farmers looked up from their work. The engine screamed toward its limits. The convertible used up the long stretch of pavement in seconds.

At the end of the straightaway the road climbed a short rise, then curved through a narrow cut in the side of a hill. Bandula appeared to have no intention of slowing for the turn, as if a Jayatilaka had no more need to heed the laws of physics than he did any other law on this, his family's island. Only as we entered the corner did he tap the brakes and downshift. The engine whined in protest but the car was still approaching the corner too fast.

With lightning reflexes, Bandula worked to bring himself back from the brink, twitching the wheel one way then the other, each move an attempt to complement and correct the last. Fighting for control, he blinked, as if only now awakening to the peril he had brought on all of us.

Fishtailing, the car drifted across the center line into the oncoming lane as Bandula let it eat up ground, trying to ease the angle of the turn.

A white car topped the rise, coming straight at us, its horn howling, the driver frantically wrenching the wheel to avoid a head-on. Surprise registered on Bandula's face, yet no fear. He hit the brake hard, once, twice, then stood on it, forcing the BMW out of its line and toward the embankment, all hope of recovering control gone.

I felt myself thrown forward against the seat belt. From the back seat Lilani let out an odd, moaning trill. The BMW hit gravel, began to slide. Bandula yanked the wheel sharply. With an odd detachment, I wondered if it would roll.

Instead, the car spun at high speed, the force gluing us to our seats. The tires screamed before losing all adhesion to the road, replaced by a strange rumbling roar as two of the wheels caught a shallow ditch at the side of the road. The car jounced violently on the uneven ground tossing me around like a rag doll as the car skipped backwards along the ditch.

The BMW slammed into the dirt bank, tearing at the earth bank. A thrill of horror. A shattering impact. Dirt. Noise. Silence.

For a long, suspended moment—five seconds? ten? a minute?—I couldn't move. The odor of hot metal and scorched rubber coiled around us like a fog. As if from a great distance, I heard a rhythmic banging and turned to see Bandula throwing himself feebly against the driver's door, trying to get out. He finally climbed out over the side of the car, and immediately fell to the ground as his legs went out from under him. He began to laugh.

I felt numb, floating. I twisted around to look toward the back seat. Lilani sat with her head down, coughing and shaking dirt out of her hair. Beside her, Kumar crawled unsteadily out of his seat and over the trunk onto the pavement. He wandered to where Bandula sat in the road, laughing.

Bandula looked up at him. "It's my mother's car!" he said, as if this were the punchline to a joke. The look of contempt he received from Kumar killed his laugh.

"You are a child," his friend spat. "Why should any of us trust you ever?"

In the back seat, Lilani sobbed, then laughed. She turned toward me and the laugh died in her throat. Her hand trembling, she reached out and touched my face. When she pulled her hand back there was blood on her fingers.

I put my hand to my face, felt it wet and sticky. "Am I badly . . .?" I was afraid to finish the sentence.

"No. I thought for a moment ..." She shook her head. "It's only a cut on your forehead."

Unsure if I had control of my limbs, I crawled out over the driver's door and onto the pavement. As I did, Jayasinghe in the embassy car topped the rise and braked to a halt beside us.

"Mr. Reid!" he cried as he got out and scampered across the road.

"It's all right, it's—" My legs folded up and I sat heavily on the hood of the car.

"Oh, Mr. Reid!"

I think I smiled. It was good. Everything was fine. A sense of peace came over me. My vision narrowed as I began to faint. Like a drowning man determined to keep his head above water, I snapped my chin up to clear my head. "I'm okay."

Bandula looked at the wreck of his car, gave another laugh and turned toward me. "We'll go on to the house in your car."

I tried to fathom whether this was a request or a command but realized he wouldn't understand the difference.

"Shouldn't we wait for the police?" I asked.

"Police?" Bandula squinted at me, puzzled, then carelessly waved at his smashed convertible, like a child turning his back on broken toys scattered across a playroom floor. "It's none of their concern."

※

We rode in silence for about twenty minutes before turning up a dirt road to a side entrance of the great estate outside Colombo. As on the night of the reception, khaki-uniformed policemen opened the gate and saluted as the car made its way up a long graveled drive ending at a paved lot occupied by two Mercedes and a couple of Land Rovers. Jayasinghe parked next to one of the Land Rovers and we all climbed out, each of us walking numbly toward the house, like drifting balloons.

In the light of day, the Jayatilakas' great house looked larger yet less interesting than it had on the night of the ambassador's reception, a huge gingerbready box with a red tile roof and a couple of small second-floor balconies.

We entered through a side door and walked down a hallway into what was clearly a young man's study, outfitted with a television, a stereo and a poster of a race car. Bandula dropped into an armchair and pressed a button on the wall.

Lilani stood in front of him, her arms crossed over her chest. "You've gone mad. What did Thilakaratne say to you that made you act like such a fool? Has he been in contact with—"

"Don't." As he had in the university parking lot, Bandula raised his hand to silence her, but the gesture spoke this time of a deep weariness, pleading to be left alone. "Don't ask me about that." He shook his head. "You must not ask me." He pressed the button on the wall a second time.

More quietly, Lilani said, "Bandula, Mr. Reid is hurt."

Bandula looked at me standing woozily in the middle of the room and winced—at my pain or his own embarrassment at not noticing, I couldn't tell. "Yes. Of course. How could I be so thoughtless, Phil? Let me call—"

"No," Lilani snapped at him. "You'll just show off and have a surgeon brought in by helicopter. I'll take care of him."

Taking me by the arm, she led me like a child down the hall to a small bathroom. She told me to sit on the edge of the tub, then wetted a towel with hot water and began to bathe the blood from my forehead.

"How is it?" I asked.

She peered at the wound. "I think you'll have a scar."

"A memory of my unfortunate …"

The thought drifted away, the dreaminess from the shock of the accident clouding my mind. With the warm towel, Lilani dabbed at my forehead. I thought I'd never felt anything so soothing as the warmth of her touch. She took the cloth away and took a closer look at the wound, leaning in so closely I could feel her breath on my lips, sensed the aroma of her skin. Overcome, unable to think clearly, I put my hand to her cheek and kissed her.

I let her go, hoping for a smile, bracing for a slap. Instead, she slowly pulled back and looked down at me.

Unsettled by her reaction, I asked, "Who are you?" She tilted her head, curious—about me, my question, the impulse that compelled me—and regarded me for a long time but said nothing.

"Who are you?" I asked again, "To Kumar? To Bandula? You're not from his world."

"What do you know about his world—or mine?" She took a bandage, gauze and tape from the medicine cabinet and, kneeling in front of me, dressed my wound. When I started to get up she stopped me with a hand to my shoulder. "You really don't understand what you're involved in." She looked at me as if she were gauging whether her words had sunk in. "And the harder you try to figure it out, the less you will know."

"Involved? Involved in what?"

She searched my eyes, but said no more. She put the things back in the cabinet and, after granting me a peculiar smile, walked out. Still woozy, I followed her down the hall to Bandula's study. A maid was setting down a tray of iced drinks—papaya and mango juices. I picked one up and held the cold glass against my head.

Bandula was sitting with one leg draped over the arm of his chair. "You will be all right, Phil?"

My lingering annoyance with Bandula evaporated at the childlike directness of the question. "Yeah, I'll be fine."

"I'm glad," the young Sri Lankan said. "I blame myself for the accident."

Lilani blew out a breath. "And who else could you blame? Who else was driving that car like he wanted to kill himself?"

Again, the tone of her voice—easing from anger into plaintive regret—took some of the sting out of her words.

Bandula looked up at her, his eyes as sad as any I had ever seen. "I don't want to kill myself," he said quietly. He reached for her hand and held it against his brow while he shook his head slowly, as if it were weighted with thoughts it couldn't hold. "No. I don't want to kill myself."

I wondered again why this rich and powerful young man accepted her rebuke without protest. A thought began to take shape in my mind that, whatever else they might be to him, Lilani and Kumar served somehow as Bandula's conscience, supplying what no one had ever required him to develop.

He saw me looking at him and brushed her hand away. He opened his mouth as if to say something, but his face went suddenly blank and he sat up straight, every muscle rigid.

From the other end of the hall, outside the room, came a woman's voice, raised in anger or excitement or exasperation or simply from a need to speak loudly, the words unintelligible, perhaps unimportant. Footsteps—high heels— tapped along the hallway, growing nearer.

Bandula whipped his leg off the arm of the chair, his eyes wide, fixed on the door.

The voice grew closer until I recognized it. Chiran Jayatilaka. Kumar shrank into the shadows of the corner in which he stood, not from fear—I sensed that fear did not exist in Kumar—but simply from a wish not to be seen, until I half expected him to melt into the wall. Lilani put a protective hand on Bandula's shoulder while he sat with his eyes fixed on the door.

With an almost physical shock, I recalled J. R. Thilakaratne's veiled invitation for me to be of some unnamed service. Could Chiran Jayatilaka have been the presence behind his unspoken request? Lilani had warned me of getting involved in something I did not understand. I felt I stood at the edge of that something, but could not penetrate the darkness veiling it. Still, the idea that the most powerful family in the country wanted something of me struck me as so preposterous that at any other time, in any other place, I would have dismissed the thought as a nasty mash-up of self-importance, paranoia and post-concussion shock. But the idea wouldn't go away.

Like the others, I found myself staring at the door, listening to the approaching footsteps, wondering what they held for each of us.

A voice called out, and as suddenly as they had approached, the footsteps stopped. The voice called a second time. Again, the sound of her footsteps came nearer, but the tap of her talons along the hallway grew hesitant, out of rhythm. She said something, a note of protest or exasperation coloring her voice. After a long moment her footsteps resumed, but now growing fainter, not louder. She was walking away. A distant door slammed shut and she was gone.

In the small room, the sense of anxiety dissipated slowly. Kumar stepped away from the corner. Bandula brushed Lilani's hand from his shoulder, his eyes darting at me then away, wondering if I had seen his weakness, seen his fear.

In that moment, I regretted that his mother had not come into the room. I wanted to know if she knew I was there and, if so, what she wanted of me. I thought again of my suspicions—or were they hopes?—that I had been singled out by this powerful figure for some special purpose. The idea gave me a strange thrill, even while I reminded myself that a yearning for distinction makes a poor lens for seeing clearly.

Bandula licked his lips and tried to recover his air of command. "Well, Phil, I suppose you will be wanting to get back to your office." Despite his effort to appear casual his voice sounded unnatural. He knew it and looked away. The invitation to lunch apparently forgotten, he waved me out of the room as if I were a servant whose services were no longer wanted.

8

A week after the Jayatilakas' reception, the heads of the embassy's various sections gathered in the basement conference room for the weekly Country Team meeting. Under Richard Donovan, the meetings were relaxed but businesslike, with each of us saying a few words about what we'd been up to during the past week and giving him a heads up about pending issues.

As always, Burt Steadman, the DCM, spoke first, followed by McWhirter. After Donovan had asked a question or two of each of them, he turned to the Military Attache, Lieutenant Commander Carl Bogdanovich, who reported that the Sri Lankans were requesting rocket launchers for their air force, despite an American policy of supplying only non-lethal aid in the war against the Tamil Tigers.

Donovan sighed and ran his fingers through his hair. "Remind me why we took sides in this mess."

A short, intense man with a habit of twisting his wedding ring as he spoke, Bogdanovich enjoyed responding to rhetorical questions. "The Tigers sent a suicide bomber against an office building two years ago, sir. Killed dozens of people. So we listed them as terrorists. So now we're required to help the Sri Lankan military."

I had discovered at my posting in Paris that if no one spoke the obvious at these meetings they wouldn't last very long.

Bogdanovich added, "The Tigers do these suicide missions because they haven't got the brains to figure out how to get their people back out."

Richard Donovan didn't smile. "If you strap enough explosives to someone it seems to me you've pretty much precluded any chance of getting him back out."

"That's right, sir," Bogdanovich chuckled, under the misapprehension they were sharing a joke. "You don't get many veteran suicide bombers."

Donovan turned to McWhirter. "You were here then. That's how they got Hamid last year, wasn't it?" he asked, referring to the country's previous Interior Minister.

McWhirter nodded. "Yes, sir. The bomber ran up to his car in the street."

"Their security didn't get him?" Donovan asked.

"They did, sir," Tony Spezza added. "They shot the bomber as he ran up. But these bombs work on push buttons. The bomber pushes down on two buttons as he makes his run. The first arms the bomb. Then he presses the second button and holds it down. When he lets go, the thing goes off. So even if you shoot 'em, *boom!*"

The ambassador shook his head. "Jesus."

Bogdanovich laughed. "The kid's head popped off like a bottle cap after he got Hamid. Took half an hour for the cops to shake the thing out of a tree."

Donovan gave him a "that's enough" look, then turned to Nancy Kawabata, the head of the Econ section. "Tell us about the drought."

Two years younger than me, Nancy was the youngest officer in the embassy. She straightened some papers in front of her with the tips of her fingers. "The fall monsoon hasn't shown up. Rice is shriveling in the fields. If the monsoon finally arrives, all this will be forgotten in a few weeks. If not ..."

Donovan nodded. "Which brings us to the inauguration of the hydro project and the Assistant Secretary's visit. We received a cable today from Washington. Catton's putting off his visit a couple of months. Something about hearings on the Hill." He turned to his DCM. "Burt, will the Sri Lankans put the ceremony off that long?"

Steadman nodded. "Yeah, they really want him here—or at least some other deep breather from Washington."

"This hydro project is one of the Jayatilakas' operations, yes?" Donovan asked, turning back to Nancy.

"They own about half." After a moment's hesitation, she added, "Actually, fifty-seven percent—"

Burt laughed. "You tried to be imprecise, but you just haven't got in you, have you?"

"—as well as fifty-three percent of the country's total electrical energy production," Nancy said as a blush colored her cheeks. "Because of the monsoon's failure, hydro-electric generation has dropped twenty-six percent in the last—"

Donovan said gently, "Nancy, it was a simple question."

She looked up and smiled. "Yessir. It's theirs."

Burt rolled his neck. "Anyway, we'll talk to the Econ ministry about arranging a ceremony. Trot out the press. The usual gang-bang."

Donovan tapped his pen on the desk and turned to me as the one in charge of press matters. "Okay, but I don't want this visit turning into a photo op for the NRP's parliamentary campaign."

"I'll do what I can," I said, but we all knew it would be largely out of our hands.

For those who hadn't been present for the event, Donovan briefly described the Jayatilaka reception, concluding with a question to McWhirter. "So, where's Chiran's husband? What's his name ... Lakshan?"

Burt chuckled. "Living in London, betting on racehorses, and chasing after pretty young men."

"Self-imposed exile?"

The pol officer shrugged. "If he'd tried to stay, someone would have imposed it on him. He's not welcome back."

"And she keeps her own name?"

"He's a Jayatilaka, too," McWhirter replied. "They're distant cousins, so it's only metaphorically incestuous."

The ambassador knitted his brows, looked at McWhirter. "Didn't you mention something about him just the other day?"

"There's a rumor making the rounds that Lakshan Jayatilaka tried to re-enter the country recently. Supposed to have arrived in the middle of the night on a flight from London. Apparently thought no one would notice."

"But someone did." Donovan said.

"Yes, someone here had to know he was coming and may have said something that found its way into the wrong ears. Anyway, he was stopped by airport officials, who put him back on the same plane he came in on. Never got out of the airport."

"So, what's this exile about?"

"Nobody says anything. Something to do with the family. Not that anyone here would make much distinction between the two."

"When was this *visitus interuptus*?"

"As I say, it's at the level of gossip. But it's supposed to have been early on the morning of the twenty-fourth."

I nearly pulled a muscle in my face trying not to react. My speech at the university, Bandula's enigmatic talk with Thilakaratne, the car crash, all of this had occurred on the twenty-fourth. The concurrence seemed too freighted with possibility to dismiss as coincidental. My gut told me they were tied together, though I couldn't see how.

"Why would Lakshan want to come back?" Donovan asked.

McWhirter frowned. "Who knows? At this point there's no love lost between him and Chiran. If there was ever any to lose. Something there goes deep. And ugly."

"You think this trip back might simply have been a personal matter?"

"There's nothing simple about this family. They could give corkscrews a lesson in being twisted. The elections are coming. Maybe he came back to embarrass her. Speak in support of the opposition."

"Tissa Sandanayake's coalition."

"It's possible."

Donovan grunted. "Well, whatever his persuasion now, he seems to have sired a son on her before he took off."

"Yes." McWhirter spoke carefully, searching for the right words. "Chiran keeps the boy out of the limelight. But South Asia's full of hereditary democracies, and that makes him a kind of heir apparent. If he's actually interested—no one knows, if he is—and understands how to fit into the mold, they'll start to fold him in, give him a piece of the action."

Donovan made a crooked smile. "You make them sound like the Corleone family."

McWhirter waggled his head. "It's been said."

Donovan turned to me. "Phil, weren't you playing basketball with him the other night while the rest of us were sacrificing our livers for our country? Tell us about him."

I cleared my throat self-consciously. "Has a little jump shot. Doesn't get back on defense quick enough."

The Ambassador chuckled. And at that moment I made a decision, or realized I had made it before I spoke. I'd come to the meeting with every intention of detailing my chance encounter with Bandula Jayatilaka at the university, my trip out to the family estate, even say a few words about the car crash, telling it all with the humor and becoming modesty that would boost my status around the table, and take me a step closer to being one of the officers who were understood to know the score in Sri Lanka. Yet, even before Donovan's smile had faded, I knew I would say nothing.

I didn't kid myself. Keeping quiet on this was no venial sin. I had an obligation to describe any contact with the Jayatilakas. If there was any connection between the events I'd witnessed and the aborted visit by Bandula's father I was holding back something important. But, for now, I would say nothing. I would guard this bit of professional capital, invest it for the future, returning higher dividends if allowed to mature. If I said anything now, more senior offices—Steadman, McWhirter—would tell me to back off, insist they would take the lead on any contacts with Sri Lanka's first family. I couldn't let that happen, couldn't let this chance slip away. Like the old bulls I'd known in Paris, I would cultivate this contact, then, when it had become a substantial relationship, I'd cash it in, writing a memo detailing and analyzing what I'd learned—the sub-rosa relationships, the hidden motivations, the buried bodies. I would file it like the claim on a gold mine. The Ambassador would be impressed. Steadman and McWhirter would turn green. My career trajectory would go up. Most of all, I told myself, it would redound to the embassy's favor. I was doing it for everyone. But, for all this to happen, I must, for now, keep it from them.

Even as I fashioned this framework of justifications and excuses, I felt on my neck the seductive breath of the hidden life, the lure of keeping a great secret, and knew that the pleasurable shudder it sent down my back was much of what drove me.

The meeting moved on to other matters, and I tried to ignore the dark gust of guilty conscience at my failure to speak truthfully the extent of my contact with Bandula Jayatilaka.

9

"Sunil Fernando's the editor of *The Times*," I told Marina, "Why should I talk to Dharmasena?"

Marina Jayawardena, my Sri Lankan press assistant, looked up from the draft article I was trying to place with a local daily—a canned op-ed from a Deputy Assistant Secretary about the wonders of open markets—and gave me The Look, the one that reminded me that of course I was the boss and I could do whatever I pleased, but I was making a mistake.

"Why?" she repeated, "Because Sunil Fernando spends half his day trying to land a soft job in the President's office and the other half drinking. It's Dharmasena who keeps the paper running."

I tried not to sigh. "Okay. You win."

"No, Mr. Reid. You win." For all her toughness, she had a smile like a movie star.

A voice from behind me called, "Mr. Reid." Chamalie, my secretary, stood in Marina's doorway. I had tried to get the staff, or at least my own secretary, to call me Philip, but they had politely refused. The culture simply didn't allow it.

Tall and gray haired, Chamalie always spoke with grave seriousness. "Post One says you have a visitor at the gate."

"A guy named Potts? Nick Potts?"

"I think so, Mr. Reid."

"Could you run down and bring him up? Tell him I'll be right back."

Nick Potts, an American working for Associated Press out of London, had come into town a couple of days earlier, making the usual rounds of the ministries and political players. I'd promised him a backgrounder on the war and its likely effect on the upcoming elections. For the moment, though, I took the stairs up to the political section.

I found McWhirter sitting at his desk, squinting at a memo he held at arm's length, as if afraid to wrinkle the French cuffs of his expensive shirt. He brought the paper closer as I came in, trying to persuade me he could still read it at that range. He flicked me the barest glance and groaned. "Oh, god, your reporter showed up."

"Chamalie's bringing him to my office." I pulled up a chair and leaned my elbows on McWhirter's desk because I knew he didn't like it. "Just give him the usual briefing. Shouldn't take half an hour."

"Do you know how much work I have?"

"Yeah. That's how I know you can spare the time."

"Tell me, Reid, did you grow up dreaming of pimping for newspaper hacks, or did the ambition come on you in adulthood?" We both knew McWhirter loved to hold forth with journalists, but he always insisted on this Kabuki-like foreplay. "You're perfectly capable of telling him the same things I would."

"But everyone knows you give good interview."

"You're trying to appeal to my vanity." McWhirter put the memo down. "Fortunately for you, that works. I'll be down in a minute."

"I won't forget you for this."

"No, I don't suppose," McWhirter sighed and returned to his memo. "Oh, Reid. They're saying the Catton visit—that power station ceremony—is firm for March. The Foreign Ministry wants to make a big deal out of it. Can you keep the press in line?"

Like most of the American officers, McWhirter held me personally responsible for the slant of every news story about the embassy.

Before I could answer, McWhirter's secretary stuck her head in the door. "Mr. McWhirter, he's here," she said.

In McWhirter's outer office a Sri Lankan man of perhaps thirty-five rose from his seat. Dressed in an impeccable tropical-weight suit, he topped six feet—extraordinarily tall for a Sri Lankan. A handsome man with a receding hairline and large, good-humored eyes, he nodded to a young Sri Lankan woman in western dress, and a short, solidly built man in a sports jacket, who both came to their feet.

McWhirter stuck out his hand. "Ah, Mr. Sandanayake, it's good to see you again."

The tall man smiled broadly. "Robert, the pleasure is mine."

I recognized Tissa Sandanayake from television footage and from photos in the opposition press. Though head of one of the parliament's smaller parties, the rice farmer's son had emerged in the last few months as the public face of the coalition challenging the Jayatilakas' NRP in the upcoming elections.

"The Ambassador's anxious to see you." McWhirter frowned to see I was still present and there was no polite way around introducing me to his contact. "Have you met our Public Affairs Officer?" he asked in a tone that said Sandanayake needn't bother.

The politician smiled broadly. "I have noticed your work for the embassy. Very sound. Very professional." He delivered the remark to McWhirter, a gift on my behalf, and turned to the young woman beside him. "Keep an eye on how he handles the press. There's much to be learned there."

I knew Sandanayake was flattering me, but I couldn't resist smiling. I'd heard of men who could change a room by their mere presence but had never met one until now.

"Mr. Reid."

Chamalie's face appeared through the half-open door of the political section, her eyes wide with anxiety. "Mr. Reid, I'm afraid this man Potts says he is going to leave. He is very upset that you weren't there when he came up." She waggled her head in that ambivalent South Asian way. "I think he's a very difficult fellow."

Reluctantly, I turned to Sandanayake and told him. "I'm sorry, but I need to go back to my office."

He grinned at me. "I think you'd better go put out that fire, Mr. Reid."

Though we in the embassy were, in principle, scrupulously neutral on internal Sri Lankan matters, I found myself wishing Sandanayake the best of luck in the upcoming elections.

The tall Sri Lankan smiled and raised his hands as if to fend off the compliment. "I thank you, but good fortune will always be yours if you work for something greater than yourself."

I knew the remark had not been aimed at me—he could know nothing of my professional infidelities—but I felt its sting.

※

Potts was pacing my office like a man fretting a late train. Well over six feet tall, he had a thin mustache and long black hair brushed straight back. An incipient gut had not yet given up its struggle with gravity.

We shook hands, though Potts seemed to begrudge the gesture of civility. "I got a lot of things to do today," he said by way of greeting.

Most reporters were genial sorts who understood that they lived, at least in part, by ingratiating themselves with their sources. Potts, though, had apparently cast himself in the hero-journalist mode and had no time for niceties.

"I've got the political counselor coming down in a minute."

Potts nodded his head in apparent satisfaction. "He been here long?"

"Couple of years."

Potts nodded again. "This is my third trip here in two years. I've covered the government's side of things better than they deserve. Now I want to go up into Tiger country, talk with Prabhakaran," he said, mentioning the Tamil Tiger's military and political leader.

I assumed a stance of professional distance. "The Embassy strongly advises Americans not to travel into areas controlled by the—"

"Yeah, yeah, I know. I've got a job to do. What's the best way of getting up there?"

I waved the journalist into a chair. Potts pulled out a tape recorder.

"There isn't any good way to get up there," I told him. Potts gave me a skeptical look. "I'm not warning you about going up there just because I have to. It's a very dangerous idea."

Potts snorted. "Okay. No one's going to blame you if I get my toe stubbed."

A.P. had a local stringer in Colombo, a Sri Lankan named Dilip, a good man and a good reporter. The fact that Potts didn't have the courtesy to bring him along meant that he probably wouldn't listen to him about how to keep from getting killed. I began to not much care about hiding my irritation. "Maybe you shouldn't get your hopes up too high. Prabhakaran doesn't speak to—"

"He'll speak to me."

His assurance surprised me. Prabhakaran spoke to no one. Was Potts bluffing or simply ignorant? Or maybe he really did have some sort of line to the Tiger leader. If so, he had to know someone with the rarest of rare connections. "Have you talked to Paul Novak?" I asked him.

Potts nodded. "The Reuters guy here."

"Talk to him. He'll tell you the same thing I'm telling you."

"But if I tell him that I'm going up anyway, he'll tell me the best way? That what you're telling me?"

"No, it isn't."

Potts nodded. I could already imagine his conversation with Novak: "That chickenshit press attaché says ... "

Before I could say more, McWhirter tapped on the door and came in. We took a few minutes going over the ground rules: no quotes by name, all attributions to "a Western diplomat." Potts wanted "an American diplomat," but I told him if that was what he wanted we couldn't go beyond official State Department policy statements, and Potts gave in.

For the next half hour McWhirter trotted Potts through the progress of the war and the current state of Sri Lankan politics. I nodded frequently, trying to show the writer that

I knew this stuff too, but in fact I always learned a great deal listening to McWhirter.

Potts grunted knowingly as he took notes, asking an occasional question. At the end of McWhirter's discourse, he asked, "So, what about this Sandanayake guy, the opposition leader? Didn't I see him coming in here while I was cooling my heels in the lobby?"

McWhirter paused, parsing his sentence carefully before he spoke. "Tissa Sandanayake is not technically the opposition leader. He is only head of a small—"

"Yeah, but didn't I just see him come in here?"

"This is an embassy. We talk to a wide variety of—"

Potts waved his hand as if clearing smoke from the room. "Okay, okay. But he's going to be taking on Susan Guneratne in the next election, right?"

McWhirter spoke slowly, as if Potts' English wasn't very good. "The next elections are parliamentary, not presidential."

"But all the western embassies have the hots for this guy."

McWhirter held up a cautionary finger. He wasn't going to let Potts push him. "Mr. Sandanayake has shown a great deal of political maturity—something this country needs. He's honest. He's smart. He's young. And he's got good judgment. Yes, he could give the President a tough fight in a couple of years."

"And he's trying to position himself for that right now. That's kind of dangerous around here, isn't it? Wasn't there an opposition leader killed here a couple of years ago?"

Potts hadn't figured out that the harder he pushed, the more cautious McWhirter grew.

The political officer looked closely at Potts. "Off the record?"

Nick Potts made a face. "How about 'One observer says.'"

McWhirter paused, looked at me. I shrugged and nodded.

"All right," McWhirter said, "One observer said it would be a good time for someone to remind the Jayatilakas that this is a democracy. Tissa Sandanayake could be the one to do it."

For a few minutes we talked about the economy and the drought. At the end, Potts flipped his notebook shut, turned off his tape recorder and grunted his thanks. Then, apparently overcome by a rogue wave of affability, he asked us if we wanted to go out for a drink. We expressed our sincere regrets and Chamalie led him back down to Post One.

10

The call from Bandula came late on a Monday morning. "I'm coming by to pick you up in fifteen minutes," he told me, giving no hint of where we were going or why, adding only, "There's something I want to show you." Nothing in his voice allowed the possibility of refusal.

Despite my irritation at his sureness that I would drop whatever I was doing to take off with him, I checked my calendar and told him I was free. Besides, I told myself that I didn't want to give the matter enough importance to invent a lie about previous commitments, or to admit that Bandula's sense of urgency intrigued me. I asked if he could meet me at the Oberoi Hotel. I didn't want anyone from the embassy seeing me ride off with Bandula Jayatilaka in whichever one of his mother's cars he hadn't wrecked yet.

When he pulled up in front of the Oberoi in a Land Rover, I was surprised to see he was alone. "Lilani couldn't come?"

He cocked his head at an angle and gave me an inquisitive look.

"Or Kumar?" I added lamely.

Bandula set his chin at a defiant angle. "I don't need them with me all the time." His attempt at toughness came off as defensive.

As he pulled out into traffic, he pressed buttons and flipped toggles, showing off the features of the big car. "It doesn't go as fast as the BMW, so I'll probably be able to keep it on the road," he said with a laugh.

And so he did. It took more than half an hour to get through Colombo traffic, then another hour driving through small villages and thick coconut groves, past wooden shops, rusting gas stations and long stretches of paddy fields, many of them dry and cracked after months of drought.

Finally, Bandula turned off the highway onto a dirt road lined with dusty palms. After a couple of miles the road ended at a wide metal arch, with letters welded to it spelling out "Kelani Children's Orphanage." Above the gateposts, a banner, billowed slightly in the breeze: "STOP THE KILLING!"

Bandula gave me a sidelong glance, anxious to see my reaction.

"Everyone wants to see the killing end," I replied to the unasked question. "It seems neutral enough."

"You haven't been here long enough. Nothing here is neutral."

We passed under the arch and pulled up before a plain stuccoed two-story building. Above its entrance hung a banner saying "CHIRAN, END THE WAR!"

Before the dust stopped swirling around the car, dozens of children swarmed from the large building like bees from a hive calling, "Mr. Bandula! Mr. Bandula!" They quickly surrounded the car, pounding on its fenders and hood, laughing in a cloudburst of goodwill. Behind the children, three women followed, advancing slowly, like farm women herding geese.

The children ranged in age from five or six to perhaps seventeen. All wore clean but faded and ill-fitting uniforms of blue and white. Whatever the condition of their clothes, the children looked healthy and well-fed.

Bandula eased his door open into the press of shouting children. "Back up. Give me room!" he shouted, trying— and failing—to look stern.

With the children hanging onto his arms and legs, Bandula made his way to the rear of the car. "Come on. Get down from there," he said to a very young boy who had crawled onto the roof of the Land Rover. In the ultimate expression of trust, the boy threw himself off the car and into Bandula's arms. Bandula set the boy down, opened the tailgate and began to hand the women the cardboard boxes that filled the vehicle's cargo space. Some of the kids pawed at the cartons, knocking one out of Bandula's hands.

"All right, that's enough!" he said, genuinely annoyed now.

Wide-eyed, the younger children fell silent and backed away. Bandula laughed at their reaction and they brightened again, though quieter now, demonstrating to him how good they could be.

One of the women picked up the spilled carton, which had come open. The children standing beside her "aahed" quietly as she pulled from the box several pairs of deep blue slacks. She gave Bandula only the flicker of a smile, as if her place in life were too humble to presume to judge his actions, even for good. She turned toward the children with the slacks draped over her arm, as a queen might show off her finest raiment.

Bandula quickly unloaded the remaining boxes, pulling from them skirts and slacks and crisp white shirts still in their plastic wrapping—enough for a new set of clothes for each of the three dozen or so children. When he had piled the last of them onto the tailgate a short, swarthy woman with an air of authority, apparently the director of the orphanage, said a few words of thanks, first in English, referring to Bandula's "many acts of generosity," then repeated her brief speech in what I recognized as Tamil.

The director—I heard a teacher address her as Mrs. Prasad—led everyone back inside the large building, where the staff had pushed the desks against the walls of a classroom to make room for a long table spread with refreshments. After perhaps half an hour of pleasant chatter, the director clapped her hands for attention. Again, she expressed her gratitude to "Mr. Jayatilaka," and included me in her thanks. I feared she took my presence as a sign of support from the American Embassy, but I didn't have the heart to tell her otherwise.

The snacks eaten, the speeches done, Mrs. Prasad dismissed the children and staff back to their classrooms. With the children out of sight, she allowed the depth of her emotion to show. Tears brimming in her eyes, she held Bandula's hands in her and thanked him once more for his generosity to the school.

Bandula tried to wave off her thanks, but I could see the effect of her words on him. We made our goodbyes and headed for the car. Still wearing a half-smile from the afterglow of the warmth shown by the children, Bandula put his hand to the car door, but stopped and said, "I'm not ready to leave. Let's walk around a bit."

We strolled the dusty grounds of the orphanage, walked past its half-dozen buildings and around the playgrounds, watched the children laughing among the trees.

"I love coming out here," he said, appearing more at peace with himself than I had ever seen him.

"They love you."

Bandula nodded and shrugged, both accepting and deprecating my words. "Most of them are war orphans. Tamils. A couple of Sinhala who lived in the north." He brightened, taken by a sudden thought. "What do you think, Phil? Maybe we could start the country over from here. Only orphans. No mothers. No fathers. No war."

He tried to make is sound as if he were making a joke. Given the reality of a country tearing itself apart, it might as well have been one, however dark. But I refused to laugh. In the short time I'd known him, I'd sensed that Bandula lacked something everyone else on the island seemed to possess in spades. Cynicism. Despite his sardonic jokes and superficial toughness, he was still capable of hope. And, in this war-wracked country, hope made people vulnerable.

He held up a hand. "I know what you're thinking. And it's true. Here I am a king, not a child. These old buildings and these bare playgrounds are my realm."

"I wasn't thinking that at all."

Bandula's smile faded. "Yet I think of it every time I come out here. Everywhere else I am just the littlest Jayatilaka— the young one, the one who can be ignored. Here I am *somebody*." The word tumbled out with a palpable weight of yearning.

"What does your family think of you running an orphanage for Tamils?"

"They don't know." He saw my skepticism. "Really, they don't. All of us in the family have some money of our own. No one pays attention to what we do with it. Some use it to indulge their vices, to pay off their parasites, to buy influence—as if they needed more. I give most of mine to a business in Colombo, which gives it to a church, which sends it here. No one would bother to trace it. But the children, they know." He made a crooked smile. "I am not a good enough man to wish to remain anonymous."

"I suppose your family wouldn't like that anti-war banner very much."

"My little act of rebellion. Way out here at the end of a dirt road. " He waved a hand at the thick groves of trees surrounding the orphanage. "Only the children and the monkeys see it."

"You don't bring your friends out here?"

"Friends? A fellow like me has no friends." Embarrassed by his note of self-pity, Bandula flung his hands up. "I make nothing but little gestures—just small enough that no one notices. Here, they think I'm a hero, but—" With startling abruptness his smile disappeared and his expression darkened. He grabbed me by the arm. "You don't know how evil she is. How crazy." His voice dropped to a whisper. "She is destroying my country. Someone has to do something about her."

I didn't need to ask Bandula who he was talking about.

"You don't understand what she has done to this island." Bandula's eyes burned into mine. "Or to my family."

"Or to your—"

"To my father?" Bandula had read my mind as neatly as a thief might pick my pocket. "My family has made its fortune from the bones of its countrymen, while the democracy my grandfather promised has been ... perverted." He spit the word out.

I didn't remind him that his grandfather, who had gained the presidency by turning one ethnic group against another,

had been the first to undermine his own pledge. Bandula was
the heir to this history, its ill-starred issue, and understood
it better than I ever would. To Bandula, it was the promise
that mattered, not how completely his family had failed in
realizing that promise. And his grandfather had paid the
price of that failure. When the unrest he created threatened
to undercut his ability to govern the country, he had tried
to stuff the genie back in the bottle by easing some of the
restrictions on Tamils. A few weeks later, while making a
speech in the town of Kandy a gunman, one of the Sinhala
chauvinists whose passions he had ridden to election, shot
him dead. The resulting crackdown on the Tamils had
led some to take to the bush and take arms against the
government. The Jayatilakas had not forgotten the lesson.
Compromise is fatal.

"They've promised fair elections this time," I said.

Bandula tossed his head dismissively. "That can only end
one way—in their total defeat. And they won't allow that
to happen."

I had heard the discussions in Country Team. Everyone in
the embassy understood that the Jayatilakas had made the
concession to hold free elections and admit international
observers because they were sure they would win. In his
hatred of his own family, and of himself, Bandula might
think otherwise, but the NRP's militant nationalism and
old-world socialism still commanded broad loyalty. It
seemed that only the family's youngest son could not see it.

Bandula made a chopping motion with his open hand,
like a professor underlining a crucial point. "When they
lose, you Americans must force them to honor the result.
You must make them. Someone has to take a stand and
stop us, stop my family, if the country is to be saved."

"Bandula, I'm not sure I can promise you—"

He cut me off with a wave of his arm. "We are of different worlds, Phil, you and me." He offered a smile to ease the breach he implied lay between us. "Yet we are very much alike. I knew from the moment we spoke, that day at the university, that you too were looking for an opportunity to do something that would make a difference. No. I realized it before that. I knew when I saw your picture in the paper, trying to save that woman."

"I hardly knew what I was doing."

Bandula shook his head. "Of course you knew what you were doing—even if you didn't realize it. You were doing what so few people here would do. Everyone here is brutalized by years of horror. It has become a part of life, like the heat or the damned crows. But you are fresh and unaffected, an American trying to do the right thing."

I couldn't help thinking how similar his words were to those J. R. Thilakaratne had spoken to me that day in his office. Yet there was a difference. While Thilakaratne had encouraged me in my hope that I could achieve great things, he could not conceal his own cynicism nor his certainty of my naiveté. Bandula, though, embraced that same hope with a purity that made me feel small. I couldn't escape the paradox of thinking that they were, despite their differences, leading me to the same place, a place I couldn't yet see.

I wondered if all of this, their shared interest in me and what I might be persuaded to do, could really have started with a photo of me carrying an injured woman in my arms.

"You know, Bandula, I'm beginning to think that while all the Americans in the embassy thought the picture made me out to be some kind of hero, everyone else in this unhappy country thinks it made me look like a damned fool."

Bandula shook his head. "Not everyone. I believe that a man who would do that wants to do something bigger. We might work together, help each other realize our goals." He said the words with a studied off-handedness that came across as anything but casual.

I felt my skin prickle. "What do you mean?"

Bandula clasped his hands behind his back and straightened his shoulders. "Mean? Nothing." He made a sad little laugh, dodging my question. "Maybe the crowd that hangs out with me is right. They let me talk and talk and talk, and tell me I'm saying nothing." Though his eyes were fixed straight ahead of him, I knew he was watching me closely.

"Maybe they don't understand how serious you are."

But he would not be drawn out and we continued to walk, the weight of unspoken words and unrevealed intentions hanging over our heads. And while we walked, something came clear to me. "Did you meet Kumar here? Was he one of the orphans?"

Bandula shot me an indecipherable glance and fell silent for so long I wondered if my question had transgressed some invisible boundary. The young Sri Lankan walked with his head bowed. I continued beside him, neither of us able to break through the silence growing between us.

But, as I began to foresee a long, silent trip back to Colombo, Bandula began to speak, the words slow and halting at first, then gaining momentum. "I've learned so much from him. Things I never knew. To me he is ... " He raised his hands in a helpless palms-up gesture, unwilling—or unable—to finish the thought.

"It's all right," I said. "I don't need to know." I tried to make the next question sound casual. "And Lilani, she came from here too?"

Bandula shook his head. I couldn't tell if he was saying no, she didn't, or that he didn't wish to talk about her. The joy that lit his face when surrounded by the laughing children had faded, and he looked tired and lost.

I clapped a hand on Bandula's shoulder, as if to take up some of the weight that bowed him down. "It's admirable. what you're doing here. I'm proud to know you."

Fearing irony or flattery, Bandula gave me a guarded look, and saw that I intended neither. "Thank you, Phil. Forget what I said about having no friends."

His broad smile returned and he swept his arm to take in the scene around him. "And here I am king!" He laughed, trying to obliterate everything he had said, and everything he had failed to say.

※

As we left, Bandula kept his eyes in the rearview mirror, watching the orphanage disappear behind us. "One day, " he said," I will no longer be able to do this—come out here on my own, go for a casual drive."

"Why not?"

"I'll be much too busy cleaning out the stables. No time for anything else."

"Stables?"

"We have to sweep out all the old guard. Fire the generals. Get rid of the leeches and cronies." The words sounded like part of a well-rehearsed soliloquy. No doubt Bandula had run this speech by the city's gilded youth until they no longer paid attention. He needed someone who hadn't grown tired of him, who would take him seriously without being servile.

"Yes, it will take a Jayatilaka to rid us of the Jayatilakas." He smiled at the irony. "One day, when I am free, I will travel and learn. I will live far from here. No family. No rank. No history. A simple man enjoying a simple life." He smiled at the prospect.

I sat silently for a moment as I reflected on the irony that each of us depended on his relationship with the Jayatilakas to realize his ambitions. Neither one of us imagined how closely—nor how cruelly—his life would follow his wish.

I tried to say the next as casually as I could. "Speaking of family, I heard that your father tried to come back into the country a couple of weeks ago."

He darted a look at me. "Who is talking to me, Phil? An embassy official or a friend?"

"Bandula, I only—"

He raised a hand, his habitual demand for silence. "Please. Don't say something neither of us will believe." His eyes on the road, he cocked his head toward me. "I have done all the talking today. Now, you talk." He sounded like a king ordering his jester to amuse him. "Start by telling me where you are from in the United States."

"I'm from California."

His mood brightened at the very word. "California! A wonderful place."

"You've been there?"

"Not yet," he replied without any loss of enthusiasm. "But one day I will. California is America. It is where dreams are born. We need to bring those dreams here, dreams worthy of a great people."

I shook my head. "California's more like the place where ideas are tried out to see if they're fit for human consumption. A lot of them aren't."

He laughed, but I could see he didn't want me to spoil his ideas about California. "So, tell me about your family. Your father works in a tall office building and plays golf?"

"No. He's a truck driver."

He blinked in surprise. "But you didn't want to be a truck driver."

"No."

Surrounded by people he couldn't trust, Bandula had developed a keen ear for the unspoken, and sensed my unease at the mention of my father. "You don't want to be like your father?"

"Do you?" I shot back.

His hands gripped the wheel until his fingers turned white, but he made no reply.

I told myself he couldn't have known the unhealed wound he had probed. It was only chance. Me? I knew I'd deliberately stepped onto dangerous ground by asking him if he yearned to be like his father.

After that we rode in silence for a while, our half-formed friendship teetering on the edge. Eventually, though, the anger provoked by my question faded from Bandula's eyes and the moment passed. The young prince of Sri Lanka drew a deep breath and waved his hand as if to take in everything around us—his island country, the relentless weight of his family's excesses, the burden of his ambitions. "Yes, one day, I will be free of all this. Then I will visit you in California."

※

As we neared the main highway, the dirt road climbed up a low ridge. At its crest Bandula pulled the Land Rover to the shoulder and got out. I followed him across the road, where we looked down at a construction site bounded by the surrounding jungle.

Below, inside a ring of cyclone fencing, among the yellow earth movers and bulldozers, stood an electrical power station, its transformers not yet connected. High, two-legged towers trailed in single file across the hills from the northeast like metal giants with a cable in each hand. A similar line led from the site toward Colombo, equally empty-handed, the cables not yet threaded.

"This is the power station your Secretary Catton will dedicate with my mother."

No point quibbling over bureaucratic calibrations distinguishing secretaries from assistant secretaries. "Your mother? I thought the President was going to dedicate the power station."

"Yes, I suppose she'll be there too," he said. "You have to remember who works for whom. This project is important to the family. My mother will want the people watching on television to remember who butters their bread—and who brought money from the Americans." He nodded. "She'll be here."

His eyes brightened with an idea. "Maybe I could arrange for some of the children from the orphanage to dance at the ceremony. Tamil children."

"Then your family would know about your connection to it."

"No, I could just have the orphanage call Susan's office"—I was struck by how casually Bandula referred to his cousin-president—"and tell them that they live nearby and want to take part. Maybe I could arrange it so that—" With a flick of his hand he cut off whatever he might have said next and looked down at the construction site, regarding it for a long time, his eyes widening and narrowing as an unspoken idea played through his head. After a few moments he glanced at me as if wondering if I could see what he saw. When he was sure I couldn't, he said, "No. You're right. My family might figure out the connection. Forget I said anything."

11

Every embassy officer faces an unending list of formal social obligations—attending everything from cocktail receptions and ministerial speeches to representing the embassy at the roll-out of a new charitable organization. They also bear an unspoken commitment to occasionally invite each other for a movie or drinks or small dinner parties. Even here, certain conventions held. Married couples tend to invite other married couples and the singles entertain each other. With my marriage in limbo, leaving me neither entirely single nor convincingly married, I kept my distance from both worlds, pushing myself ever further away from the embassy community. No one mentioned my separation from Jean, but everyone knew, and they chalked up my behavior to a broken heart and I did nothing to make them think they were wrong.

The closest I came to a real friendship was with Tony Spezza, the embassy's other recluse. We occasionally met for a beer at the Galle Face Hotel or went fishing, hiring the skipper of a small boat to take us a few miles down the coast. Even on the water, just the two of us and the skipper, we never said much, each of us sensing the contours of our own pain in the reflection of the other. Tony would have a beer, then one more, until some light in his head would go out. Nothing in his manner suggested drunkenness, but his gaze would turn slowly inward. His silence at these times struck me as a gesture of trust. His job was to ferret out secrets. My deepest impulse drove me to keep them, achieving an odd sort of balance.

If Tony was one of the less frequent dinner hosts, he had proven one of the best, making a point of inviting the admin and visa section wretches and the secretaries, the ones that others forgot—all done with no shadow of condescension, only a feeling that the evening had been dialed down a couple of notches for comfort.

Even at home he wore the same ruthlessly ironed short-sleeved white shirts he wore to work. His only concession to the informality of the evening was to take off his tie, revealing a wedge of spotless white T-shirt. His shoulders squared and his back straight, he looked more than ever like one of the old Mercury astronauts on a day off.

And it would be Tony who wouldn't hire a cook for the evening, as the rest of us would have done, but instead made *coq au vin* and scalloped potatoes—where did he get potatoes in Sri Lanka?—with a salad of cucumbers and tomatoes, rounded off with homemade mango sorbet. When we sat down to dinner Gwen, the ambassador's secretary, took the seat across from me. "I was going to sit next to you," she said, "but I hear you splash your soup."

Tall red-haired, unmarried, somewhere beyond thirty, Gwen belonged to that contingent of women who join the foreign service like men join the Foreign Legion, to leave behind something unspoken. She handled her front-office duties—part secretary, part hostess, part den-mother—with quiet good cheer, giving everyone she dealt with the feeling they held a special place with her. It had taken a long time for us to realize that none of us knew her well.

Like Tony, Gwen had been an exception to my avoidance of embassy social life. We had gone out for dinner a couple of times at restaurants seldom frequented by other Americans. She never asked me about Jean and, in return, I let her talk around anything of importance in her life. When I saw her in the front office the next morning she would act as if nothing had happened between us, and I'd realize nothing had.

Looking around Tony's table, I thought again that an anthropologist should study the peculiar social life of a small American embassy. In the States, friends, neighbors, colleagues, and lovers occupy special orbits, each one discrete from the others. In the world of a small embassy, though, we revolve on a common path, simultaneously filling all of these varied roles, making for a claustrophobic intimacy that leads to endless circles of gossip, most of it terrifyingly accurate. Marital troubles, money worries, drinking problems, office romances become common property. Mike Jarreau, the admin head, had once groused, "A guy can't even have the squits without everyone knowing about it." If the embassy were to install glass walls in every house, few of us would notice the difference.

At a sensible hour, the guests began to make their farewells until the dinner party shrunk down to Tony and me lounging in opposite armchairs with Gwen on the couch between and, like us, a beer cradled in her lap. Maybe it was inevitable that the evening would come down to the three of us, the ones who most held back from the others.

I thought of how lovely Gwen looked, her hair ever so slightly out of place, her stockinged feet propped on the coffee table. She must have caught something in my eye because she turned away, trailing a flickering smile. A little embarrassed, I made some going home noises and started to get up from the chair.

Before I could get to my feet, Tony lifted his eyebrows. "Why don't you stick around a few minutes?" The invitation sounded so casual that I could almost have missed its insistence.

"Uh-oh," Gwen said, "sounds like it's time for some guy-talk." She fumbled for her shoes. "I've got to get up early anyway."

She smiled at Tony's half-hearted offer of coffee. "See you fellas 'round campus," she said and closed the door behind her as she left.

In the renewed stillness, Tony slurped the foam from the neck of a newly opened bottle and didn't quite look at me. "I ran that security clearance by the Interior Ministry today." I'd been trying to hire a part-time translator in the press section and needed a security check. "Clean record. I'll get the papers over to personnel."

"Thanks."

Tony blew out a breath, giving up the pretense that he wanted to discuss bureaucratic ephemera. "I forgot to ask, what was that bandage on your forehead a couple of weeks ago?"

Reflexively, I touched the red line below my scalp. "Cut myself shaving?"

The embassy security officer—for I knew that's who I was talking to now—smiled. "Maybe you had a little traffic accident?"

I could see the scene in the drivers' room: Jayasinghe, afraid that people would hear of the crash, and fearing that he would somehow get blamed, had preemptively related his side of the story to the other drivers and it had drifted like smoke up to Tony's office. We both knew I should have reported it.

I stalled, wondering how much Tony really knew.

"And with one of the Jayatilakas maybe?"

He knew a lot.

I felt a sharp barb of guilt, knowing I had repaid Tony's trust with bad faith. He would care little about my concern that if the people upstairs—the Ambassador, the DCM, McWhirter—learned of my secret cultivation of Bandula Jayatilaka they would tell me to introduce him to themselves then shove me away from what was rightly a political section contact. To confess to Tony my craving for advancement, my need to ride this horse to the finish line of praise and promotion would, for Tony, hold no more merit than a drunk's craving for another beer.

"Y'know, Philip, if our press attaché gets killed riding around with the black sheep of the country's most powerful family, who's going to spin the story to the newspapers for us?" Tony chuckled as if he weren't dead serious.

"Black sheep?"

"Maybe he's a little young yet to qualify for the title," Tony said. "But he hangs around with a bunch of well-heeled deadbeats—and some Tamil kid who looks like trouble. I'm not sure these are the people you want to be running with."

Tony left me a silence that we both knew I needed to fill. I used it to switch the talk to other subjects—work, the drought, and, after a look at my watch, the lateness of the hour.

"Okay." He made the barest of nods. He had to know I was hiding something but maybe, figuring it didn't relate directly to security, he chose, for friendship's sake, to give me a pass this time.

I thought it fortunate that a wave of shame is nothing visible. But I should have been thinking that anything that made me feel like this could only end badly.

When I rose to leave a few minutes later, he stood in the open doorway and clapped me on the shoulder. "Look, Philip, on this thing with the Jayatilaka kid—I'm not exactly giving you a warning. Not laying down the law. Just some friendly advice."

"Sure. Thanks, Tony." I knew I should tell him everything. I felt a twist in my gut at the realization that if I didn't soon tell Tony—or Steadman or McWhirter—I would pass the point at which this secret, rather than serving as my lever to advancement, would start to become my master and me it's slave.

Yet I said nothing but "Goodnight" and walked out to my car.

12

On Friday evenings the Hilton's nightclub became a haven for ex-pats who found themselves in Colombo during a smoldering civil war. Here, Korean engineers jostled for space on the dance floor with German pharmaceuticals execs; French tourists bumped elbows with Chinese manufacturing reps and Indian bankers, while Sri Lankan elites, and well-heeled British cricket fans ogled the girl singer of the Filipino quartet on the bandstand. Though Tony didn't like large gatherings of Americans in such a public place, that evening a group of us from the embassy sat around a couple of cocktail tables in a corner of the room.

I hadn't particularly wanted to go, but didn't want to attract the inevitable attention of once again refusing an invitation for a night on the town. So I straddled the line of my ambivalence by leaning back in my chair and pretending I wasn't there—until Barb Sproul, the Econ secretary, put a hand on my shoulder and startled me back to the present. "Philip, we just never see you."

I knew this was a barely-veiled reference to my no-show for drinks at the Sprouls' place a couple of weekends earlier.

She shifted her San Antonio twang into a soft purr, like a cat trying to persuade you it has no claws. "And when are we going to meet that wife of yours?"

Meow.

For months, I'd been expecting to hear that Jean had filed for divorce. But the moment hadn't come, and I didn't know why. Maybe she hadn't yet forced herself, as I had, to face the unhappy fact that our marriage was over. Whatever the reason, I sure as hell didn't want to discuss it with Barb Sproul. So, I cupped a hand over my ear and nodded helplessly at the amped-up band. Before she could repeat herself, I felt a hand on my arm. It was Gwen, bless her heart. Knowing Barb, she sensed I needed bailing out and had come to rescue me. With a double-wide smile in Barb's direction, she squeezed my arm and nodded toward the bandstand. Offering Barb a shrug of counterfeit regret, I followed Gwen onto the dance floor.

We shouldered our way through the throng until we were obscured from view by the other dancers. After a quick peek to make sure no one from our tables could see us, Gwen put her mouth to my ear and asked, "What's up? Barb hitting on you?"

"She's asking where Jean is."

"Ouch. Low blow, Romeo." She pulled back until she could look me in the eye. "But you can't be surprised. If you don't make yourself part of the club, you're looking for the wrong kind of attention. Anyway, forget it. Let's dance."

The band switched to a slow number and I started to put my arms around her, but she took my left hand and raised it into ballroom position. "You've got enough people talking behind your back without that," she said and gave me a conspiratorial wink to ease the blow.

Content with the world, I looked around the dance floor, taking in the scene around me as part of the bouquet of the moment. As I did, the crowd parted for an instant and I thought I caught a glimpse of Nick Potts walking across the hotel lobby with Bandula Jayatilaka.

As quickly as the gap had appeared, it closed again and I lost sight of the two men. Knocked off-center by the idea of the AP correspondent, who said he was headed for Tiger country, talking amicably with the scion of the Jayatilakas, the Tigers' most implacable foes, I told myself that, no, I must have been mistaken; it didn't make any sense at all.

13

One of the pleasures of serving as the Public Affairs Officer was the chance to oversee the American Library, housed in a former villa a mile or so from the embassy. The graying head librarian, Shirani Jayasekera, was one of the stars of the embassy staff, as smart and capable as any of the American officers.

A few days after the evening at the Hilton, I went over to her shop to attend one of her weekly staff meetings, which she ran with the solemnity of a Security Council meeting. After she had summarized library activities over the last week, I gave the staff my regular rundown of what was going on in the other sections of the embassy. Usually, I left at that point, but decided that day to stick around. For a few minutes I leaned back and forgot about Bandula and Tony Spezza and that sonofabitch Potts and listened contentedly to discussions of book orders and movie screenings and circulation figures. When the meeting ended I headed toward the door, strolling through the reading room and book stacks, past the students studying for exams or talking quietly in an atmosphere of thoughtful calm.

Like a tune playing quietly in my head, the image of Lilani had lingered in my mind since the day of the accident, her face often before me as I went through my day—so often that when she finally stood right in front of me, browsing through the fiction stacks I almost took her for a mirage.

But she saw me clearly.

"You don't have enough Henry James," she said, stopping me with a smile before softly adding "Philip," as my heart flipped over.

In a relapse of the blissful daze I'd suffered when she dressed the cut on my head put my arms around her and kissed her on the top of the head.

I felt her laugh and suddenly remembered where we were. As if burnt by a flame, I quickly pulled away and looked around to see if anyone had been watching.

"Ah, it's kisses all around for patrons of the American library." She laughed at my embarrassment. "Whose circulation is it you wish to increase?"

My face reddened and I stammered, "I… I'm…"

Her smile wavered. "If you apologize I'll slap you right in the face."

"Are you here alone? Do you have a car?"

She looked into my eyes and nodded wordlessly.

"Let's get out of here."

Outside, I told my driver to go back to the embassy, and drove with Lilani to the Galle Face Hotel, where I asked for a table on the lawn overlooking the sea.

※

A fresh wind whipped the edges of the checkered tablecloth and the coconut palms swayed overhead. Whitecaps on the normally quiet sea added their grace note to the pleasant turmoil in my mind. We chatted about nothing in particular. I told her a bit about my life—though not about Jean, it was too early for that—and described my work, conscious that I was trying to impress her. I talked of California, my years at college, of teaching high school, of road trips, and hiking in the Sierras. She listened closely, watching my face as I spoke, as if searching for a truth beyond my words.

When I finally wound down, I wanted her to say, "What an interesting life," or "You've done so much." What I got was, "But why have you not told me who you are."

In another setting it might have been seemed inconsequential, even an invitation to flirt. But I heard the echo of that day at Bandula's house, when I had asked her the same question. She turned her head away slightly and looked at me out of the corner of her eye, as if only a skewed look, a stolen glance would suffice to see me correctly. "You are a man who likes to keep his secrets."

My face burned. "What makes you think that?" The clumsiest of dodges.

She pivoted away, but her eyes never left me.

"Philip, who do you trust with those things you don't tell anyone else? There must be someone. Your brothers and sisters?"

"No brothers. No sisters."

"Your mother, your father."

I tried to make a joke of it. "No. In the U.S. at least, the last people we tell anything to are our parents."

Her face darkened and I regretted my flippant tone. So I talked about Mom, her warmth, told how she cared for her plants throughout the hot, endless summers, how I laughed at her flightiness. I told her how, when I was a boy, she had developed cancer, was told she would likely die.

"I couldn't take it in. At that age we think our parents are indestructible. There was a part of me that was terrified, but I knew I couldn't talk to anyone about it, so I kept it inside."

"But lived."

"Yes. She lived."

"Because you kept your secret."

"Well, not because—" Then I understood what she was saying, and I couldn't speak.

"But you have two," she said.

"Sorry?"

"You have two parents."

"Well, yeah, sure."

"Your father," she prompted.

"My dad." I leaned back in my chair, unconsciously putting distance between us. "He's a truck driver."

She waited a moment. "That's all? You tell me all about your mother, but about your father you say, 'He's a truck driver.' Nothing more."

In my mind I saw again the vital, big-bellied man who drove a set of doubles for one of the farms that covers the wide, rich earth of California's central valley, saw him leaning over the big steering wheel, remembered him grunting as he hauled himself in and out of the cab, joking with the other drivers in that deep authoritative voice, slapping backs, lending his strong back and wide shoulders to the guys loading his truck with tomatoes and lettuce and peppers. I regarded him as if he were a mythic creature, like Hercules or the Minotaur, taking his energy from the sun, renewing himself through the sweat that dripped off his arms and face and turned his shirt black.

Even while I tried to persuade myself I'd said enough, the words came stumbling out, haltingly at first, then with greater sureness. "When I was a boy, he let me ride with him in summer. He wasn't supposed to. Company policy. So I couldn't just go with him down to the yard and hop in. Instead, he'd tell me to take a bus out to some little crossroads in the middle of nowhere and I'd get off and wait. God, it was hot, waiting, but I knew he wouldn't let me down."

These weren't the words I'd thought I would say to her about my dad. It seemed they had chosen me and I wasn't sure I could continue. "I'd see his big truck coming down the road. He'd pull over, reach across the cab and pop open the passenger door. And I'd be looking up at him, way up there, smiling down at me. Then I would climb up in his cab. He had a thermos with cold water, and he'd give me a long pull. I remember how it tasted of the coffee he'd filled it with in the morning, but I didn't care. It was cold, and it was my dad's." I found myself smiling at the memory.

But no, I wouldn't let him beguile me again. I waved a hand to make it go away. "A long time ago."

"You talked a lot on these trips? Just father-son."

Not wanting her to see how I was struggling, I knew I had to continue—found that I wanted to. "Couldn't talk. The truck was ancient, no a/c, so we had to roll the windows down and the short exhaust stack was right by my ear. Even shouting, we could hardly hear each other. No, we didn't talk much." For a moment it all came back so strongly that I was no longer sitting at a table on the edge of the Indian Ocean, but back in that big noisy Peterbilt, riding through the San Joaquin Valley next to my dad. "Maybe the whole ride was a conversation," I said, more to myself than to her. The longing to go back and start life over was so strong that my voice faltered.

"What happened?"

"What do you mean?"

She looked at me steadily.

I'd heard the question, knew what she was asking. I shrugged like it was no big deal. "Happened? Nothing really."

We both knew I was lying, about my dad, about me. I wanted to tell her everything, but I couldn't, the need to keep it back, to hold onto the secret, too ingrained. Finally, I could only look away and say. "You grow up. Find out things aren't like they seemed when you were a kid. You move on."

I had pulled away from her when she first asked about my dad. But as I told her my story I found that I had gradually leaned forward as I told—and didn't tell—my story, until my face was only inches from hers. Abruptly, I retreated again. "But enough about me. Let's talk about you." I trotted out the cliché for a laugh and I respected her for not smiling. "You and Bandula are close, yes?" Though I had tried to pose the question casually, I knew, the moment the words were out of my mouth, that my question could not have been more blunt.

It didn't come easily for her, any more than it had for me. She opened her mouth to speak, but then closed her eyes tightly, as if pain had taken her voice. When she opened them again, I thought they were the saddest eyes I'd ever seen. "It's already started," she said, her words barely a whisper.

"Started? What are you talking about?"

"Our secrets are driving us away from each other."

I felt a hot wave pass through me, a wave that might have been shame, might have been fear. "Which ... what secrets?"

She knew I was evading her, just as I sensed she had, in her way ever since we met, been evading me.

"Philip, I told you once that you don't understand what you were getting into."

"By knowing you? By taking the risk of getting close to you?" I reached across the table and took her hand.

It was too much. Lilani pulled her hand back. She murmured something, but the wind snatched her words away and I caught only, "I'm sorry, but I have to go."

She rose from her chair so quickly I thought she might start running.

"Now? Just like that?"

"Yes, I …" She tried to laugh it off, but the laugh died in her throat. Then she leaned across the table and gave me a lingering kiss to the cheek, like a promissory note on an unknown debt.

As she walked away she looked back twice, once to smile at me again, and once to make sure I wasn't following her.

14

It took nearly three hours to cover the seventy-five miles from Colombo to Kandy, a slow tedious journey compensated by our escape from the heat and humidity of the coastal plain. The hazy, humid air grew cooler, and I breathed it in like a balm to the lungs as the road twisted among the hills, covered by dense tropical forest.

Yes, a slow and tedious journey, except when it was absolutely terrifying.

I suppose the highway might have been perfectly adequate at one time, but its two pot-holed lanes now struggled vainly to channel four or five meandering streams of traffic. Overloaded trucks tilted alarmingly, seeming to run forward and tip over at the same time. Sardine-can buses muscled their way through swarms of three-wheeled tuk-tuks, the beeping horns of the tiny vehicles as incessant and annoying as the buzz of mosquitoes. Sprinkled among these little pests, plodding oxcarts and wandering cows cluttered the road like moving roadblocks. And, like a vision straight out of Rudyard Kipling, the occasional *mahout* walked along the shoulder of the road with his elephant, searching for work at a construction site or timber camp.

Behind the wheel of the embassy car, Jayasinghe smiled as if at a little joke each time he dodged the onrushing apocalypse of buses, cars and trucks that jumped into our lane as they passed slower-moving vehicles. Meanwhile, I sat in the back seat, twitching and gasping at the unending string of near misses.

Jayasinghe looked in the mirror and smiled. "This won't last much longer, sir."

The frightening ambiguity of his promise only increased my anxiety.

Eventually, we topped the last forested ridge and looked down on the town of Kandy, lying within a bowl formed by the surrounding hills. A lake dominated the center of the town. On its shore stood the island's most revered Buddhist temple. In the days of the old kingdom, before the British had come, Kandy had been the island's capital. The old palaces and offices of state had crowded around the temple's thick walls and flaring rooflines, dissolving any distinction between spiritual and temporal order—or, more accurately, lending the government the mandate of heaven by its proximity to the temple complex. For the island's Sinhala majority, overwhelmingly Buddhist, the temple represented the navel of the world, its physical and spiritual center.

Though the last kingdom ended with the takeover by the British, Kandy remained an important regional capital and I had booked two days of appointments with local government officials, civic leaders and administrators of the local university, ending with the visit I looked forward to the most, a call on the editor of the *Kandy Herald*, one of the few newspapers published outside of Colombo. I enjoyed the *Herald's* small town feel and admired its earnestness even as I puzzled over its syntax, coming to cherish such quirks as the headline for a story about an activist civic association that read, "Kandy Ass. Deserves Respect."

By the time I'd run through my first day's appointments, Colombo's clogged and bafflingly crooked streets had come to seem as straightforward as an interstate compared to those in Kandy. I ran behind schedule all day. The local figures I met took my tardiness with good grace, pouring me endless cups of tea until I thought my kidneys might shut down. I filled a notebook with their views, and was struck by their perspectives on politics, the economy and the war, all of which differed greatly from those of their counterparts in Colombo.

By the end of the day, I was charmed, better informed, and exhausted, happy to head back to my hotel.

※

I leaned against the wooden bar of the New Orient Hotel, situated a couple miles outside of town, swirled the ice in my gin and tonic and took a deep, unsatisfying breath of the heavy night air coming off the Mahawela River.

An acquaintance at the Australian embassy had once told me that it was the rulers of the British Raj in India who had invented the gin and tonic. "The tonic, y'see, was used to ward off malaria," he explained.

"And the gin?" I'd asked.

The Australian had laughed at my denseness. "To get you so facking drunk you forgot you were in facking India."

The drink also proved to be one of the compensations of living in the tropics. The sharp tonic, a touch of bitters and a generous pour of gin could, for a moment, push back the weight of a muggy night, affording a momentary safe harbor in a sea of sweat and heat. That night its gentle haze also cushioned the pounding of tropical drums and the jangling of copper bracelets from the local dancing troupe performing on the veranda outside the bar.

With their billowing red pants, bare chests and fey-looking metal headdresses, the young men twirling on the terrace appeared determined to prove that they could smile as vapidly as any troupe of Las Vegas chorines. Yet a seriousness clung to the performance, a lingering echo of the day when their dances served as an offering, intended to propitiate powerful spirits rather than amuse foreign tourists.

And after a couple more drinks, I told myself, I would know exactly how the gods felt about it.

A tap on the shoulder interrupted my search for meaning. I looked up to find a familiar mustachioed face smirking down at me.

"Well, Nick Potts, what a total drag to see you here."

Something about this tickled Potts—probably the mistaken notion that I was joking—and the AP reporter settled onto a stool next to mine. "Why don't you get rid of that pin-striped suit, Reid? Makes you look like a wandering Mormon."

"I thought you were going up to Apache country or something. Change your mind?"

Potts' eyes shifted away. "Maybe."

Fine, I thought. I wasn't going to try to beat the truth out of him.

"I came up to write a sidebar on Kandy. Cultural capital and all that stuff," Potts said, nodding at the dancers on the terrace.

The drums made real conversation impossible, and after

a few minutes I could see that Potts was only half there anyway, his words coming in short careless snatches as he glanced at his watch and looked over his shoulder toward the lobby.

The dancers ended their performance and exited past the hotel swimming pool while the bartender turned the TV back to the cricket match they had interrupted. Potts ordered another scotch and looked again at his watch. He didn't object when I asked for the tab.

It struck me as strange. Visiting correspondents usually tried to pump me for off-the-record stuff until I almost needed a crowbar to pry myself away from them. But Potts seemed oddly incurious, even anxious for me to leave.

When I paid for my drinks and turned to say goodnight to Potts, I found the reporter looking once more toward the lobby, not, this time, as if he were searching for someone, but as if he had found him.

I followed his gaze and saw, just inside the hotel entrance, a young man in a threadbare shirt and faded slacks. Already, the concierge had come out from behind his desk to shoo this low-caste hustler back outside.

"A friend of yours, Nick?" I was laughing, but he couldn't have understood why.

"Huh?" Potts jumped as if he'd stuck his finger in a socket. "No. Just some guy who said he'd show me around the town."

"It's ten-thirty at night, Nick."

"Yeah, well ..." Potts said avoiding my gaze, "We're just going to arrange things for tomorrow."

"Y'know, I need someone like that myself to guide me around Kandy. I'd like to meet him."

Potts chuckled uneasily. "He's just some kid guide.

Probably not worth..." His voice trailed off.

By now the concierge had the protesting young man halfway out the door. Potts, with a last distracted look my way, rose and hurried toward the lobby.

Hands in my pockets, enjoying myself now, I sauntered after him.

"Ah, Mr. Potts," the concierge said with a smile as he saw the American approaching from the bar. "Do you know this boy? He insists that—"

"Yeah, yeah, he's fine," Potts said and waved the concierge back behind his desk. He frowned when he saw I'd come with him. "Maybe I'll see you in the morning, Reid."

"Sure," I said.

I had been in Sri Lanka long enough to know that I should simply accept certain things, rather than try to understand them. Why should I let on that I already knew his guide? After all, despite the suspicion I saw in his eyes, Kumar didn't let on that he knew me. Finding him here with Potts startled me into catching, behind the play-acting, a glimpse of the truth. The facts hung together almost too neatly. Kumar's presence in Kandy, Potts' certainty that he would get an interview with the Tiger leader—and the sight of Potts walking with Bandula through the lobby of the Hilton the previous Friday. I was sure now that I hadn't imagined it. Bandula, with Kumar as his agent, would gladly serve as Potts' means of getting through the Tigers' lines up north. The question I couldn't answer was "why?"

"Look, Reid," Potts said, "I think I can handle this by myself now."

Tormenting Potts was fun, but probably a vice. I could confront the two of them with what I suspected was the truth and listen to them deny it all night long, but it was getting late, and I decided to let it go.

I'd said goodnight and turned to head toward my room when a long, thundering boom, like distant thunder, rolled across the sky. Everyone in the lobby looked out the picture window toward the center of town, two miles off. Only with the fading of the rumbling concussion did we realize we had all, a couple of seconds earlier, caught the sight of a distant flash.

It seemed everyone in the room had stopped breathing.

I looked at Potts. "I've got a car and driver."

The reporter nodded. "Let me get my camera. I'll meet you out front in three minutes."

15

The embassy car's diplomatic license plates got the four of us—Potts insisted on bringing Kumar—through two hastily thrown up checkpoints that blocked the roads near the lake. At the third roadblock an army officer stood in front of a waist-high metal barrier and told Jayasinghe we couldn't go any further. Behind him, black smoke, faintly lighted by flames, billowed into the night sky from around the temple.

I got out and pressed into the mob jammed against the barricade, all of them shouting at the officer that they wanted or needed or absolutely had to get through. Sirens echoed from every direction. I elbowed my way as far as the barrier and flashed my diplomatic ID at the officer. Some of the people pressing against me registered my suit and my white skin, and their importuning took on an almost frantic note as they saw that some Westerner, living in his world of unearned privilege, was about to trump them once again.

The Sri Lankan officer's eyes darted from the besieging throng to me, then darted back at the crowd, apparently hoping that if he ignored me I might go away.

I shouldered aside a large woman who had been sticking her finger in the officer's chest.

The soldier shouted at me over the noise of the crowd. "What do you want?"

With a little bump of surprise, I realized that I wasn't sure. I had come, in part, out of curiosity—perhaps morbid—and, in part, from a desire to be the man on the spot for the embassy, to gather information on a momentous event. That I had missed my chance after the bombing at the bridge on the day of my arrival made me all the more determined. Lurking under this, I sensed something else—a perverse yearning to impress my will on this soldier, to force him to let me through for the simple fact that he wished to stop me.

Drunk on this volatile mix of motivations, the only thing I knew for sure was that I had come too far to back down. "I have a report there are injured Americans over there," I lied.

The officer raised his chin in a little gesture that somehow looked more defensive than defiant. "No one is allowed past this point," he said. He was a slim man, very fit, with the kind of posture that made him look taller than he was. Behind him, a corporal, picking up on his lieutenant's growing agitation, unshouldered his assault rifle and waved it at me. A drop of sweat ran down my back, reminding me that the young, poorly-trained draftees were known to fire with little provocation.

"You are required by diplomatic conventions to let us through," I told him, compounding my previous lie with a new one, feeling the danger grow as I pushed the already unnerved officer further into a corner and, at the same time, ratcheted up the aggravation of the machine gun-toting corporal, who had wrapped his finger around the trigger. I felt my pulse quicken with the increasing peril, and worried that I was beginning to enjoy the danger.

The officer licked his lips and put his hand on his sidearm. Fear—not physical fear, but the fear of doing something wrong—came off him like heat from a furnace, feeding his anger.

The corporal pulled back the action on his gun. My knees began to shake. A trembling thrill of adrenalin-fueled exhilaration ran through me, a sense that I had landed in the middle of a movie that a moment ago I had simply been watching. Pushed by a perverse wave of elation, I nearly laughed, but knew for a certainty that the corporal would shoot me if I did.

"C'mon, Reid!" Potts shouted, leaning out the car window, "It's not worth—"

"Shut up," I told him, even as I wondered why getting through this barrier had become so important to me that I would risk getting killed for it. I looked at the officer, urging him, daring him, to make a decision, any decision.

A pickup truck full of policemen pulled up behind the embassy car. Its driver leaned on the horn and shouted something out his open window. From behind the barricade, the corporal looked at his officer, pleading for a command.

Potts shouted, "For God's sake, Reid!"

The driver of the police pickup again laid on his horn. I looked at the officer, communicating to him what I was sure we both knew—he wasn't going to shoot a diplomat, a Westerner, a white man, simply for wanting his way. And he hated himself for it. It was the self-loathing that made the moment dangerous.

Once more the policeman leaned on the horn of the pickup. The officer trembled with indecision.

I nodded at him, even dared to give the man an easy smile, as if we were sharing a joke.

With a strangled shout, the officer drew his pistol, crying out something that I wasn't sure was intelligible in any language. But he waved the pistol at the police car, not at me. Furious, he barked a command at his corporal, who looked at him for a long moment, then, with an expression of disdain, turned toward the two soldiers manning the barricade and ordered them to roll it out of the way.

※

The tire tracks told the story. The bomber's truck had left the road a hundred yards back and sped toward the temple along its deserted promenade. The driver, maybe too excited, coming too fast—who could fathom the mind of a man who knew he was about to die?—had let a couple of wheels drift onto the grassy verge, tearing up the turf. Running along the wall of the temple complex for perhaps fifty yards, he had wrenched his small truck onto the great moonstone, the flat carved stone, itself holy, that sanctified the entrance to the temple. Then he had detonated his bomb.

We got out and I told Jayasinghe to stay with the car. My legs still trembled with the madness of the encounter at the barricade as I walked toward the temple entrance. Potts followed a few steps back, his camera on a strap over his shoulder. Kumar trotted a couple of paces behind, just close enough that no one would doubt he belonged with us.

Near the entrance to the temple complex I flashed my diplomatic ID at a soldier and braced for another confrontation. He waved me through without a word. I gestured that Potts and Kumar were with me.

The force of the explosion had blown the truck's back wheels twenty yards across the grass and twisted the still-burning hulk of the cab. Shattered stone from the arch over the moonstone had fallen into the truck's broken bed. Headlights from a dozen official vehicles—police cars, ambulances, a fire truck—cast a cat's cradle of crisscrossing beams on the flames and smoke. A few onlookers who had sneaked through the cordon around the site stared dumbly at the burning wreckage.

Trying to look resolute and purposeful, men in uniform milled around the destruction, arrived too late to do any good. Their anger at their own impotence cast an ugly mood over the scene.

Within the temple grounds lay piles of broken stone and a few scattered heaps of saffron cloth—the bodies of priests unlucky enough to have been standing near the entrance when the truck exploded. Under the vehicle lay the sacred moonstone, shattered by the blast, the very portal of paradise violated.

Ignoring the still-sputtering flames from the truck, several soldiers crowded around its cab. With a collective roar they wrenched open the twisted door and yanked out a long, bloody pile of cloth and flesh that a short time ago had been a human being.

They dropped what remained of the bomber onto the ground and gaped at his mangled corpse, as if he had been made momentarily holy by the enormity of his crime. Then one of the soldiers gave the body a kick. Quickly, the others joined in, viciously kicking the shattered body, channeling the fury of their offended gods.

A television crew turned its camera on the soldiers who, bathed in the camera's bright light, began shouting at the newsmen. A large man in a police uniform ran up, waving his arms and shouting at the TV crew. When they ignored him, he struck the cameraman on the side of the head with his baton.

Potts rapidly snapped pictures, his camera's flash freezing the action into broken pieces.

I needed to warn him that he was quickly turning himself from observer to provocateur. "Hey, Potts, maybe you'd better not—" But I was interrupted by another shout from behind us.

A couple of the onlookers had somehow recognized Kumar as a Tamil—I never understood how Sri Lankans could instinctively sense each other's identity—and rushed him from behind. One of the men, clad only in a sarong, hit Kumar with a looping blow that dropped him to one knee. Scrambling to his feet, Kumar backed against the hood of a police car, like a cornered boxer leaning on the ropes.

Before they could hit him again, Potts shoved himself between Kumar and his attackers, shouting, "No! No! He's mine."

Two soldiers came out of the darkness, lashing out at whoever stood within range of their rifle butts. Potts held up his hands, but got only as far as, "American journ—" before taking a blow across the face, then a heavier one in the gut that knocked him to his knees.

Like sharks drawn to blood, more soldiers ran up out of the darkness.

Blinded by headlights, I waved my diplomatic ID, shouting, "Stop! Stop!" at the shadows moving around me. The elation from my confrontation at the barricades had vanished and fear came on me like a fever.

In front of me a dark form blocked the light and I felt a blow to my ribs, then another to the side of the head. I dropped to the ground and curled into a ball.

In their adrenaline-spiked confusion, the soldiers now turned their rifle butts against the men attacking Kumar—not out of any urge to protect the young Tamil, but only to reassert their monopoly on violence. If there were any beatings to hand out, they would be the ones to deliver them.

When one of Kumar's attackers crumpled to the ground with blood gushing from his head the others ran. The soldiers chased them into the darkness and our small corner of the night's events fell silent again.

I tried to take a deep breath and gasped in pain from the blow to my ribs. As I struggled to get to my feet, hands grabbed me under the shoulders. Fearing another beating, I swung my elbows furiously, crying out from the pain as I did.

"Mr. Reid, it's me!"

"Ah. Jayasinghe, help me," I gasped, humbled by the abject tone I heard in my voice. Fighting a wave of dizziness, I stumbled over to Potts and with Kumar's help brought the reporter to his feet. For a long while Potts stood with his head down, his hands on his knees, panting with anger and residual fear. He dabbed at his face with a handkerchief and nodded to himself when he saw no blood.

"We should get you to a hospital," I said.

Potts shook his head. "Where's my camera?"

Jayasinghe found it lying on the pavement, still in one piece.

"Good," Potts said between gritted teeth. "I got my pictures. I need to get back to my room and file a story." He saw the expression on my face. "It's okay. I've been hit before."

"You're nuts," I told him, not without admiration.

On the ride back to the hotel my shaking legs gradually fell still. Gingerly, I felt around my bruised ribs and decided I probably hadn't broken anything. Next to Jayasinghe, Kumar sat staring into the darkness, unmoving, only his eyes alive. Potts leaned weakly against the window, his hand over his eyes.

"You okay, Nick?" I asked.

After a long moment he grunted, "Yeah." The flicker of a smile crept across his face. "I almost forgot to thank you for a lovely evening."

I tried to laugh, but it hurt too much.

16

Back at the hotel, we stumbled out of the car while the valets shook their heads and "tsked" worriedly. Potts refused the concierge's offer to call a doctor, but agreed to let Jayasinghe help him to his room. As the two men limped slowly into the hotel, Kumar began to walk off into the darkness.

"No," I told him, "You're coming with me."

※

The act of turning the room key felt like a fresh blow from the rifle butt, but I got the door open and stumbled over to the mini fridge, where I took out a bottle of cold water and placed it against my ribs. Kumar stood in the open doorway, his face a mask of hostility and uncertainty.

"Come in. Shut the door," I said. When I heard the door close I expected to find Kumar gone. But he had stayed, standing in the middle of the room, shifting awkwardly from one foot to the other as if he might yet run.

I tried sitting in a chair but found I could only manage the pain by lying down on the bed. I nodded Kumar toward the chair but he didn't move.

"Tell me why you're helping Potts," I said.

Kumar only glared at me.

"Look, I'm not the police. I'm not the CIA. I'm not going to have you arrested. I only want to know what's going on."

His hands balled into fists, Kumar's eyes searched for enemies in the shadows around him. His English wasn't strong, and I didn't know how much he understood of what I was saying. It was strange speaking to a man in one language, knowing that he was thinking in another.

Daunted by my task, I nearly gave up, certain that the chasm between us, made up of language, culture, status—of everything that mattered—would never allow us to understand each other, no matter what words we used. On the other hand, that flash of craziness I'd shown at the barricades might have lent me a madman's not inconsiderable stature. I decided to press whatever advantage it gave me.

"Don't worry. Potts didn't say anything. I happened to see him with Bandula a few days ago and put it together. I know this is Bandula's idea, not yours. Do you know someone with the Tigers? Or maybe Bandula just figures any young Tamil can find a way to make contact with them."

Kumar said nothing.

I remembered the Tamil's hostility at the basketball game on the night of the reception, undercut by his oddly respectful handshake. For all his defiance, Kumar could not shake the habit of deference, born of a lifetime of submission to those whom he had always been told were his betters. And, like the officer at the barricades, he would despise himself for it.

Could that be the thread that bound Bandula and Kumar together—that when they looked in the mirror they both despised what they saw? And the only way they could avoid self-destruction was to turn this contempt for themselves into anger and direct it outward.

I tried to act more at ease than I felt. "It's just that I don't understand. Bandula wants Potts to go up north, get an interview with Prabhakaran. He wants Potts to write an article. One that no Sri Lankan would be allowed to write. One that will make his mother look bad in the western press."

When Kumar broke his silence he spoke quietly, barely above a whisper, as if afraid someone might overhear him even here. "What do you know about anything?"

"Maybe nothing. So, help me understand. Does Bandula really hate his family enough to—"

"His mother is an evil person," he said, almost shouting, as if he knew his few words could not convey the depth of his hatred. "You don't know anything."

Kumar's rudimentary English could not disguise how closely his thoughts paralleled Bandula's or how, for both of them, the dark twins of anger and fear twisted around their hearts.

"Kumar, I'm not your enemy. Sinhala, Tamil—I don't care. Okay, I sound like some naïve foreigner. But maybe you could use some naiveté around here. All I know is that in a couple of years I'm going to leave Sri Lanka behind and move on to my next post. That'll be a lot easier to do if I can say to myself that I accomplished something while I was here, did something worthwhile." I didn't add, "and got promoted for it."

He glowered at me, said nothing.

Start over, I told myself.

"Okay, you met at the orphanage, yes?" Did he understand the question? Did he understand anything of what I had said? "You lived in the orphanage when you two met. I can see why you would be friends. He'd lost one parent. You'd lost both. In the war. Am I right?"

"Yes!" The word came at me like a bullet. Kumar's eyes widened. "No!" He tried to regain his pose of silence, his control over himself, but the words poured out, expelled by the pressure of a tormented heart. "No. Not in the war. There wasn't any war. Not yet. Then this man, Jayantha"—I recognized the name of Bandula's grandfather, the former president, Chiran's father— "this man turned his people against us so he could be president. He put his gangs against the Tamils. In all the cities. In Colombo. His gangmen came to my house and took my father, my mother into the street. All the Tamils got taken out to the street by the gangmen. And they beat them. They fell. I saw them beat my father, but he wouldn't fall. They got angry when he wouldn't fall and they beat him. His head and his face—all blood. My mother, crying, and they beat her until she's dead. And my father falls and they kick him and kick him. They kill him and then they kicked him more."

I remembered the soldiers kicking the dead bomber that evening and wondered what kind of hatred and terror made even death an insufficient punishment.

Kumar struck himself in the chest—once, twice, three times—pounding home the point he was not sure he could make with his words, hitting himself hard enough to grunt with pain.

Could self-destruction prove the only avenue strong enough to exorcise the ghosts that haunted him?

"But I didn't cry." He strangled on the words. "I want to help my father, help my mother, but I can't. I saw and did nothing. I will not cry."

He stopped speaking as abruptly as he had started, radiating fury and hate. His heavy, rapid breathing, like that of a man who had run a great distance, filled the quiet room.

He had watched his parents murdered in front of him while he could do nothing. Could he ever admit to himself that there was nothing he could have done?

I thought of the two men, Kumar and Bandula, and the fact that it was the dark twins of hatred and grief twisting around their hearts that bound them together. The circumstances of their despair—for Kumar the death of his parents, for Bandula his father's abandonment—made for a dangerous bond.

"So you ended up in Bandula's orphanage," I said quietly, as if ending a story.

"It was not his then. We were both too young."

Too young for what? I sensed Kumar meant something other than their ages.

"He came later," Kumar continued, his voice calmer now. "He is the best man I know. He came to the orphanage and made our lives better. I was the oldest one there. We were the same age. We talked many times. We walked together."

And what more? I decided the answer to that question didn't really matter. It all made sense—two young men trapped in childhood fears—falling into each other for protection from the rest of the world.

Kumar lifted his chin. "I understand then that every Sinhala is not bad," he said. "But not everyone he knows is good like him."

"Are you talking about Lilani?"

I sensed that the hardness in Kumar's eyes came not from anger but jealousy. Jealousy of her influence over Bandula?

Sexual jealousy? Perhaps the jealousy of a tortured man toward anyone not burning in their own brand of hell?

"Who is she?" I asked. "Who is Lilani?"

A sneer came over Kumar's face. "She is a half-person." He had gathered himself together now and could channel the emotions roiling within him. "You Americans want us to love you. But we hate you. You could make things come good here in my poor country. Then we would love you. But you don't. Why don't you help the brown man?"

The little speech struck me as both so false and so true that now I was the one who could say nothing.

When I made no reply, Kumar turned and walked out, leaving the door open behind him.

17

Bothered by the pain in my ribs and even more by my conversation with Kumar, I slept poorly and rose late. After some breakfast I called my secretary, Chamalie, in Colombo

"Oh, Mr. Reid," she said in a high tremolo, "I was so concerned about you." The temple bombing had led every news report in the country that morning, some making it sound as if the whole city had been blown to pieces. After assuring her I was all right, I asked her to reconfirm my appointments set for that morning. She called back half an hour later to tell me everyone had canceled, pleading pressing duties.

Jayasinghe was already waiting in the car when I stepped outside the hotel. I slumped into the back seat and told him to head downtown. Fearing that Rohan Jayawardene, too, would refuse to see me, I decided not to phone the *Kandy Herald* but simply stop by the newspaper offices.

I looked dumbly out the window as we drove through town, my head working slowly, my thoughts turning like a sinister carousel ridden by Potts, Kumar and Bandula, circling the shattered moonstone, all of them connected in ways I could not fathom.

※

It took some time to find the offices of the *Herald*, located in a peeling wooden building at the back of an alley. Jayasinghe parked on the sidewalk while I climbed up to the paper's second story office.

I explained to the middle-aged woman who met me at the front door that I had an appointment. She nodded and led me across a large room filled with old-fashioned desks topped with modern computers. At the far end of the room she parted a thin curtain that set off a space as an office for the *Herald's* editor and publisher.

Behind a cluttered desk sat Rohan Jayawardene, a short, soft-bellied man with a gray, fleshy face framed by a tangle of graying hair. His baggy eyes, swimming behind thick glasses, blinked in different directions, one aimed at me, the other wandering off toward something else, both of them reflecting a deep weariness.

He tossed his pen onto the desk, nodded me into a chair and rubbed his eyes. "Forgive me for not getting up. I've been working all night." Nodding toward his newsroom, Rohan said, "I think we've just about wrapped up the reporting on this bomb." He stared at a couple of hand-written pages on his desk. Though it was only nine in the morning, his breath smelled of alcohol. "Now all I have to do is write my piece making sense of it all." He turned his bloodshot gaze on me, his wandering eye drifting in its eccentric orbit. "So tell me, Mr. American Press Attaché, how do you explain madness? These Tigers . . . What kind of movement is this? What kind of liberators are they? Our Tamil brothers have real grievances, but these fellows run around out in the bush with guns in their hands or bombs strapped to their bellies, thinking they can kill their way to a solution."

I tried to think of something worth saying. "What do the Tigers hope to gain by this?"

"Gain? Our hatred. That's what they thrive on. They need our rage in order to survive. They feed off death—their own and ours. And we help them. We'll take our revenge for this monstrous act, kill some of them, lose a few of our own—just enough that we never lack for scores to settle. And each death drives us closer to the abyss." The old editor looked at me. "People speak of dancing on graves of others? Here it's the dead who dance on the graves in which the living have chosen to bury themselves."

"There are elections coming," I said, "Perhaps someone can beat the NRP."

"Ah, yes. Tissa Sandanayake. Everyone looks to him as the savior. In my weaker moments, even I believe. Childish dreams." He made a dismissive wave of his hand, snapped off a piece of chocolate from a bar on his desk and popped it in his mouth. "In the meantime we have the NRP, the Jayatilaka family's exclusive club. Members only. National. Reconciliation. Party." He ticked the words off on his fingers like an umpire calling out a batter on strikes. "We didn't have much to reconcile when they formed it. Now we have plenty." Rohan coughed deeply, winced in pain. "And all the while the Jayatilakas sit in Colombo perfecting colonialism."

I blinked.

His harsh laugh ended in a coughing fit. "It's true. Exploiting the native people for the benefit of a distant ruling class. We've simply traded foreign colonists for domestic ones. These new ones all went to British schools, speak English among themselves, drive German cars and drink French wine. They spend weeks, months in Paris or London or Rome each year. It's colonialism with a home-grown face. They're just not as competent as the old colonists. The cracks show. Things fall apart."

"But you have a newspaper, a voice."

Rohan blew out a breath. "Ah! The American comes into our offices and calls for a change. Tells us to undertake great acts and set everything right."

I flinched as Rohan's shot hit home.

"My renowned newspaper," he scoffed. "It's too inefficient to call it a business, but I need the income too badly to call it a hobby." The aging editor rolled his shoulders against the weight of his burdens. "I get to write my editorials, publish my paper. It's like wetting your pants in a dark suit. It makes you feel warm all over—and nobody notices."

"I'm told you're an historian."

The journalist eyed me with a weary smile. "If you miss a deadline by a couple of days you're considered lazy. You miss it by twenty years, you're an historian."

Rohan made a sweeping gesture that took in his office, his city, his country. "I should just fold up this damn thing. But I haven't got the courage to admit that my life's work has been a waste." As if calling to someone a long time gone, he whispered a single word. "Serendip".

I waited, but finally had to ask. "Serendip?"

Rohan Jayawardene looked at me as if he had forgotten I was there. "An ancient name for this unhappy island. Serendip. The Island of Serendipity. My god."

The pain in his smile made me want to look away.

Rohan leaned over his desk and drew his hand through the air like a knife. "You come here, you Americans, and all the others. You fall in love with our exotic island, the swaying palms, the azure sea, the charm of the dusky natives. How strange, how quaint, how romantic it all seems, how ready for your guiding hand. The very clever ones among you can perhaps see the obvious. Not one of you sees beyond it. Believe me, none of you understands what you're doing."

I thought of Lilani's enigmatic warning. "So I've been told."

"Then you should listen!" Rohan shook his head and held up a hand by way of apology. "I understand," he said. "I am not young and an American. I know what it's like to have history on someone else's side. Sri Lanka and its people are ancient and small. We are tied to this rock, and history crashes over us in waves. 'History is a nightmare from which I cannot awake.' Your James Joyce—an Irishman, another fellow from an ancient and tragic island— he knew." The old man sighed. "We are not like you. We are not optimists."

"And so you end up with this private club, these local colonists, in charge of your country."

Rohan spread his hands to express the obviousness of it all. "If it was a real government, Susan Guneratne would be in charge. But she just administers things for her auntie. It's Chiran's club now." He peered over his glasses. "You've met her?"

I nodded.

"Charming, isn't she?" The old editor's smile plumbed the depth of his sadness. "The poor girl." He saw my surprise. "Truly. The poor girl. I knew her as a happy young woman. But she has lost everything—her father, her husband, her boy. She wants everyone to love her. That's what she really wants. And all she gets is envy and hate and it's driven her mad." Rohan looked at me. "But they're all charming, the Jayatilakas. All of them charming and mad."

A long silence filled the room. Weighed down by the transfer of some quantum of Rohan Jayawardene's despair from his shoulders to mine, I struggled to my feet. As I was about to pull the curtain aside, I turned and asked him. "So, who will take over from the aunt?"

"From Chiran? She's still a young woman—at least to an old man like me."

"Yes, but someday it will be someone else. Who? Will her husband come back one day, take charge?"

"No, he has managed his escape. Someone said he tried to come back a few weeks ago. I don't believe it. Why would he? No, he's gone to Europe, where it can't touch him." Rohan nodded. "He's paid his price. If anyone speaks of him at all anymore, they call him a pervert, a coward." He shook his head. "I wonder if he gives a damn."

"Then her son, Bandula. Perhaps he will be the one."

"The young one?" Rohan shook his head. "Too wild. Too many conflicts with mama." The old editor shook his head and shrugged. "They have more intrigues than the Borgias." He paused. "But a charming young fellow. Just like the rest of them. Charming and mad."

18

Richard Donovan gazed out his office window toward the sea. A lid of thick clouds lay over the Indian Ocean. He tossed a pile of newspapers with their towering headlines across the coffee table, took off his reading glasses and twirled them between his fingers. "So, where's this Potts guy now?"

"I saw him in Kandy before I left." I said. I had got back from Kandy the night before and hardly got into my office that morning before getting the summons to come up to the Ambassador's office. "He told me he was catching tonight's flight back to London."

I had briefed the Ambassador on what I had seen of the attack in Kandy. Like a third chair musician granted a solo, I enjoyed my momentary prominence as the only officer on the scene of the island's most dramatic event in years. In fact, though, I had little to add to the news stories other than my personal experience—and even that only mirrored Potts' first-hand account, which hit the wires soon after he'd filed his story from the hotel. Still, it was fun to see McWhirter chafing at the need to listen for a change. I barely even minded when he interjected, "That's been in the papers," at nearly everything I said.

Tony Spezza, sitting next to McWhirter, leaned forward and asked. "You think Potts planned to go up north?"

"That's what he said."

"Why did he change his plans?"

"Something about his editor calling him back after filing his report. Another assignment."

Even from the crest of this heady moment, I could see the dangerous trough waiting for me. I couldn't mention Kumar's presence in Kandy, or my own certainty that Bandula had asked Kumar to help get Potts through the lines. If I did, I would have to explain much else besides, starting with my unreported contacts with Bandula and my vague suspicions about how he might have something to do with Potts' trip to the north. Tony would then feel compelled to say that he had already told me to stay away from both of them. The Ambassador, I was certain, would order me to cut my contacts and leave the Jayatilakas to himself and the political section. I would lose my hold on the thread connecting me to the most powerful people in the country—and the advancement this contact represented. I would lose, too, my chance to know better the woman whose image played constantly in the back of my mind.

No, my secrets had become too precious to surrender, at least for now.

So I said nothing, and took one more step outside the protective circle of the embassy, a step that would not be easily regained.

Burt Steadman snorted and looked at the ambassador. "That sumbitch Potts was probably going to go up there and write some story about the Tigers being a bunch of misunderstood idealists," he drawled, "Make Prabhakaran out to be George Washington in a sarong."

When people started talking tough, especially the people who wrote his yearly work evaluation, McWhirter didn't like to get left behind. "I did *not* like this guy Potts when I met him. We shouldn't have given him the time of day. An article like the one he wrote from Kandy could prove deeply embarrassing to our host government."

Richard Donovan smiled faintly. "Maybe a little embarrassment would prove salutary for them."

The pol chief cleared his throat and said, "Sir, with all respect, we've listed the Tigers as a terrorist organization. They've killed innocent civilians and—"

Donovan held up his hand and sighed the sigh of a man who can't make a quip without someone taking him literally. "You're duty officer this week?" the Ambassador asked me.

"Yeah, I'll be taking all the after-hours calls," I said.

He rose and patted me on the back. "Let's hope for your sake it's a quiet week."

The meeting ended with Donovan telling me, "Good work," and assigning me, not McWhirter, to write the reporting cable on the attack in Kandy. I felt a glow of validation, a glow immediately snuffed out by the sense that I had already betrayed the trust I had been given.

19

Like everyone else, I took off my shoes before entering the temple, Colombo's largest and most revered. I felt faintly ridiculous as I hopped on one foot then the other while I untied my laces and pulled off my black oxfords.

In front of me, a woman in a red sari held her son's hand as they slipped out of their sandals with barely a change of gait. The contrast of their grace with my awkwardness suggested an inescapable truth: they belonged here, I did not.

After my meeting in the Ambassador's office, the torments of conscience, amplified by the fear that I would be found out before I could turn my knowledge to any kind of advantage, left me so agitated that I could not return to my office. Instead, I borrowed a car from the motor pool and drove aimlessly until I found myself near the temple. Like a drunk who spots a tavern, I pulled over and practically ran into its precincts.

I had peeled off my socks and I felt oddly naked, standing in my suit and tie and bare feet. I added my shoes to the long row that lined the stone step and entered the temple through one of its towering arches.

Within the cool and shady interior of the temple's thick walls, the heat and the sounds of the outside world faded away. I looked up at the soaring vault and sensed the lifting of the oppressive weight on my soul, as if, within the temple, gravity surrendered a bit of its hold.

The smooth stone felt warm and moist under my sweating feet as I padded across the floor, strewn with flower petals. For the span of a couple of deep, cleansing breaths, I absorbed the temple's colors and shadows, taking in the rich mustiness of coconut oil, tropical flowers and incense. Before me rose an altar covered with flowers, their blue, red and lavender blossoms glowing with the light of small votive candles nestled among them. Behind the flowers and the flickering candles lay an immense recumbent Buddha, lying on its side, its head propped on one hand, its face lighted by a beatific smile. The startling colors of the figure's clothes and features—yellows, reds and oranges, bright as breakfast cereals—made the sculpture look like a huge toy, and I felt sure that only the self-imposed limits of my western mind made the Buddha's smile appear a little mischievous.

The woman in the red sari placed a handful of blossoms on the altar and made a quick palms-together reverence. The boy did the same, looking to his mother for the assurance he had done it correctly. She said a short prayer then turned and slipped quietly out of the temple, the lightness of her step making me feel earthbound and heavy. The tranquility I had felt a moment earlier evaporated, leaving me vaguely disturbed by the unfamiliar images around me.

As if my unease had tripped some spiritual intruder alarm, a priest in robes the color of melted butter quietly approached. A short, fleshy man with a shaven head and a smooth, untroubled face, he could have been anywhere between forty and ninety years of age.

"Would you like a tour of the temple?" the priest asked in the musical cadence of the local English. The drape of his robes left bare one shoulder and much of his chest, a demi-nakedness that struck me as utterly innocent, yet somehow slightly indecent. "Behind you here ... " He indicated the wall opposite the altar, which rose high into the shadows of the temple, its surface covered by simple illustrations laid out in square panels like a page from a comic book, their radiant colors echoing those of the recumbent Buddha. "... you find incidents from the many incarnations of the Buddha."

The priest pointed out a few of the panels and briefly told their stories.

"You mean he did all this in a single lifetime?"

Coming from someone else, the priest's smile might have seemed condescending, but his pacific gaze and the simplicity of his manner disarmed me. "One lifetime, many incarnations. The five hundred and fifty incarnations of the Buddha. The Buddha remains eternal, always *enlightened*"— he spoke as if he had only now coined the word, the odd emphasis both alien and apt. "Yet he has come to us in many manifestations. Ever-changing, always the same, the one true reality. He is our guide out of this world of *illusions*, our lives seemingly full, but finally *empty*."

The priest's mild eyes, unblinking as a baby's, held me in their gaze until I feared he could feel the weight of my betrayals, the vanity behind my secrets, the emptiness of my ambitions. I made a show of regarding the pictures before me so that I could turn away.

"You too have known many other lives," the priest said, his smile an invitation to reflection and candor.

I thought of my secret forays as a boy into the delta country near home and of wandering the great farms that covered the valley like a patchwork quilt. Finally, as if those images had pulled him from my mind, I thought of my father. Boys are born reconciled with their mothers. With their fathers they must earn it, and once lost it is lost for good. I thought of my days at the university. Then Jean and love. And Paris and loss. Now here, and the double life I had chosen for myself.

Slowly, my thoughts returned to the temple and Sri Lanka and this priest's benign countenance.

"Many lives?" I smiled, repeating the priest's question. "No. Just the one."

The priest regarded me, waiting for a more truthful answer.

"I'm sorry," I said, putting on my most genial, business-like manner. "But I need to go now. I'll be late for an appointment."

The priest opened his arms to embrace all the demands that constrain men's wishes. "Yes. Come back when you have time. We will speak again."

20

I groped in the dark for the ringing phone that had startled me from a deep sleep. "Mnmh ... yeah?"

"Mr. Reid?"

"Yeah."

"Sir, this is Sergeant Taylor at Post One. You're duty officer this week?"

A tickle of apprehension began to stir me awake. "What is it, Cal?"

"Sir, I just received a phone call about an injured American and figured I'd better call you right away."

"Another traffic accident?" I asked. There had been two in the last few months involving American tourists

"No, sir. The call came from the military."

"The military?"

"Yessir. Army says one of its patrols up near Habarana jumped a group of Tigers trying to cross from the south back into their own lines last night. There was a firefight and the Army drove 'em off."

I sat up and rubbed the sleep from my eyes. "I don't understand what that has to do with ... "

"When this patrol starts to pursue, first thing they find is some guy on the ground who's taken a round."

"American?"

"Yessir. Says he's a journalist."

I closed my eyes and muttered an oath.

"Sir?"

"Where is he?"

"They're choppering him down to Colombo right now. I guess he's already been in the air for a while. They say he should be at the airport in about a half hour."

"What time is it?"

"Almost oh-four-hundred."

"They're taking him to the military hospital?"

"No sir, Nawaloka Hospital, downtown."

Fully awake now, I swung my feet out of bed. "Okay. Who's the duty driver?"

"It's Gita, sir."

"Send him over here right away. Tell him we're heading for the hospital. Is there a backup driver?"

"I can get one."

"Have him pick up Kathy Beecham, the consular officer, and meet me—"

"Mrs. Beecham's down in Galle until tomorrow, sir, seeing some American who got hisself thrown in jail down there."

"All right, but someone needs to call her right away. And we'll need her assistant, David Gunawardene. Have the backup driver take him straight to the hospital. David'll know what to do."

"Shall I wake the Ambassador?"

"No. There's nothing he can do right now. But he gets up early—call him at the residence at six-thirty."

"Yessir."

"Can you patch me through to Marina, my press assistant? She's going to have to call A.P."

"I'm not sure this guy's with A.P., sir."

"I am."

※

Even in Colombo the streets are nearly empty at four in the morning and Gita made good time to the hospital. I'd hardly stepped out of the car when an army ambulance pulled up to the emergency entrance. I watched orderlies transfer Potts from the ambulance onto a rickety gurney. Blood covered his shirt and he held a hand over his bandaged face. The squeaking of a balky wheel sounded like a child's whimper as the orderlies rolled him toward the emergency room.

I'd turned to follow Potts inside when I heard a voice. "Sir?"

An army officer got out of the ambulance and slowly put on his cap as if he couldn't speak until it was in place. "You're with the American Embassy?"

"Yes."

"We need to talk."

"Talk?"

"This gentleman was caught trying to cross our lines into a restricted part of the country with a group of terrorists last night."

"He's a journalist."

The military officer raised his chin. "Journalists are not exempt from the law, sir. His actions are also a violation of his visa."

My gut twisted with exasperation. Getting pissed off at Potts was my prerogative, and I didn't want to share it with any Sri Lankan army officer. "What are you going to do, arrest him?"

The officer spread his feet slightly and clasped his hands behind his back. "That's a very real possibility."

"Fine, but I've got no time for you right now."

"Sir— " the man started, but I had let the hospital door close behind me and was following the sound of the squeaking gurney.

※

The emergency waiting room smelled of sweat and disinfectant and sickness. Discolored paint and dingy linoleum added their dram of gloom to the half-dozen or so people who sagged in plastic chairs set against the wall.

Potts lay on his gurney, unattended.

I walked over and put a hand on his arm. "Potts, it's Philip Reid."

"Reid," he said to me, his voice barely audible. "How do I get out of here? Just get me on a plane."

"I don't think you're going anywhere for a while." I ignored Potts tired sigh. "You told me you were going back to London."

"Yeah, well ..."

"So, how you feeling?"

"Terrible." Potts paused, licked his lips. "Took some grenade shrapnel."

"I heard you got shot."

He shook his head slightly as if afraid it might break. "You heard wrong."

A woman of about forty with a stethoscope around her neck walked briskly into the room. "Are you with the American Embassy?"

"Yes. Philip Reid."

She gave my hand a quick shake. "Doctor Dharmasena. Who is going to be responsible for this man?"

"What do you mean?"

"We can't treat him until we know who's going to pay for the treatment." She wasn't joking.

Her expression told me there was no point arguing with her. I took the clipboard from the doctor's hands and scribbled a note saying that, on behalf of the American embassy, I took full responsibility for Nick Potts' treatment. I had no idea if I had the authority to make such a commitment but knew that I couldn't let an injured American—not even Potts—lie on a gurney without medical care.

The doctor read over the note, then looked at me quizzically. "Do I know you?" she asked.

I frowned, knowing where this was going. "No. We've never met."

"Ah, I have it now," she said. "You're the man who got that inured woman onto a stretcher."

"That was months ago."

"I was on duty that afternoon. I was sorry I couldn't save her."

Her words were clear, but I couldn't take them in. "You couldn't ..."

"She was dead by the time they got her out of the ambulance."

How many times had I deprecated my actions on that day, telling people that anyone could have done what I did? Yet in my heart, I had accepted their praise. I was bound for great things. I was, after all, an exceptional guy. I had saved a woman's life.

She saw my surprise and gave a little shrug, as if to say we should be used to such things. Then she called for an attendant, who wheeled Potts towards an elevator. Absent as a sleepwalker, I followed.

※

The ancient elevator groaned its way up to the third floor, where the attendant wheeled Potts into an alcove outside a large pair of swinging doors, then walked off. I stood dumbly beside Potts, reordering my idea of who I was and what I had done. All my dismissive comments about my supposed heroism had proven true. I had achieved nothing.

Potts drew a deep, slow breath. "Reid?"

"Yeah."

"Thanks for coming up here with me."

I didn't want to tell him it was simply my job. "It's okay, Nick. Besides, I wanted to get away from some military guy down there. Real asshole. Said he wanted to arrest you."

"Yeah, he mentioned something along those lines on our way down here in the chopper." Potts breathed quietly for a few moments. "He's a good guy. Been with me all night. Saw I got patched up. Flew down here with me."

I wondered if I would ever get anything right.

"I guess I was a little impatient with him. Maybe with that doctor, too. I didn't get a lot of sleep."

"Yeah, I've had a rough day, too." His faint smile cracked the dried blood on his cheek.

Another orderly came and took Potts away to get some x-rays, then brought him back. A doctor appeared, a short, youthful man with an assured smile. He shook hands with me and then said to Potts, "You're a lucky fellow. You could easily have been killed." The shrapnel had broken his nose and cheekbone and there was some damage to the eye, he told us. "But I will make it all right again," he said with modest pride, "You'll come out looking more handsome than ever." The doctor laughed in the certitude of his abilities, then disappeared through the swinging doors that led to surgery.

I pulled up a chair and leaned in toward Potts. "Nick, is there anyone you want me to call?"

"Thanks. No."

"Wife?"

"No wife."

Your parents? A brother or sister?"

"Haven't got anyone to call." He smiled, embarrassed. "Yeah, you could call my editor," he offered. "Guy named Simon Brown. A.P. London. Dilip, our guy here, can give you the number."

"Someone's already called Dilip. He should be on his way."

"Thanks."

We both knew where the conversation had to go.

"You told me you'd gone back to London. What were you doing up there, Nick?"

"Going after a story." He raised his eyebrows. "I guess I got one."

"I know Bandula Jayatilaka made the contacts to get you up there. I saw you with him at the Hilton. Why would he do that? What's in it for him?"

His hand still over his face, Potts turned his head toward my voice. "You know how to keep a secret?" he whispered.

"Yes." I leaned closer.

"So do I."

I let the ensuing silence build a foundation for the next question. "Do you think you were set up?"

It was odd watching Pott's thoughts reflected in the set of his mouth, the only part of his face that I could see. The journalist frowned, but I could see the uncertainty my question had caused him. "Set up?"

"After getting you up there, could they have arranged for the Tigers to lead you into an ambush?" Potts' mouth opened in a wordless sigh. I pressed in. "You know, 'American Journalist Shot By Government Troops.' Makes everyone look bad."

"They sure left me behind in a hurry once I'd been hit." For a long time, Potts thought it over. "Sonsofbitches," he said without vehemence.

David Gunawardene, our Sri Lankan consular assistant, arrived before they wheeled Potts off to surgery. He spoke with the doctors, asked Potts if he felt well enough to sign a couple of forms. The journalist struggled to get up on one elbow. When he took his hand away to steady himself I could see swelling around his eye, the caked blood, the torn flesh.

David spoke in the calm, efficient manner of a family doctor. "As soon as I can, I'll ask how long you'll be here. Then we can start working on a flight back to London."

I nodded toward the entrance. "There's some military guy outside, says they might try to arrest him."

David waggled his head in a deprecating way. "I met him on my way in and we spoke. He says we can deal with that later."

Dilip, the local A.P. guy, showed up a few minutes later.

I remembered the sound of relief in Cal Taylor's voice on the phone a couple of hours earlier when I'd taken from him the responsibility for the injured American. Now I felt something of the same emotion as I pulled back and let David and Dilip and the hospital take it from there.

I shook hands with Potts, told him that Kathy Beecham or I would be back later in the day, then went downstairs and left the hospital through a side door. I longed for fresh air, but the morning was already heavy and damp.

I went home and back to bed for a while but couldn't sleep and drove into the embassy only a little late.

※

I got a call from Sig Appleton, the *New York Times* correspondent in New Delhi, who wanted something on the story of the injured journalist. "Sig, I can't. The guy makes his living by telling what happens to him. I can't just hand his story to someone else."

Appleton made unhappy sounds but promised to take me out to lunch next time he was in Colombo.

Later that morning, I briefed the Ambassador, Steadman and McWhirter on what I knew. They, too, suspected that someone had arranged Potts' trip north and at the same time arranged an ambush to make sure he never got there.

Burt Steadman threw his arms along the back of the couch and said, "You know, this Potts guy has already overstayed his visa—not to mention breaking its terms. He knew he wasn't supposed to go up there. The government has every right to throw him in jail."

Donovan nodded. "Assuming the surgery goes well, I'll visit him tomorrow. If I have to, I'll call the Foreign Ministry and try to persuade them that it isn't smart to arrest a badly wounded man who can place his grievances in half the newspapers in the world." He shook his head and looked at me. "This guy has given you quite a week."

"Sir, you don't know how glad I'll be when he's gone."

21

After her return from Galle, Kathy Beacham, the consular officer, visited Potts daily and reported that the
doctors had saved his eye, but he would be in the hospital for
some time. The A.P. writer quickly became yesterday's news.

In the meantime, for everyone in the embassy, the rhythm
of work accelerated with the approaching elections. Though
the vote was still several weeks away, the island's political
temperature was already climbing. Like the sections of a
malignant orchestra beginning to tune up, party-controlled
thugs armed with rocks, knives and clubs began to square
off in small battles, breaking heads, ransacking political
offices, laying down markers of terror and retribution to be
redeemed later in blood.

Not wanting his embassy chained to the opinions and
personalities found in the capital, Ambassador Donovan
assigned me to go with Nancy Kawabata and the defense
attaché, Carl Bogdanovich, on a tour of outlying districts.
"See what's going on," he told us. "Listen to what people
are saying. Don't ask a lot of questions. Let people talk—
and keep your eyes open. Bring me back some truth."

There was a lot of truth out there. Stories in the opposition
dailies accused the NRP of killing one of its candidates near

Kandy. The NRP papers countered that opposition toughs had shot to death a party leader on the southern coast. In the north, a couple of Tamil office-seekers who had dared to say that the Tigers did not represent the aspirations of the Tamil people were blown to pieces under what one paper boldly described as "suspicious circumstances."

When I thumbed past the major headlines toward the back pages of the newspaper I found signs of a more disturbing disintegration—accounts pointing to an epidemic of wife-beatings and sexual abuse, too many stories about young women hanging themselves for no apparent reason and of young men killing their best friends in drunken fights, stories of burglars murdering every member of an impoverished family before escaping with barely enough money for a pack of cigarettes. The air had become weighted not only from the incessant heat and humidity but from a deep sense of despair that had stationed itself over the island paradise like an immovable and oppressive weather front of the soul.

Embassy officers asked their contacts which party they expected to carry the elections and whether a win by either would advance the prospects for an end to the war. Most shrugged and said that, while they personally favored Tissa Sandanayake and his coalition, Susan's auntie would see that the NRP won, even if they had to do it fair and square. As for peace? No one could imagine it.

※

Even at night, the oppressive heat and humidity never dissipated. When we were home, most of us who worked at the embassy turned the air-conditioning on high to get some relief, and to lay down a thick layer of insulation between ourselves and the world outside our doors. We seldom thought, at least consciously, of the unrelenting weight of living in a foreign land, an alien culture, forever the foreigner, constantly adapting to new people, new languages, new customs. But its weight wore us down. Still, if foreign service officers share one common characteristic it's the ability to adapt. We are shapeshifters of the first water. We speak whatever language is required of us as we move from country to country, culture to culture, and try to remember we're Americans, representatives of our government and people, not simply well-paid nomads. It comes at a price, of course, and after a while we can begin to act oddly. We choose at times to try to make it all go away, create a little sanctuary, no bigger than a cozy room in our tax-payer furnished homes, where we can hide, where we can pretend we're somewhere else, somewhere familiar.

So, that night I sat in my study watching a Celtic-Lakers game I had recorded off the satellite. I had the a/c cranked up so high I had to put a blanket around me, though I didn't want to reflect on the fact that it was Sri Lanka itself I was trying to keep at bay.

I must have done a pretty good job of it, because I didn't hear the doorbell ring, nor the knock on the door of the study, and I jumped as Madhu, my housekeeper, poked her head in the room.

"There is someone at the door for you, Mr. Reid. Someone sent by Mr. Jayatilaka." Her eyes widened as if she had invoked Beelzebub himself.

I went downstairs and found, like the spirit of my bad faith, Bandula's driver, Peter, a beefy moon-faced fellow, filling the open doorway. "Good evening, sir," he said, smiling. He motioned toward the car. "Mr. Bandula would like the pleasure of your company at the Rama."

"The Rama?" I asked.

"A night club in Wellawatta. He is waiting in the car."

In the driveway, the passenger door of the big Land Rover gaped open for me. In its shadows, I saw Bandula waiting for me in the back seat.

Even though I wanted to say no, wished to make clear to Bandula that I wasn't one of his lackey's, ever-ready to do his bidding, I couldn't bring myself to do it with him sitting in his car waiting for me, couldn't hurt his feelings like that.

And Lilani. Though I didn't see her in the car, I hoped, like a lovesick teenager, that Bandula might lead me to her.

So I grabbed my wallet and followed Peter out to the car.

I hadn't seen Bandula in a couple of weeks, but he barely nodded as I got in the car, as if he had something on his mind.

We said little as Peter weaved through traffic on the Galle Road, which we would take to Wellawatta, a few miles down the coast. I knew not to ask about Lilani. I had come to believe that speaking of her diminished the possibility of seeing her. Kumar's absence, too, went unmentioned. Finally, impatient with the wall of forbidden subjects, I ran right at one of them and asked him if he knew who had arranged Potts' attempt to cross into Tiger country. Bandula played it cool, letting out a scoffing laugh. "I have no idea what you're talking about," he said.

Feeling the need to start paying off the debt I'd incurred by my double-dealing with the embassy, I began subtly, or so I thought, to bring up politics, asking Bandula how his president-aunt hoped to fend off the opposition challenge in the upcoming elections.

As he had when I'd mentioned the rumor of his father's attempt to return to the island, Bandula looked at me quizzically, a slight smile on this face, and asked, "Why would my aunt talk to me about that?" batting my question back at me, like a skilled tennis player volleying with a novice.

I groped for a way to shake his maddening show of aplomb. "I keep thinking of something J. R. said when I met with him. He asked me who I served. Funny question. It made me wonder whether your mother wanted to use me in some way. That she had something in mind for me. And I …"

The words died in my mouth as Bandula's look of amused detachment vanished. "You have no idea, do you?" he said, "You honestly think that my mother—" Bandula forced a laugh, but his hands twitched oddly.

In my exasperation, it was easy to dismiss him as an immature manchild resenting the apron strings he couldn't bring himself to untie, easy to miss how smart he was, brought up in a household that breathed politics like most of us breathe air. It had given him a keen sense of what others wanted, what motivated them, catching nuances of meaning the speakers themselves did not grasp. So we conducted our little fugue of variations on a well-worn theme. Behind his evasions, his claims of ignorance, I sensed his mind at work on something I could not see, waiting for me to say the right thing, ask the right question. He knew of my lofty ambitions, and knew he was the means by which I could realize them. Still I couldn't understand what he needed of me.

Finally, he waved away my questions and asked, "Tell me, Phil, don't you have a girlfriend, a lover? You, a good-looking young diplomat with money in your pocket. Single and footloose. The girls must come flocking to you." He said the last with a conspiratorial smile.

We both knew he was talking about Lilani.

"Actually, no," I said.

He laughed. "What? You're telling me the local girls show no interest—"

"I mean I'm not single."

His face went blank. "What?"

So I told him about Jean, about our separation, its permanence.

"You're married," he said slowly. I could see him recalibrating his ideas about me, recalculating his sense of who I was.

"Married? If you want to call a marriage something where we live on the opposite ends of the earth and have no contact, then, yes, I'm still technically married." It struck me that, for all my efforts to draw him out, it was always me who revealed himself. "I don't understand why she doesn't file for divorce. I keep expecting a letter from a lawyer, a phone call. Something. I'm beginning to think she enjoys letting me hang in the wind. Her ounce of revenge."

"Maybe she wants you to come back."

I shook my head. "She knows I can't do that. Won't. Her life is there. Mine is here."

We drove slowly through the eternal traffic jam of Colombo, giving me plenty of time to regret my decision to come.

※

The Rama is located in a beachside hotel beyond the southern end of the city. Bandula said something about meeting friends there. With gut-twisting dread, I imagined him holding court with his crowd of young Sri Lankans who chased boredom with money, introducing them to his tame American diplomat. Even in my current state of fear and loathing, my desire to exploit this contact with the Jayatilakas would be nicely matched by the enjoyment Bandula's friends would gain from patronizing me.

What I found when we arrived at the Rama made me realize how little I knew Bandula.

Coming in the door of the dimly lighted club, my vitals shook with the pulsing World Beat music pounded out by the band onto the dozens of couples happily twisting and jumping on the crowded dance floor.

Bandula led me to a table set in a shadowed back corner of the room. To my surprise, the table, instead of bearing a crowd of Colombo's gilded youth, was empty—but for one person.

I searched Lilani's face, wondering if she had changed since I'd seen her last. Was her hair a little shorter? Her dress new? Was I meeting the girl who had smiled when I impulsively kissed her in the library, or the troubled young woman who had left me at the table on the lawn of the Galle Face Hotel?

Our eyes met. Then, with excruciating deliberateness, she turned away.

To keep from crying out, I bit my lip as she drove this icicle through my heart. I searched my mind for some sin of omission or commission that might have caused her to cut me so. Had I pursued her with so little apparent ardor that she doubted my sincerity? Or perhaps I had mistaken her kindness for affection and she wished to show me she did not share my feeling for her.

Without a word of greeting, Bandula sat down in the chair next to her, leaving me to stand, near them but not with them. Once again, I tried, and failed, to understand the relationship between them.

I grabbed a chair from another table but sat a long arm's length from the table, snared by the invisible webs we had spun between us, webs that kept us from coming too close but would not let us escape.

Why had Bandula invited me to come with him this evening? And why had he made sure Lilani would be there? I had come to understand that, with the possible exception of the day I had run into her at the library, I only saw her when he wanted me to see her. When it didn't serve his purpose, she wasn't there. And he had to know I didn't have any way to find her, could only see her at his sufferance.

He must have sensed how sick I had grown of this game of emotional hide-and-seek, seen I was ready to cut through the barriers of polite restraint we had constructed between us and ask him what the hell he was doing, what he wanted from me, from Lilani, from himself. For I had hardly sat down when he pushed away from the table and walked to the edge of the dance floor. His arms crossed, his face radiating resentment and self-loathing, he looked out at what normal, happy couples did, standing only a few feet from them but as distant as the moon.

In his absence, the few feet separating me from Lilani might have been as many miles. The best thing to do was leave. I stood to go, but instead, pushed myself to cross the short gap and the measureless chasm between us. In the pulsing din of the crowded room I would have had to shout to be heard, and I wasn't going to shout. So I simply put my hand out toward Lilani, inviting her to dance. Only the fact that she turned further away made me sure she had seen me.

I took a step closer, my hand still extended.

When she looked up at me, I saw on her face violent crosscurrents of uncertainty and hope—and as so often, sensed the eloquence of her silence, speaking to me in a language I could not understand.

Some spans of time can't be measured by any clock, and I have no idea how long we looked into each other's eyes, searching for answers. I stood beside her, trembling like a man on a high wire, insisting she acknowledge my presence. And at the moment I thought I would fall, when I would have to turn away and never come back, she reached up and put her hand in mine.

While other couples gyrated and jumped to the frantic beat coming from the band, I led Lilani onto the dance floor and put my arm around her waist. She rested her head on my shoulder and, paying no heed to anyone else, we slowly danced to a tune of our own. Gradually, I felt her relax in my arms, and I knew that, however incompletely, however tentatively, she saw the first hints of an answer to the question I had read in her face.

As the song ended, I feared she would break our embrace, leave the floor and return to the table. The band jumped into a new tune with defiant ear-splitting chords and no attempt at melody, possessed of only a driving beat that told everyone they had better dance or get out of the way. Its challenge seemed to liberate something in Lilani, who began to shake her shoulders and roll her hips to its irresistible rhythm. Unready to allow herself a full smile, she bit her lip until she saw that I too had accepted the music's insistent message. Sure now, she danced with alluring freedom, giving me only a sly smile and sidelong looks, but she was with me now, no longer holding herself back. Driven by the music and freedom and the moment, she inched toward me, dancing a bit closer, then a bit closer yet.

Then, without warning, she bumped into me violently enough to set me back a step. For an instant I was happily impressed by my own magnetism, but soon realized she had been hit from behind by another dancer, one of several thrown at us on a wave of disorder.

I looked for the epicenter of the shock wave that had propelled the dancers into each other, even knocking down a couple of them, and found that an empty circle had formed in the middle of the crowded dance floor—empty, that is, but for a young Sri Lankan couple and Bandula, his eyes burning, his hands gripping the arm of the young man's girl.

For a moment, the band kept playing as Bandula spun the girl around trying to force her to dance with him, but she was too frightened to make any move but those he forced on her. While the other dancers froze, the young woman looked beseechingly to the boy she had been dancing with.

The young man, a burly fellow half a head taller than Bandula, took a step toward him, fists clenched. Bandula dropped the girl and squared around, ready to accept the fight he had provoked.

The guy looked more than capable of giving Bandula a beating, and I sensed that, for some twisted reason, this was what Bandula wanted. But when the boy recognized who had pushed him, his gesture died as quickly as it was born. Quivering with anger and frustration, he turned to walk off the dance floor.

Bandula couldn't let it go at that. It wasn't about the girl anymore, if it had ever been. It was about humiliating the young man and daring him to do something about it. In two quick strides Bandula caught him and gave him a two-handed push to his back that sent him sprawling.

The musicians dropped their instruments and scurried off the bandstand. The other couples on the dance floor backed further away like a school of fish fleeing a shark.

A silence fell on the room as palpable as the music that had filled it a moment earlier. With a deep groan of rage, the young man, his face purple with anger, sprang to his feet and came at Bandula. Before he had taken two steps, though, he came to a sudden stop, his attention captured by something behind me.

I looked over my shoulder and saw two men I had not noticed when I came in, wearing suits that fit tightly over their thick arms and barrel chests. A bulge under the shoulder of one of the men made clear they were bodyguards who had accompanied Bandula on his night out. They emerged from the shadows near the corner of the room and took a few precautionary steps toward the dance floor.

With a cry of frustration and disgust, the young man swept his arm through the empty air, a shadow of the punch he dared not throw, then walked out a side door into the night.

Before the door had shut behind him, the frightened nightclub manager scurried to the edge of the dance floor and waved at the musicians to pick up their instruments and resume playing. Hesitantly, couples began to dance again, but the joy had been sucked out of the room and the dancers now mostly worked at maintaining their distance from the young Jayatilaka and his unhappy partner.

For a few awkward moments Bandula made a repellant charade of dancing with the frightened young woman. The terrified girl moved in odd jerky motions and looked at the dancers around her as a drowning woman might look for rescue. Then, as abruptly as he had seized her, he abandoned her without a backward glance, stalked off the dance floor and slumped into his chair, alone now at the table we had briefly shared.

As Bandula sat glowering at the dance floor, the manager rushed up to him, speaking urgently while making broad fawning gestures of chagrin. A line of sweat glistened on his forehead.

With a sneer of contempt, Bandula waved him away. His eyes swept the dance floor and I knew he was looking for Lilani and me. For all I pitied him—that was the only emotion I could feel toward Bandula at the moment—I didn't want anything to do with him and, taking her by the hand, led Lilani out of the club through a fire exit.

We came out on a landing above the hotel grounds, felt the night air, warm and close, the sky lighted by a quarter moon. Below us lay a grassy park-like refuge, dotted with coconut palms. After the din of the club, the sound of the distant surf kissing the sand, eased our hearts like a great, slow metronome. We were alone. I looked up into the night sky and savored Lilani's presence.

When she spoke, I could hear in her voice the sadness I had seen in her when I first arrived. "Sometimes the sky seems empty when I look up," she said, "I know the stars are there, but I can't see them." She looked deeply into my eyes and when I met her gaze she did not turn away.

I drew her close and kissed her, a long and serious kiss, full of promises and questions. With an uncertain smile flickering on and off, she turned her head and leaned against my chest, "Ah, yes, the stars. I can see them now."

Through her thin dress, I could feel the curve of her back against my hand and the flatness of her belly against mine, the swell of her breasts. I felt how perfectly she fit against me. We stayed like this a long time, easing into the night and a clearer sense of each other, awakening to the idea of the two of us together.

"I still don't know you," I whispered. "Tell me something about you, anything."

"About me? There's nothing you would want to know."

I laid my head against hers. "C'mon, make it easy for me. You were born in a certain place. School was whatever. Now you live in another place." I looked down at her and saw that she understood the seriousness of what I was asking. "You always appear out of nowhere and when you're gone I don't know what it is you go back to—or who."

For a long, suspended time she said nothing. Then, "Yes, I was born in a certain place. School was ... whatever. Now I live in another place." She looked up at me. "But I go home with no one. No one waits for me. There's no one there."

I almost asked, "Not even Bandula?" but knew the question would have been nothing but a confession of my own insecurity. She stirred in my arms, pulling away ever so slightly. I looked into her eyes. Where I hoped to find affection, even love, I saw fear.

"What is it?"

She shook her head, and I knew not to press for more. In return, she gave me something of herself. "I live in a cottage on the Jayatilaka's estate," she said, "A little place where he—they—let me stay." Lilani leaned into me again, though I could feel in her tense back and her tight embrace she was holding back far more than she'd told me.

"You've always lived with the Jayatilakas?"

"Yes. No."

I tried to smile. "Well, that's clear enough." I drew her close again, trying to somehow erase the distance between us. "You don't have to go back there tonight."

I knew it was no good even as I spoke. Her silence was her answer. In fact, our entire conversation had been formed more of silences than words, and the silences had carried more meaning.

When she spoke her words came slowly, as if she needed to pull them out one by one. "I can go to a place in the mountains."

"You have a home there?"

"Home?" She weighed the idea. "It's a place I can go. It belonged to my . . . my father."

I felt her hesitancy but didn't understand it. "Your father?"

She ignored the question she had herself raised. "I can wait for you there." She looked at me as if she had invited me to a hanging rather than a tryst. "Do you know where Haputale is?"

"Up in the mountains, in tea country. Tell me when to come."

I heard the laugh hidden in her voice. "How soon can you get there?"

"I have to take a trip upcountry for the embassy in a few days. On the way back, I can have them drop me off there."

With a blast of noise and stale air, the door from the club burst open. Bandula appeared in the doorway, standing unsteadily, his eyes dead, his hands gripping the doorframe like a man fighting the urge to jump off a cliff.

"He apologized to me. That worm of a manager. I do all … *that*, and he apologizes to me." He laughed as if he might weep. "My head is so full of great things. Yet every moment of my life is like … like …" His arm cut through the air. "Like *this*. Nothing I do is allowed to have consequences. Everything is covered up. My actions, good or bad, are all undone. Erased. Like I'm a child followed around by a genie that snaps his fingers and makes everything I do disappear." He made fists as if he might strike himself, as Kumar had done in the hotel room in Kandy. But even this gesture remained incomplete. "Do you understand me?" he asked. I couldn't tell if the question was directed to me or to Lilani—or perhaps to himself. "Do you understand what I'm trying to say?" A terrible frustration distorted his voice.

I could only speak the truth. "No, I don't understand at all."

Bandula writhed in the doorway as if stabbed. Raising his eyes to the night, he turned his head away and thrust out his hand toward Lilani. "Come on. Both of you. We're leaving this place." He had said nothing about finding us in each other's arms, but I was sure he had taken it in.

Lilani's mouth curled in distaste. "You're drunk," she said.

"Of course I'm drunk." He tried to laugh, but it came out as the groan of a man unquiet in his grave. "Come on, the driver is waiting."

The young Sri Lankan locked his gaze on me with a yearning that looked disturbingly like madness.

I felt a flicker of interest and almost told him I would go with him if he would promise to finally make clear what he wanted from me. Instead, I told him, "I'm going home. I've had enough of you for one night."

A look of confusion passed over Bandula's face. I told myself that I must try never to hurt him. It was too easy.

"That's fine," he said, his chin at a defiant pitch. "Go home! And tell the embassy how one of the Jayatilakas made a fool of himself at a nightclub on Saturday night."

"I've told you, I haven't said anything to the embassy about knowing you."

His eyes narrowed. However drunk he might have been, he possessed a canniness that never relaxed. "No? But you will. You will."

Again, he thrust his hand toward Lilani. She hesitated. Would she look to me to save her? No. Her face a study in resignation, she took his hand and followed him through the door, leaving me to call a cab and go home.

23

For the first time that afternoon I forgot about the heat and the hardness of my folding chair and how badly the last round of oversweet, milky tea had set on my stomach. Even the members of the journalists' union attending their annual convention in the cramped meeting hall of a second rate hotel stopped their chairs squeaking and sat up a little straighter as Tissa Sandanayake came into the room.

Charisma is a quality that can't be measured, but its presence changes the atmosphere in a room. Relaxed, confident, Sandanayake stood beside the podium, one elbow resting casually on its lip and spoke to us of the need to reconcile Sinhala and Tamil, Hindu and Buddhist, past and present, of the need to open to the world rather than hide from it, to ease the burdens on the poor, to end the culture of privilege.

It hardly seemed like a speech at all, but more like one of those moments in a conversation when a friend speaks plainly of what is on his mind and in his heart. Several of the reporters forgot themselves, ceased writing and simply listened, their pens still poised over their forgotten notebooks.

When he had finished his brief address many of the union members rose to their feet before catching themselves violating their professionally-imposed neutrality and sheepishly settled back into their chairs. But their applause carried the pent-up fervor of a group of people not allowed to express political views except as ordered by their editors.

While a few of the reporters filed off toward lunch, others crowded the podium, impelled to stand a little closer to Sandanayake, even to reach out and touch him, neverminding for a moment that those of them who worked for the Jayatilakas' papers would later be required to attack the very speech that moved them.

I was attending the convention to work my journalistic contacts and show the embassy's support for the union. Yet I was no more immune to the pull of Sandanayake's persona than were those around me. Trying to look casual, I worked my way toward the speaker through the knot of star-struck writers, but their excitement was contagious.

Sandanayake caught sight of me over the sea of his admirers. "Ah, Mr. Reid."

I hoped I didn't betray how flattered I was that this man, perhaps the next president, would recognize me and call me by name in front of his admiring crowd. Yet even as I enjoyed his unspoken compliment a twitch of caution reminded me that this was how great figures bent others to their will.

Jostled by the crowd and by two staffers trying to push Sandanayake toward an exit, he called over his shoulder, "Come, Mr. Reid. I need to talk to you," and gestured for me to follow him out.

A couple of the writers glanced curiously at me then, as flowers follow the sun, turned back toward the magnetic presence in their midst.

The stoutly-built young man I'd seen with Sandanayake outside McWhirter's office shouldered a hole in the crowd and pulled the politician through it by the arm, allowing him to appear reluctant to leave. I followed through the gap he created.

Outside, Sandanayake shook off the last of his well-wishers and got into a waiting car. The stout young man opened the door on the other side and, to my surprise, nodded at me to get in beside Sandanayake. The young woman I had met at the embassy that day got in beside the driver and glanced at a stapled two-page document in her hands. "We need to be in Galle by five-thirty," she said, leaning over the seat.

Tissa Sandanayake leaned back in his seat, clearly fatigued. "Preparing for these parliamentary elections is exhausting work, Mr. Reid. I can't imagine what running for the presidency might be like."

I wanted to ask if this was confirmation of his candidacy, but knew that I would not get, nor did I deserve, a straight answer.

He ran his hands over his face and let out a long sigh. "Maybe this kind of campaign, the indirect kind, is harder." Abruptly, he sat up, his eyes clear and focused, as if renewed by that single sigh. "I understand you're heading upcountry soon." Sandanayake saw my surprise and laughed. "Ambassador Donovan mentioned something about it last week."

"Yes, I guess I am."

"Then over to Badulla, yes?"

The Ambassador had insisted that Nancy and Carl and I make a call on Sandanayake's parents in Badulla, on the eastern side of the mountains. President Guneratne had been implying that the United States favored the NRP in the upcoming elections even while she whipped up anti-American sentiment to appease the left wing of her party.

Word of a visit on the Sandanayakes by members of the embassy would travel through the networks of political gossip more effectively than any press release, undercutting the Sri Lankan president's gamesmanship.

"Listen, Philip, I need to talk to you. Not here. Can you meet me tomorrow evening about seven thirty out in Battaramula, off the Pelawatta Road?" He looked toward the young woman in the front seat. "Margaret, will tell you how to get there. When you arrive, if I haven't come out yet, just wait in your car." He paused a moment. "You don't need to tell anyone about this, of course." He saw the question on my face. "I'm sure the ambassador would understand."

We both knew the ambassador wouldn't understand at all. My life had become a series of secrets and deceptions, each one, like a Russian doll, emerging from the one before it, and I could not stop—did not want to stop— now. Despite what Lilani might think, I told myself I was beginning to understand how things worked in Sri Lanka, was even becoming a part of it, a familiar presence to the most powerful people in the country. I waved aside the twitch of uncertainty I had felt earlier. I told myself I could set everything right, could prove that my approach to my work, however questionable, would redound not only to my benefit, but to the embassy's too. I was doing this for them.

"I'll be there," I said.

Tissa Sandanayake smiled, and with that smile sealed my complicity.

※

When I returned to the embassy later that afternoon Chamalie rose from behind her desk. "There's a contractor in your office," she said, adding, "From Virginia," as if that state were a dubious proposition I might not approve of.

For a moment it looked as if the man on the ladder had come all the way from Virginia to clean my windows. Then I saw that, rather than scraping anything off the glass, he was smoothing something on—a thin sheet of plastic that filtered the blue sky to gray.

The man, tall and lanky with a mop of sandy hair, saw me and waved at the window. "Mylar. Keeps the window from blowing into a thousand pieces if there's a bomb." The man must have seen something in my face, because he laughed and added, "Don't worry. We're doing this in every embassy. Just routine."

24

Plagued by misgivings about my agreement to meet Tissa Sandanayake the following evening I slept poorly that night and got to the office late. But work proved only a waking continuation of my restless night. Drugged by a potent cocktail of sleeplessness and guilt, I accomplished little. Reading a warning in my uneasy silence, my staff avoided me.

Late in the afternoon, I drifted down the hall to the cramped lunchroom that faced on the sea through a couple of salt-encrusted windows. Among the local employees, the higher ranking and better paid ate in the embassy cafeteria, leaving this room to people like Ajith, a slight, graying man who made copies and ran errands. He had distributed two press releases that day and was only now sitting down to lunch.

As I made myself a cup of coffee, voices sounded in the hallway and two burly guys in grease-stained overalls from the maintenance section lumbered into the room. One, a tall, balding mechanic from the motor pool, I had seen before. The other, a short man with thick, powerful arms, was unfamiliar to me. I was standing behind the half-opened door, so the two men didn't notice me as they sat down at the far end of the table for a cup of tea and a bit of cake.

Without a word or even a glance at the other men, Ajith ducked his head between his hunched shoulders, nervously folded his half-eaten meal back into its greasy newspaper and walked out.

"Good day, sir," he murmured to me as he passed.

The two maintenance men turned toward me in surprise. Apparently embarrassed that I had witnessed this little scene they put on a friendly air and the shorter one of the two waved toward Ajith and called to him, "Come. Sit. Sit."

I felt sure the man was speaking English for my benefit.

Ajith ignored them and disappeared down the hall. The two men, after one more glance my way, went back to their tea and cakes.

I felt oddly disturbed by this seemingly inconsequential moment and asked myself what I had just witnessed. Was Ajith of the wrong caste? The wrong ethnic group? Perhaps, within the obscure hierarchy of the local employees, he lacked the status of the two maintenance men, making him unwelcome at the table. I had no idea.

The incident—if it could even be called that—brought home to me once more that, like all American officers, I came and went over the course of a couple of years, pretending to direct the work of people I never understood. All the while, in fact, I drifted like flotsam on a tide of time and culture, with little awareness of the deep currents that flowed under me.

The folly of what I was doing struck me like a blow. I'd been certain I was where I had worked so hard to put myself, on the threshold of important things, primed for advancement, ready for my career to take off. Yet, beyond that teetering threshold everything lay obscured. Even while I kept my own secrets, I realized that I lived within a web formed by the secrets kept by others, secrets of which I knew nothing.

With the sudden shock of a revelation, I saw for the first time the terrible damage I might cause, thrashing around in this darkness. Pushed by a wave of shame and panic, I knew I no longer wanted to stand outside the embassy's grace. I understood what I needed to do.

※

I knocked at Tony's front door and waited. In the lengthening silence, the feeling of righteousness that had buoyed me since my epiphany in the lunchroom, the relief of knowing I had finally set out to do what I should have done weeks earlier, started to slip away.

I knocked again. No response.

I had lifted my hand one last time, to console myself with the half-truth that I had tried, when I heard the click of the lock. The door opened a few inches.

"Gwen." I wasn't able to keep the surprise from my voice.

The shaft of late-afternoon light slicing through the half-open door gave her hair the tone of muted gold from an old painting. I tried to tell myself that the little blow of disappointment I felt was absurd. Despite a couple of dinners in out-of-the-way restaurants, Gwen and I had shared no relationship, outside the dubious one of having made no commitment to anyone else. Finding her here made perfect sense. Gwen and Tony could join their solitudes with no questions asked, from each other or anyone else. Yet it hurt in a way that must have shown on my face.

She offered a tentative smile that I could read as apologetic if I wished and opened the door wider.

"Is Tony here?"

"I'm sorry. No, he's not."

She didn't need to say that Tony wouldn't have told her where he was or what he was doing, and that she would not have asked.

"Ah." The fact that she would be alone in his house spoke of an intimacy I wouldn't have guessed at. I wondered if she had quietly moved in with him, somehow managing to fly under the radar of embassy gossip.

She cocked her head in silent query.

"I called his office, but he wasn't in. I thought maybe ..."

"You can wait for him if you want," she said, but remained standing in the doorway.

I had never believed in fate. Most Americans don't. We think we control the heavens, not the other way around. But in coming to Sri Lanka I had arrived in a world with an entirely different range of possibilities, where life was painted from a different palette. Here, most people believed the positions of the ever-moving heavenly bodies ordered the course of their lives. Or they held to the unknowable dialectic of karma stretching across uncountable incarnations. Either way, they saw their lives as leading along a fated track, determined before birth.

Perhaps by living here, surrounded by the beliefs of millions, my life too had slipped out of the illusion of control and become ordained by fate. No matter what time or which day I had come, Tony would not have been at home and I would lose the spur of resolution that had brought me to his door. I had weeks ago started down a rogue path and would now have to walk it to the end.

"I know you, Philip. Something's wrong."

I wanted to say, "I was at the office and I realized that we'll never understand what we're doing here. We stumble around, making things better or making them worse in ways we don't intend or even see. Everything would be better if we didn't do anything at all." Instead, I asked, "What time is it?"

"Nearly seven. Philip, are you in trouble?"

"I'm not sure." I tried to say it lightly, as if making a joke. "No need to tell him I came by."

She looked at me, puzzled and worried, for I was her friend. "All right, if that's what you want."

She shut the door, and I walked back to my car.

25

Seven thirty had come and gone and the setting sun had made an oven of the embassy car I'd parked on the side of the dusty, treeless dirt road. The road lay empty but for the swirling dust devils that rose like unhappy portents above the bare fields. The silence of the empty spaces seeped into my ears until only the sound of the occasional car passing on the highway, a half mile away, reassured me I had not gone deaf. Across the road, the gates of the spike-topped wall that surrounded the large stuccoed house remained shut.

I turned the radio on, then turned it off, glanced at my watch and thought again that the embassy sedan, with its diplomatic license plate, looked as conspicuous as an armored car on the otherwise empty road. For the third time since I'd arrived I decided I'd waited long enough. The wrong set of eyes might see me, and the embassy would hear that one of its officers had been sitting by the side of the road in front of a house owned by— Well, who? I had no idea. I started to turn the key in the ignition, then stopped. Give it a few more minutes, I said to myself.

The sweat that trickled down my hands felt oily and oppressive, tracing the path of my own bad faith. I wiped my palms on my pants legs. A crow took a couple of skittish swoops over the dusty road, then landed and began picking at something—garbage, a dead dog, something—in the bottom of a ditch.

The groaning of the steel gate startled me out of my funk. As the gate slowly swung open, I caught a glimpse of an impressive house and a gravel drive with two cars—and the figure of J. R. Thilakaratne. The shock of finding this most stalwart of Jayatilaka loyalists at the place where I had agreed to meet its most noted opponent caused my mind to blink out like an overloaded circuit.

Even on this hot evening, the Government of Sri Lanka's Official Censor wore a dark suit and carried himself with all the dignity of a self-regarding bishop. The gate shut behind him as he walked across the road toward me. Thilakaratne looked somehow less out of place here than in his own office, more plausible as a conspirator than as a bureaucrat, his demeanor as natural as on that day in the university parking lot when he relayed the still unknown message that had provoked Bandula into crashing his mother's car.

He leaned his arms on the open window of my car and said, "I do not understand what you are doing here."

Caught in some sort of psychic echo chamber, I heard my own thoughts expressed through this other man's words. Yet I was sure he was lying. My presence hadn't surprised him. He'd known I was outside the gate, waiting.

He tried again. "I wasn't expecting— "

"To see me. And I'm supposed to believe that."

The Sri Lankan shrugged and nodded toward the house. "The party I assume you're expecting will be out momentarily." The slight smile that had lingered on Thilakaratne's lips faded and his habitually mournful expression reasserted itself. "Mr. Reid, the way we do things here occasionally seems peculiar even to us." He cocked his head to one side, as if wondering whether I could understand what he was saying. "What appears as betrayal often proves to be the height of fidelity."

Again, his words seemed plucked from my own mind, expressing the sophistries I had leaned on to justify my behavior

On this cue, the steel gate again groaned open on its hinges. Tissa Sandanayake's bodyguard emerged and stood just outside the gate, his hands clasped casually in front of him, his eyes taking in everything. After a pause just long enough to take a deep breath, the man himself strolled through the gate, smiling, carrying a manila envelope in his hand.

Thilakaratne retreated a few steps, as if pretending he were not there. Perhaps it worked, I thought, for Sandanayake walked past the other man as if he did not exist.

For an unsettling instant, I swore that Sandanayake's step had taken on the peculiar rolling gate of my father as I had seen him so often, climbing down from his truck at some heat-blasted loading dock in the San Joaquin Valley. At the shock of this thought, the blood rushed to my face and I knew why I had come out here to meet him on this deserted road. I wanted to trust Tissa Sandanayake, as I had once trusted my father. At this revelation of my own tormented motivations, I almost started up the car and drove away. But I didn't.

A cloud of dust appeared in my rearview mirror, approaching from the main highway. As it grew closer it resolved itself into a small expensive sedan, which stopped on the side of the road directly behind me.

"It has been very nice to chat with you," Thilakaratne lied one last time, then climbed into the back seat of the car and, with a peculiar wave, drove into the gathering dusk. He did it all without looking at Sandanayake, as if he might yet convince me that the two of them had not been meeting together in the house behind the wall.

"Well, Mr. Reid. Philip." Tissa beamed as he held out his hand. "I'm sorry to have kept you waiting so long. Thank you for your willingness to come all the way out here." The politician spoke forcefully and quickly, apparently trying to derail whatever train of thought his appearance with Thilakaratne might have set in motion. He hefted the manila envelope in his hand. "As I said earlier, I understand that your upcoming trip will be taking you to the home of my parents in Badulla. I am grateful to Ambassador Donovan for this gesture. It's ..." He paused, tapped the edge of the envelope against the palm of his hand and rethought whatever he'd been about to say. "I would consider it a very great service if you would give this envelope to my parents. It's nothing terribly important. A letter. No great matter." He held his hands open in a gesture of frankness. "Some things are too personal to trust to the vagaries of our mail system." Despite his assurances, his smile faded under the weight of something unspoken.

Perhaps he saw that I had registered his uncertainty, for he quickly recovered himself and his smile, the one he turned to the public, his emblem of confidence and strength. "However, if one can't always have faith in the mails, one can have faith in certain people."

A still-feeble reflex warned me to beware of the flattery of great men, but I thought, yes, he's right; despite everything, I am trustworthy.

If Thilakaratne and Sandanayake would lie to me, why shouldn't I lie to myself?

When I reached for the offered envelope, Sandanayake seemed unable to let it go, as if this normally decisive man were afflicted by second thoughts.

He shook his head to cover his discomfort. "Of course, you might feel awkward delivering private messages while on official duty. I understand. And I'm . . . certain you won't want to mention this to anyone." His attempt at an off-hand manner failed and, with uncharacteristic uncertainty, he groped for words. "I know how discreet you have been regarding your relationship with our friend, Mr. Jayatila-ka. I understand what a risk you have taken regarding your standing within the embassy." He looked at me steadily un-til he was sure I had taken his meaning.

The words fell like a deadbolt locking a door behind me.

Sandanayake's smile bent into something like a grimace at his oh-so-obliquely expressed threat of disclosure. How he had learned of my friendship with Bandula was immaterial. Perhaps it was something Thilakaratne knew of and for some reason had mentioned to him. The only thing that mattered was that my relationship with Bandula had become a known commodity outside the embassy and, like any other com-modity, could be traded, but only on a very private market.

I wanted to tell this last best hope of Sri Lankan politics, "You didn't have to do this. I would have done this favor for you anyway." But that didn't matter now, and I said nothing, even as I again fought the urge to drive away before Sandanayake could overcome whatever scruple or apprehension kept him from handing me the envelope.

Even as these questions raced through my mind, Tissa's face relaxed. The moment had passed. There would be no going back. He let out a slow breath. "No doubt you can find a private moment with my parents in which to give this to them." He looked at me intently, and when he saw whatever it was he sought, he let the envelope go. "As I say, its contents aren't of any great importance, so you needn't tell anyone about it."

"It's all right. I wouldn't—" I stopped. Of what value is a promise that my betrayal will only go so far?

At this sign of hesitation, a cloud crossed the Sri Lankan's face, as if he too had doubts about what he wished me to do. But the cloud quickly passed and he bestowed upon me his broadest, most magnetic smile. Yes, I can see that you are the man for the job."

We both bit hard on the bullet of irony to get through this parlous moment. He patted me on the shoulder then turned back toward the house and walked away as the iron gate once more groaned open. What questions might I have asked if I'd known that this was the last time I would ever see him?

I started the car and headed back to the city, arriving in darkness.

26

On a hot, humid afternoon—there were no other kind, even in early December—a Saturday, Bandula's driver, Peter had come to fetch me for a basketball game at the Jayaytilaka's house. I recognized most of the players from the night of the reception, including the pudgy player Kumar had knocked over, though I was surprised to find that Kumar himself was absent.

Without the goad of the young Tamil forcing them to play their best, the game became more decorous than competitive, with lots of high fives and little scoring. For me, the familiar weight of the ball in my hands, the simple joy of running, the streams of sweat rolling down my back gave me a sense of liberation from everything beyond the basketball court.

We played for more than an hour in the hot, heavy air until we all felt the pleasant exhaustion of hard play. Afterward, the other players stood around for a bit, striking poses as they drank from logo-splashed water bottles before going home in their chauffeur-driven cars.

Wiping his brow with a towel, Bandula steered me toward the house. "Go into the kitchen and ask for a drink while I shower. I'll be down in a couple of minutes."

With dinner still hours away, the kitchen was empty of its usual troupe of cooks and servants. A lone woman wearing curlers in her hair and the simple white dress of a housemaid had the kitchen to herself. She stood with her back to me, peering into the oversized refrigerator. Humming a tune to herself, she reached toward a back shelf, knocking something over as she did. "Oh, damn," she muttered, and reached for a sponge to clean up her mess. Only when she shut the refrigerator door and turned toward me, a plate of cold chicken in her hand, did I recognize her.

The uncrowned queen of Sri Lanka laughed at my surprise. "Oh, you have caught the great Chiran Jayatilaka raiding her own fridge." She took a tall glass out of the cupboard. "You look perished, Philip. You need a nice glass of mango juice."

I accepted the drink, aware of Chiran's eyes on me, and groped for something to say, "I wouldn't have thought you knew who I was."

"Ah! Don't you think the guards around this house keep me informed of everything?" She continued to smile even as her words chilled my heart. "So, what do you think of our little place?" She laughed when I didn't answer immediately. "But I'm fishing for compliments. Next, I'll be asking you if you think I'm pretty."

I started to say something, but she put up a hand, a gesture her son had apparently taken from her. "No, please. Not a word." Her smile fading, she gazed at me. "You're a good friend to my son. I'm grateful. He has so few real friends." She began picking at the chicken on her plate. "Oh, he has a bunch of spoiled children he hangs around with, but they think of nothing but themselves, of what they can get out of him." She looked at me closely. "You don't think I have a normal mother's concern for her son's happiness? That I don't worry about my boy? Especially when he spends so much time with that slut. What is her name? Ah, Lilani. And, my god, that K-K-K—"

"Kumar."

She looked at me as if I'd uttered an obscenity, but recovered quickly, hiding her sudden vulnerability behind the smokescreen of a beguiling smile. "But you, you're his friend. I know this. You have his best interests at heart."

"Your son's a good man."

She shook her head. "He's still a boy," she said, then cocked her head like a curious bird. "So, tell me, what do you want?"

"Sorry?"

Again, she smiled, but no longer amused. "Want. What is it you want?" she repeated. "Everyone wants something. Access. Information. A bit of gossip. Don't be ashamed. Friendship doesn't prevent that sort of thing. So, what is it you tell your people at the embassy after you've been here?"

"I haven't told them anything. They don't know." I'd felt the need to prove her wrong, but immediately regretted revealing anything she could use.

"You don't expect me to believe that," she scoffed. As attuned to others' moods as a shark to troubled waters, she sensed my uneasiness and spoke with a coaxing, conspiratorial hush. "Of course you tell them things. You have to think about what it can do for your career. You're ambitious. Ah, you didn't think I could tell. But I'm surrounded by ambitious men. I know that vice when I see it. I use their ambition to make them do what I want."

Though not a beautiful woman, there was something sensual, even seductive about her, and I fought against a strong, if horrifying, attraction that I was certain she was aware of.

She laughed. "Oh, I don't blame you for wanting something. Don't be ashamed. It's just politics," she said, looking at me demurely.

But it was too late now. Like a mouse awakened to the snake's mesmerizing charm, I put myself on guard.

"Everything's politics, isn't it?" she said, looking over my shoulder, addressing these remarks to someone else.

When I turned to follow her gaze I found Bandula, his hair still wet from the shower, standing in the doorway, his fists clenched. I wondered how long he had been listening.

Chiran Jayatilaka smiled. "Ah, here he is now. We were just talking about you and your friends."

Bandula looked at me, his face distorted by the fear of betrayal.

His mother laughed. "No, your friend told me nothing. I think perhaps he was about to, but you walked in at just the wrong moment." She waggled her head. "No, he's a real friend—not like that Tamil boy you waste your time on. I can't imagine what you two do together all the time. Up in your room." She looked at me. "Of course, you've met him, so you know what I mean."

"Mother!" Bandula cried.

I wondered where such cruelty came from. What could Bandula have done to her to deserve this? He was simply the son of her husband. And, of course, that was enough. I was certain her cruelty toward Lilani stemmed from her friendship with him. I would find out later how nearly right I was, and how greatly wrong.

"No, don't be upset," she cooed. "I've only asked your friend what he wants out of you, and he won't tell me."

His eyes grew wide, on the verge of tears. "Can't you see?" he shouted, "He doesn't want anything."

I felt my stomach drop, knowing I was hearing the repetition of my own lie.

Chiran looked at me, then at her son with an expression of fond pity. "Well, don't be upset with *me*. I've already said that I know he's your friend. And do tell him that this filthy girl he fancies is only trying to use him."

Bandula balled his fists like a frustrated child. "Leave him alone."

She turned her eyes on me, but I sensed that somehow she wasn't really looking at me anymore. "You see how it is?" she asked, her smile cold as a steel knife. "Now, be sure to tell them in the embassy that I know everything that's going on." Almost imperceptibly, she shook her head. "Tell them that I know they won't let me rest in peace. I know of their love for this farmer's boy. This boy, Sandanayake. Tell them that his star has risen as far as it will rise, and he has nothing left to him but to fall." Her voice rose, like a storm gathering strength. "I keep an eye on everything that happens. Even the fall of a sparrow. 'If it be now, 'tis not to come; if it be not to come, it will be now.'" She laughed, and with that laugh I knew she was mad. "You all want to know why the war continues, why it goes on and on. I know. I know why there's a drought. Everything has gone wrong, but don't worry. It's only a test of my strength. I'll put it all right again."

With a strangled cry, Bandula ran from the kitchen. The slam of the door resounded like a bomb.

27

Forty miles out of Colombo, the road to Kurunegala turns north off the Kandy highway and enters a dense forest. The tops of the trees merge over the narrow two-lane blacktop, filtering the sunlight to perpetual dusk. Here, dozens of reed-thin men in threadbare clothes line the road along the fringes of the forest, standing at their rickety tables, offering to passing motorists identical selections of coconut, jackfruit and roasted nuts. They dry the nuts on grills over smoldering fires, the smoke rising moodily through the trees, adding a sad and dreamy touch to the scene.

Our fact-finding mission was only a couple of hours old, but already I sensed we were traveling through another country, one divorced from the vitality and wealth of the capital, as well as from its cabals and politics. Over the next three days I would find how right—and wrong—I was.

Not wanting to wake Nancy and Carl, who were dozing in the back seat of the embassy Land Rover, I leaned toward Gita and asked, "How can any of them make a living when they're all selling the same thing just a few yards from each other?"

Gita seemed at first not to have heard the question, then shrugged and said, "They always do this, sir."

A few months earlier his response would have struck me as no answer at all, but I had learned that in a culture as tradition-bound as Sri Lanka's the answer to "why?" is always "because." I had come to learn, too, that when I didn't understand a response it was because, in a very real sense, I hadn't understood my own question.

Without taking his eyes off the road, Gita said quietly, "Something is troubling you, sir."

I opened my mouth to deny it, but the lie would not come out.

"I am sorry, sir. I should not say anything. But you are forever looking behind us. I assure you that no one is following us. There is no one there."

I wouldn't have known how to tell him that I was not searching the road behind us, but had been unconsciously looking toward the back of the car where my bag was stowed, thinking of Tissa Sandanayake's letter hidden in its pocket, wondering what secrets it held. Just as I had told no one of the errand he had given me, he had told me nothing of the letter's contents—a secret wrapped in a secret.

We continued in silence and soon left the comforting shadows of the woods.

※

Driving long, slow hours from town to town, dashing wearily from appointment to appointment, the up-country trip became a series of snapshots, their discontinuity reflecting the fractured nature of the country.

In Kurunegala, Nancy's statistics-crammed luncheon speech to the Chamber of Commerce acted like a soporific on the overfed businessmen. They woke up a bit when, her remarks finished, she asked them why they thought the country's economy fared so poorly. Someone cited the lack of infrastructure investment by the government. Another faulted export policy, while the man next to him said the problem was import policy. A couple of the businessmen blamed the educational system. One after another the ideas bubbled up from the drowsy audience. Not one of them blamed the war that was tearing the country to pieces.

※

We stopped for the night at a tourist hotel near Dambula. Wearied by the long day, we all went to bed early. I was asleep two minutes after my head hit the pillow.

Sometime deep into the night I woke with a start, my heart beating wildly, certain that I had heard footsteps on my third-floor balcony. I held my breath, listened. I began to tell myself that it had been a dream, I heard it again, a thumping scuffling sound from outside that grew closer, then stopped. Was it only my troubled conscience that made me believe someone was spying on me?

I looked toward the balcony—my room faced out on an empty plain, so I had not pulled the drapes—and saw shadowy figures moving in the dark.

Blood rushing to my head and limbs, I leaped from bed and grabbed a chair. As I raised it high, ready to swing at whoever was peering in on me, I finally saw my intruders clearly and gently let the chair down.

By the light of the moon, a string of monkeys squatted on the balcony railing, fascinated by the opportunity to watch a human in his natural habitat.

My knees buckled in relief. But when I returned to bed I found I could not get back to sleep.

I rose again and crossed the room. From the pocket in my bag, I drew the manila envelope that Tissa Sandanayake had entrusted to me. The flap was secured with a red string wrapped around a cardboard disk. Within the large envelope I felt the outlines of a smaller one.

I stood like this for a long time, tempted to open the larger envelope to see if the smaller one gave any clue to its contents. What was one more betrayal now?

My willingness to betray Tissa's confidence raised a wave of self-loathing in me and stopped my hand. I stuffed the envelope back into the pocket of my bag and yanked the blinds closed. The monkeys scattered into the darkness, chattering with fright.

※

Anaradhapura lay at the northern limit of government control. Beyond it was Tiger country. We all felt the sense of entering a city under siege. Barbed wire checkpoints guarded every route into town. In Colombo, solitary soldiers stood a relaxed guard at various points around the city. Here, they clumped in nervous knots, idling uneasily around major intersections and government buildings, their hands on their rifles.

※

At the local university I crossed the strangely empty campus and spoke to a group of young students about American foreign policy. Afterward, while drinking tea in his office, the rector halted midway through his description of the university's excellent academics and sunk his head in his hands. He confessed the students were not his but from a local boarding school, brought in to hide from the American diplomat the fact that the campus had been shut down because of the violence wrought by a pro-government student gang. He had been ordered that morning to reopen the campus and reinstate the members of the gang or he would be fired. "This government. This country," he said, weeping.

※

As Public Affairs Officer, part of my job consisted of watching local TV, especially the news, even while traveling. In the evening, I lay in bed in my hotel room and switched on the television, which opened me up to the nightmare paradox that, while I thought constantly of Lilani, the one I saw was Chiran. She presided at charity balls held in her honor, opened conferences at the university center named after her father, attended the openings of children's health clinics bearing the family name. Though others might serve as cabinet officials, members of parliament, even as president, it seemed that it was her presence, not theirs, that loomed over the island like watchful, potentially vengeful, deity.

※

The following day we drove for several dispiriting hours past fields of dried and cracking earth. We allowed ourselves only one quick break along the way to visit the ruins of one of the island's ancient capitals. We wandered for a few minutes among stacks of shattered stone and broken brick, the remains of fallen temples and ruined palaces, their walls entwined in a living quilt of vines and creepers.

Amid the chirping of cicadas and the sigh of the wind, we noticed after a while a faint but steady buzzing, like a lingering vibration from the dead city and its vanished population.

Curious, we followed the sound until we came to a dusty fountain that looked as if water had not run through it since the surrounding lanes had rung with the sounds of its long-departed inhabitants. Around the fountain, moving in a grave and ponderous circle, walked half a dozen Buddhist monks, their orange robes glowing like flame against the gray stone, chanting in eerie unison, slowly shuffling around the ruined fountain, as if their endless circling might bring it back to life.

※

We arrived in the provincial town of Polonnaruwa in the early afternoon, just in time for another whirlwind of appointments, each of us going our separate ways for the day.

After dinner with Nancy and Carl in the hotel restaurant, I excused myself before the dessert, pleading fatigue. I couldn't confess the truth that I was driven by my obsession with the letter concealed in my bag, its presence as ineluctable, and disturbing, as Poe's telltale heart.

I fairly ran back to my room and entered it like a thief, too hurried to turn on the lights. I crossed quickly to my bag, unzipped its pocket and retrieved Tissa Sandanayaka's letter, running my hand once again along the edges of the large envelope, tracing with my fingertips the contours of the smaller envelope within.

It took only a moment to unwind the string that held shut the larger envelope and shake its contents out. Without bothering to turn on a lamp, I felt along the flap of the smaller envelope and found that it was sealed shut. I knew I could not bring myself to tear it open, but could see there was something written across its face. I drew back the curtain and read by the moon's faint light the single, handwritten line: *TO BE OPENED IN THE EVENT OF MY DEATH.*

I grunted as if someone had punched me in the stomach, and an irrational horror came over me that in reading the tall block letters I had somehow killed the man whose secret I carried, as surely as if I had shot him myself. For a long time, I stood in the moonlit room, not moving, barely breathing. Then I placed the letter back into the large envelope and once more wrapped the string around its flap.

28

After the yellowing plains and parched fields of the north, the countryside around Badulla glowed with abundance. Here, on the eastern slopes of the island's central mountains, water still poured from artesian springs, and the rice paddies glowed like emeralds. It seemed the last corner of Sri Lanka in which life still thrived.

Road-jaded and stiff, Carl and Nancy and I climbed out of the Land Rover and made our way up the walkway to the door of a white house set among the rice fields.

I had pictured the Sandanayakes as an aging and weathered farm couple, dressed in sarongs, living by the generosity of their accomplished son, in a modern house. So I felt a rush of shame when we were greeted by a graying but attractive woman in western dress, carrying herself with the same quiet self-possession that I had seen in her son. "Please, come in," she said, "I am Nili Sandanayake, Tissa's mother."

"Ah, our callers from the American Embassy!" called an enthusiastic voice from the living room. Ranjith Sandanayake, a vigorous barrel-chested man in his sixties, came into the tiny foyer. He firmly shook Carl's hand and mine, then took Nancy's as if it were the first flower of spring. "Come in. Come in."

Tissa Sandanayake's political career had been cultivated in the fertile soil of his family's longstanding political engagement. Years earlier, his father had made himself a leader in the farmer's movement, demanding justice from the overlords in Colombo. The older man still carried a limp testifying to a leg shattered by landowners' thugs. But he had pressed on until the farmers' movement he started became the small but dynamic Renewal Party, now led by the couple's son.

The elder Sandanayake waved us toward a couch. He eased into a well-worn armchair and offered us coffee rather than tea, saying, "I know Americans."

Nancy, shy and bold, looked at her hands and spoke first. "Mr. Sandanayake— "

The old activist leaned forward in his chair and waved away formality with a sweep of his hand. "Call me Ranjith."

Nancy coughed as if this would take a little effort. "Ranjith. We wanted to come here today to— "

Ranjith Sandanayake held up his hands to stop her. "Look, I'm too old to sit here and pile up words with you. You came here so that I would tell the local press about your visit. That will get into the national papers and let Susan Guneratne and the NRP know that they're not the only game in town." He laughed and raised an eyebrow at her, coaxing a confession. "Am I right?"

Nancy blushed. "Well, that may play a part—"

"That's it exactly. And it's smart. I hope you've let some of the editors in Colombo know about this visit. They're the ones who count."

I told him, "Yes, we're letting out the word on this."

"Good. Good," Ranjith said, striking his fist into the palm of his hand. "That's how the game is played."

As Ranjith beamed from his armchair, clearly delighted to be at the center of some political elbow-throwing, Nili returned bearing a tray of coffee cups.

The three of us, sat on the couch, holding our cups in our laps, looking like the hear-no-evil, see-no-evil, speak-no-evil monkeys on a coffee break. I glanced around the small living room, noting its furniture, solid but not showy, a bookcase full of cloth–bound volumes, tall windows letting in light and air. I felt sure the internal furnishings of this couple were much the same—practical, straightforward. How different it was from the Jayatilakas' great mansion outside Colombo and from the strange and unhappy lives that passed within its walls.

For all the differences between them, though, the sons of these two families had committed themselves to change. I couldn't help but think that, compared to Tissa Sandanayake's leadership and his call to political reform, Bandula's dreams seemed childish and half-formed.

Carl leaned forward on the couch. "We're grateful you've allowed us to come, sir. Frankness is a rare commodity around here, and—"

Ranjith beamed. "And your presence here is the most important message you can carry. We will all make sure that the word gets back to Colombo. Then we can—"

"Ranjith," Nili Sandanayake said.

Her husband stopped mid-sentence and glanced at his wife with an apologetic smile. "I'm not letting them talk, am I?"

Nili moved her hands from the arms of the straight-backed chair into her lap—the simplest of gestures, but it quietly shifted the focus to her. "All we have wanted is the chance to have a real election," she said. "Your embassy has put pressure on these people, helped to make this happen. But we fear that the run-up to the election will set off a wave of violence that will make a mockery of the election itself. One can see it beginning already." Her quiet thoughtfulness perfectly complemented her husband's enthusiasm.

Carl raised a reassuring hand. "I hear you. We're doing everything we can to see that the whole process is as open as can be."

The graying woman nodded. "An election between those who are simply fortunate enough to have survived the campaign does not make a democracy."

Ranjith Sandanayake sighed and ran his fingers through his hair. "There is a candidate whose name you will never find on the ballot, but it tops the electoral list of those in power. His name is fear. Fear dominates the debate. Fear speaks first and last at all the rallies. Fear writes the editorials. Fear of disorder, fear of the Tamil Tigers, fear of the future, fear of the past." He looked steadily at us. "Yes, we fear even the past because we have made enormous mistakes and are terrified that these errors have foreclosed our future, that it no longer belongs to us. We fear that the future has nothing to offer us but extinction. So, we end up chasing a ghost—the ghost of ourselves."

"How do you create a better future?" I asked.

The old labor leader leaned forward as if to make sure that not a word was missed. "We must restore the past if we hope to live in the present. We must make amends, reconcile ourselves to our history so we can have a future."

The candidate's mother spoke with quiet and compelling strength. "Many say that our son can lead us there. I believe it's true. Tissa sees a future in which we live in peace with each other and, more importantly, as Ranjith says, live in peace with ourselves."

We spoke for a few more minutes about the election and the drought and shared some political gossip from Colombo. When we finished our coffee, we rose to go.

After we said our goodbyes and started to climb into the Land Cruiser, Nancy looked at me quizzically. "Didn't you have a coat?"

I had counted on her noticing, and made what I hoped looked like an authentically chagrined smile.

"I will get it, sir," Gita said. But I was already out of the car and making my way up the walk. Nili did not look surprised to see me when she answered the door. Ranjith had my coat in his hand. I made sure the door had closed behind me before taking the folded envelope from the inside pocket of my coat and handing it to Ranjith.

The old man gazed at his son's handwriting on the outside of the larger envelope. Without looking up, he said, "He told us to expect this." He made a small smile. "It's nothing all that ..." Like his son before him, he attempted to make light of the letter with a dismissive gesture, but he couldn't finish what he was going to say, and the envelope shook slightly in his hands.

I understood. He knew its contents. "I'm happy to be of service," I said.

Nili put a hand on my arm. "Tissa lives without fear. That is why the government hates him. He refuses to be afraid. That is *their* fear—a man who can reconcile the past and finally leave it behind."

Ranjith nodded vigorously. "Tissa can do that." The note of a proud father faded into a worried sigh. "If he is allowed. If he is allowed."

The enthusiasm drained from his eyes, and he took his wife's hand. They exchanged a look that told me the NRP's candidate, fear, had not overlooked the parents of its greatest opponent.

29

Tea covers the slopes of Sri Lanka's mountains like a great green carpet, spilling over the steep ridges and running down to the streams that trace the bottoms of the rugged draws. From a distance, the blanket of tea bushes appears as smooth and lustrous as a well-tended lawn. A few trees dot the hillsides, as if planted to perfectly set off the even rows, making the slopes pleasing to the eye and soothing to the mind.

What looked from a distance like multi-colored beads scattered across the fields became sari-clad women dragging their long cloth sacks along the narrow paths between the rows of tea. In contrast to the bright colors of their saris, the women were hollow-eyed and sunken-cheeked. The beauty of the land hid the difficult lives of those who worked it.

We arrived late in the morning to Haputale, a small town set within the tea country's rugged hills. Here the mountain air tasted fresh, like clear water, so unlike the coast where breathing is like sucking air through a wet dishrag. In a few hours, by late afternoon, Gita and the others would be out of the mountains, onto the coastal plain and back in Colombo. But I was stopping here.

A large, irregular square formed the center of the small town. I told Gita to drop me off along the curb. He pulled to a stop in front of a row of vegetable stands. I got out of the Land Rover, opened the tailgate and took out my bag. Funny how much lighter it felt without the letter in it.

Nancy turned and leaned over the back of the rear seat. "And you want us to just leave you here?"

We exchanged a look, but she knew I would say nothing. Before we had departed Colombo I'd told them that I would be leaving them here to do a little tea tourism. Nancy never believed me and had tried several times to coax my secret from me. Now she leaned over the back seat, rested her chin on her hands and batted her eyes at me. "This 'Philip Reid, Man of Mystery' thing is getting old."

I had to laugh, but shook my head, refusing to rise to the bait.

White with car-sickness from the drive through the twisting mountain roads, Carl muttered, "Leave the guy alone."

I avoided Nancy's gaze as she waited for a last-minute confession.

Defeated, she sighed with exasperation. "And people say *we're* inscrutable." She laughed and gave in. "Okay. See you 'round campus." She waved through the back window as the embassy car pulled away, leaving me standing on the pavement. I picked up my suitcase and began to walk.

Half a mile from the center of town, I found the lane I'd been told to look for, one that led me out along the crest of a narrow ridge. To my left, the ground fell away sharply for more than a thousand feet, a dizzying drop overlooking the distant checkerboard of rice paddies and woods stretching for miles into the hazy distance. Far to the west, a wandering line of trees marked the course of a river meandering toward the Indian Ocean. To my right a gentler slope, heavily wooded, led down to a stream, its burbling just audible over the sigh of the wind.

Children stopped to watch me pass along the dirt road, giggling at the sight of a Westerner carrying his own bag. I smiled back, causing the smaller ones to run off laughing in a rush of pleasurable fright.

After half an hour of walking in the cool December air, I stopped at the bottom of a drive that rose to my left, where the ridge jutted above the road. Panting slightly in the thin mountain air, I walked to the top of the drive. Here, the broken ridgetop widened just enough to allow space for a white cottage, glowing in the sun, and a wedge of lawn that ended at a rocky point.

My knock echoed within the silent cottage. When no one answered I let myself in. The air inside was cool and fresh and still, and I knew that I was alone.

Large windows looked out over the vista to the west while the sun beamed in from the opposite side, making the front room bright and pleasant. A tiny kitchen held a propane range and a refrigerator. The sun glittered off a freshly washed knife on the counter. Across the hall a small study contained shelves filled with hard-backed books and a wooden desk covered by a layer of dust. A world globe on a stand showed boundaries and names washed away in a wave of headlines years earlier. An open window had not entirely aired out the faint smell of bookish mildew.

I set my bag down in the bedroom, the largest and most comfortable room in the cottage. Tall windows stood open to the breeze, and the sun gave the room a sense of cozy spaciousness. On one side lay a large bed covered by a thick quilt. Next to it was a dressing table backed by a mirror, clouded with time. On the other side of the room stood a small table set for tea.

I didn't hear her enter but turned toward the presence I felt behind me. In her arms she held a bunch of flowers picked from the grassy slopes below.

She laid the flowers on the bed and sighed as I put my arms around her, barely touching her at first, then closing her in a tight embrace, feeling the warmth of her body against mine. She leaned her head on my chest and I thought again how perfectly she fit against me. Something that I had kept wrapped tightly within me started to relax.

She wore a wool sweater in the mountain air, and I ran my fingertips just under its edges, where the swell of her hips began, the skin soft and downy and warm. She shivered and I held her more tightly.

"It's not that I'm cold," she whispered, and I could hear the smile in her voice.

She raised her chin and we kissed, tentatively at first, then stronger, surer, more comfortably, and I slowly ran my hands up her back, pulling off her sweater. She began to unbutton my shirt.

She turned back the quilt so that we would not have to feel chilly as we began to make love, but we soon threw it off, scattering the flowers onto the floor.

※

Afterwards, I ran my hands over her smooth belly and the softness of her small breasts. I ran my tongue along her ear and felt her shiver again, like the aftershock of an earthquake. I had never in my life felt freer from everything that had come before—not as if nothing had ever happened to me, but as if none of it mattered anymore. The prison door of the past swung open, beckoning me to leave and not look back. Our nakedness was both fact and metaphor. Each of us had laid ourselves naked before the other.

It seemed the moment to say something that had long flickered at the back of my mind. "I was always afraid you didn't care for me. I hoped, but you hardly said a word to me."

She nestled her head against my shoulder. "In my mind I said so much. But I was afraid."

"Afraid? Of what?"

"Of you— "

"Of me?"

"—and what you might mean to me. I was afraid to hope."

We held each other wordlessly for a long time, the need for talk in abeyance for now.

Lilani rose from the bed and went to the kitchen, returning a few moments later with a papaya and a mango and cold water. We pulled the quilt over us and lay with our limbs intertwined. I looked around the room, thinking that, no matter who had been here before, it was ours now. It belonged to no one else.

As if in answer, the old house creaked.

Lilani jumped at the sound and turned toward the door.

"You expecting someone?" I laughed.

"Why should I be—?" When she saw I was joking she tried to laugh. "No, of course not." But she appeared unsettled and her laugh was forced.

Her uneasiness crept into my heart like a shiver of poison, but I let it go, deciding it was my imagination, a last remnant of anxiety from carrying Tissa's letter. But I had fulfilled that obligation and could relax. It was all behind me. Only the future mattered now.

"Is this a place you come often?" I asked.

"Sometimes."

She saw me waiting for more and after a moment added, "I come here by myself, to be alone."

I kissed her and whispered, "There was a time when I thought I wanted to know all about you, where you came from, who you were. But now it doesn't matter. I don't need to know."

She brushed the hair from my forehead and looked into my eyes, unsmiling. "Yes, you do," she said. "You'll have to know, so that there will only be truth between us." She looked at me as if her eyes were her sole means of expressing the truth she needed me to know. Never in my life had I understood how much love and sadness could look alike.

※

I was laying wood in the bedroom fireplace that night when I heard the front door open then softly close. I told myself not to follow too quickly. I took a moment to build the fire and light it, watched it burning well, then crossed the empty house and went outside.

I found Lilani sitting at the top of the stony point that rose at the end of the lawn, jutting out over the precipice below. I climbed onto the rocks and found a place beside her. For a long time we sat without speaking, looking out over the darkness as from the deck of a great ship sailing on the night sky.

A few lights shone from solitary farmhouses, blinking in the distance as if the stars lay not only above us, but below us as well. To the west, where I thought to find only the blackness of the night, I saw a bright light that quickly blinked out before reappearing a few moments later and fading once again.

"That is the lighthouse at Kalutura," Lilani said.

"But that must be … "

"Almost eighty kilometers away."

We contemplated for a moment that great distance, and the diminishing distance between ourselves.

She tried to look me in the eye, but could not.

"What is it?" I asked.

She turned away, then abruptly turned back, her eyes penetrating deeply into mine. "Philip, Bandula told me you're married."

Her words came as a relief. I felt the weight of the un-asked question, sensed its importance to a young woman living within a traditional culture, and began to understand the risk she was taking to be with me.

Leaning close, I said, "You don't have to worry about that. It's over, been over for a long time." I'd never said this to anyone, never pronounced the end of my marriage. In hearing my own words, I felt their finality. "She returned to the life we had come from. I stayed with this one," I told her. "I never hear from her. She'll file for divorce at some point, and that will be the end of it."

Slowly, she leaned her head on my shoulder. I put my arm around her and felt her breathe deeply, letting go of something she had held inside. For a long time I watched the beam from the distant lighthouse, and thought how comforting its sight must be to those sailing on the ocean's dark waters.

30

In the morning I woke to sunlight streaming through the window. For a disorienting moment I couldn't remember where I was, in what bed or house, or even in what country. It came back to me only gradually, as if I were fading from one dream and into another. Still blinking awake, I smiled to myself at the sound of Lilani's feet padding along the hallway from the kitchen and thought, this must be love, finding joy in hearing another's footsteps.

She wore a white robe and carried a tray with a teapot and bread and jam.

"Come on, lazybones. Get up and have something to eat." She said, setting the tray on the table in the sun. She laughed and I thought how brave she was, trying to be like an American girl for me. I had not thought of her accent in a long time, how musical it sounded to my ear, or of the darkness of her skin, the color of tea against the whiteness of her robe. They seemed perfect here. Would they seem so in another country?

What was I doing in this world? The quiet joy I'd felt a moment earlier faded, replaced by a familiar fear that whatever I did here, whether I worked or loved or found the food to feed my ambition, I would do it without any real understanding, and so it would be doomed before I started. Somehow I knew from the way she set out teacups and buttered the toast that she had thought about me, about these questions long before I had and had dared to love me anyway.

"Come back to bed."

She shook her head. "No. We are going to eat and then take a morning walk."

"Into Haputale?"

She poured the tea. "Into the countryside." She looked at me, suddenly serious. "There are things I need to show you. Things you need to see."

※

The sun felt lighter in the mountains than in Colombo and its warmth sat easy on my shoulder as I walked with Lilani along the narrow dirt road below the cottage.

At this altitude there were pine trees and we walked in their shade, lovers now and the world ours. A faint wind sighed in the treetops.

I imagined that we could be walking along some back road in California, in the northern Coast Range, above the great valley where I had lived most of my life. In a moment we would top a rise and see in the distance the blue Pacific, and I would be home.

Instead, when we came out of the pines we found long carpets of tea rolling down the slope to our right. A wooden sign gave the name of the tea plantation and carried the logo of a British tea company. Scattered along the slope, a ragged line of pickers worked among the plants, their orange and red and blue saris bright as jelly beans against the green of the tea bushes. At the top of the ridge, to the other side of the road, stood a large stone house within a grassy lawn—a thoroughly British home, landed like a spaceship on a hilltop in Sri Lanka.

Lilani took my hand. "It was built for the overseer and his family when tea was first planted here a hundred years ago. They came all this way—a father and a mother and two children—and were so homesick that they built a home just like the one they had left. A cold house for a cold climate, yet they built it here in the tropics." She gazed at the house as we passed, then looked at me. "You must get homesick."

I sensed something larger behind the question. "There's nothing I want—only to be here with you."

She blew out a breath, resisting the urge to believe me.

Below us and to the right, the rugged hills formed a bowl within which lay a village of low, white-walled cinder-block houses crowded together within a crooked network of dirt lanes.

"Funny to see a village right in the middle of these tea fields," I said.

"It's one of the plantation's towns," Lilani said. "These are for the Tea Tamils."

"The Tea Tamils?"

"They are different from the other Tamils on the island. They came at the same time the English built that house. The English planters transported the Tamils here from India because they were experienced at picking tea. They brought them here to these company-owned villages. And here they have stayed."

I looked at the village below and thought of the hard lives of its inhabitants. "Why don't they find other work? Move somewhere else?"

She laughed, but her eyes were stony. "You can only say that because you don't understand. How can they remove themselves to somewhere else? They have no money, no friends, no family in the cities. No one would hire them to do other work. No one calls them slaves, but they receive almost nothing for doing work that kills them while they are still young. Most of them live and die in the same company villages where they are born."

I stood at the edge of the road and stared down at the village, trying to take it all in. "Can't they—" I didn't know what it was I thought they could do.

"Complain to the government?" Her mocking tone hurt. "They don't have the same rights as others. They are barely citizens, the lowest of underclasses. No one stands up for them. No one is their champion. Not even the Tigers fight in their name. They are disowned by everyone."

A short distance further on, Lilani crossed the road and took a dirt path that led down to the settlement. I followed.

Up close, the village lost what little charm it had held from a distance. Mangy dogs barked and made as if to attack, but when I looked at them they shambled away, whining in the backs of their throats.

An unwholesome stew of shameful odors clung to the dirt lanes and I struggled not to put my hand over my nose. The inhabitants, mostly children and old women at this hour of the morning, flicked curious glances at us, too shy to stare.

As if assessing things that needed doing, Lilani looked closely at the condition of the whitewashed shacks, the open drains, the muddy pathways.

"Does the company let aid agencies in here?" I asked her.

"No," she said, scoffing. "That would be too great an admission of their own meanness. They allow a few individuals to help. Quietly. That's all."

A wooden cart leaned against a mud-brick wall. A young girl passed with a jar of water on her head. I thought what a shame it was that poverty should be so picturesque.

While the majority of Sinhala are Buddhists, Tamils are generally Hindu and the village's small central square was dominated by a Hindu temple, its two towers a frozen fugue of countless fantastical figures—grinning demons and grimacing angels in hallucinatory colors I had no names for—standing one atop the other, stretching toward the sky, reflecting the chaos that abided within the dialectic of creation and destruction.

Lilani led me around the hamlet's dirt lanes until we stopped before one of the hovels that lined the narrow streets. She glanced back at me with a complex semaphore of expressions. Before I could begin to decipher them she spoke into the dark interior of the house. She must have received an answer for she entered. I followed, stooping through the low doorway.

An unglazed window set high in one wall allowed a shaft of light into the single-room structure, revealing a few spare furnishings and, sitting at the edge of a low bed, a small woman, thin as a bird, with weathered skin and a sunken face collapsed around a nearly toothless mouth.

Lilani bowed and made the traditional palms-together gesture of greeting to the woman, who returned the gesture and nodded at us to sit down. I sat on a rough wooden chair. Lilani took a small stool at the woman's right hand.

The older woman's sari lent her a poignant grace and contrasted sharply with Lilani's slacks and tennis shoes.

The differing styles implied not simply a divide between generations but between worlds.

The woman's face testified to the hard truth that those who worked in the fields grew old by a different calendar than the privileged class of this island. I searched her withered cheeks and bony nose, the dark, toughened skin and watery eyes for some trace of youth, some hint of lost beauty amid the wreckage of years. No. Nothing.

The two women talked quietly for a few minutes. To my surprise, they spoke in Tamil, which I could recognize but not understand. Living as she did with the very avatars of Sinhala nationalism, I had always assumed that Lilani belonged to the ethnic majority. Once more, the illusion that I had begun to understand who she was dissolved like a reflection in water stirred by the wind, and I was faced again with the fact that she remained a stranger to me.

While the two women spoke, Lilani at first translated little phrases for me, such as, "She welcomes you to her home," and "She is honored to have a visitor from so far away," but after a while the two women talked only to each other, their voices barely audible. Once or twice the older woman glanced at me, and I assumed I was one of the topics of their earnest conversation.

After they had passed perhaps a quarter hour in this increasingly deep dialogue, Lilani again bowed her head, placed her palms together, then kneeled next to the woman and embraced her. The old woman looked up at me, wondering, I think, if I had any manners. I repeated the simple palms-together gesture and we departed.

We left the village behind and walked in silence up the steep track to the top of the ridge. When we had regained the road I said, "You do charitable work with this woman?"

"What I'm allowed, yes," Lilani said, then looked at me in surprise, as if I had misunderstood something she thought perfectly clear. "Who do you think she is?" she asked.

I realized I had no idea. "That she is someone you . . ." My voice trailed off in uncertainty.

"Her name is Lakshmi." She looked into my face for a glimmer of realization. "She is my mother."

We stood facing each other across the narrow road, its width suddenly much greater than the three paces it would take to cross it.

"This is what I wanted you to see," she said. "I needed you to meet her."

I started to ask why, but the answer came to me before I could speak and I was compelled to consider with new gravity who we were, Lilani and me. A curtain in my mind pulled away and I finally began to get a glimmer of things I had not understood before. "The cottage on the ridgetop," I said, "you said it belongs to the Jayatilakas. But before that, you said—"

"That it belonged to my father." Lilani resumed walking along the road. Something in her manner, remote and fragile, persuaded me to keep to the opposite side of the road, walking parallel to her but no longer entirely with her, the closeness we had felt that morning not ended, but suspended. After a long silence she began to speak.

"Though you wouldn't know it to see her now, my mother once had a beauty that would attract the attention of any man. She was charming and bold and many of the young men in the village wanted to marry her just to see if they were strong enough to live with her, could keep her happy. She felt she could take her time, consider them all, and choose at her leisure. But one day the son of the Sri Lankan family that owned the plantation saw her in the fields as he was passing in his car. He often came here from Colombo, staying in a large house on the other side of Haputale, where he would have boys and young women brought to him for his pleasure. From the moment he saw my mother he decided he had to have her. When his driver came down to the village for her the next day, she didn't dare question his right to take her. And, the next day, when the man sent her back to the village while he returned to his mansion in Colombo, she knew there was no one to hear her protest.

"When he returned a few weeks later, he had her brought to him again. This was against his custom. Usually, when he had taken his pleasure with someone, he never wanted to see them again. That changed. No longer were others brought to him. Despite everything he was born to, he had fallen in love with her, an impoverished Tamil tea worker. I think she was the only person, man or woman, he ever really loved. He had the cottage built for them, and she lived there even when he was away.

"A year or two later he married someone else, a woman of his own class. But he saw no reason to stop seeing my mother. After all, he had not married for love, but for power and wealth, and his wife looked the other way when he drove up here, not caring about his past rapes and abuses, not knowing that he now saw only one woman when he came."

Her arms crossed tightly over her chest, Lilani nodded up the road. "I was born in the cottage. It was—is—my home. For several years he kept us both here, until his wife finally found out. She could accept him abusing boys and young women. But when she found out about my mother she wanted to tear the sky in two in her rage. I've often wondered why she was so angry. What was it to her? She didn't love my father. I can only think it was from finding out that he could love while she could not. That part of her doesn't exist. She wanted to murder my mother. But my father said he would kill her if she did. She knew he meant it. So, she forced my father to send my mother back down the mountain to the village from which she had come, back among the Tea Tamils. But now the young men would have nothing to do with her, partly from disgust, partly from fear of the wealthy man and his family." Lilani looked at me. "Do I need to tell you who these people are?"

It took me a moment to piece it together and I spoke slowly as it came to me. "Then Bandula's father ..."

"Is my father, too. Bandula and I are brother and sister. Or half." She blew out a bitter laugh. "Half this, half that."

Lilani took a deep breath as if bracing for hard work. "The only price my father could exact from Chiran was to bring me back with him to Colombo and raise me as his daughter. She hated him for it. And she hates me even now. Even before the civil war started, war had torn our house apart. As a young girl I somehow thought that the two wars were the same, one waged outside our house, one inside. I knew I was considered a Tamil, no matter my father's name. I asked my father if Chiran's armies were fighting their war in order to get into the house and kill me."

She stopped in the middle of the road, the emotions swirling within her so strong she could no longer walk if she were to speak these truths. "When my father couldn't stand it anymore he left—and left me alone with Chiran. I didn't understand why he would desert me and leave me with my deadliest enemy. I still don't. Chiran told me that my father left because he was a coward. I've come to think it's true."

We had gradually drifted nearer each other as we recommenced our walk. I started to put an arm around her shoulders. She pushed me gently away, making clear that she had not finished.

"A lot of terrible things have been said about my father, and many of them are true. But he was always kind to me, and I loved him." She lowered her eyes, her head shaking with emotion. "To love someone is not a wise thing to do in this country." She swallowed hard, trying to maintain control of herself. "When it became clear that my father wasn't coming back, Chiran threw me out of the house. She wanted to send me back here, but I only went as a far as a guest cottage on the property because Bandula wouldn't let her send me away. He was only thirteen, two years younger than me, but he stood up to her. He has always accepted me as his sister." She let a smile cross her face. "Sometimes I am more like a mother to him, his real mother, a woman who will love him and teach him how to act like a man. Chiran hates me for that too, because she will never let him be a man. There is so much good in him. I think you see it too. But will he ever be allowed to grow up enough to use that goodness in the way he dreams? Chiran would be content to let him remain a child, under her thumb, would let him dream his life away." She tilted her head back and took a long breath, let it out. "Sometimes I wonder why she is so full of hate, but most of the time I don't want to know."

"Why not?"

"Because I don't want to feel any pity for her."

We resumed walking along the narrow road, through the pines and back along the ridge. The wind had come up, strong and warm off the sea, and we walked a little apart, as if the force of her story had separated us.

I almost asked about the one she had not mentioned—Kumar—but thought I understood that part now. In Kumar's eyes, Lilani came half from the family that had caused his parents' death and half from the only people he could look down on, the Tea Tamils. While he had somehow forgiven Bandula for being of the same family, he could not forgive it in her, perhaps because of what they had in common rather than how they differed. "Half a person," he had called her that night in my hotel in Kandy. And hadn't Lilani herself said she was "half this and half that," condemned to live half a life?

Soon the cottage appeared on the peak of the ridge, but I saw it differently now, as the place where Lilani returned time and again, trying to reconcile the torn pieces of herself.

It struck me with sudden clarity. They were all war orphans—Bandula, Kumar, Lilani—orphans of a war that divided both a family and a people, a war that divided the souls of all three of them. Each of them had been abandoned and longed to be made whole.

31

That evening we lay in bed, still sweating, our limbs carelessly entwined, our breathing slowly returning to normal. The setting sun shining through the tall windows made its slow transit of the room as Lilani drifted into sleep.

I felt the relief of a mind freed from thought, from any sense of time, from any place other than this. For the moment, I lived only in the senses, thinking of nothing—which made Lilani's quiet stirring, the trembling of her hands, as startling as a sudden cry.

"What?" I whispered, hoping she would not answer, fearing she could see more clearly than I what barriers lay ahead of us if we were to truly love and allow ourselves to be loved.

She did not wake, but her hands stirred again, plucked by some nerve that could not rest. Then her eyes opened, made bottomless and unquiet by some deep dread. "You keep so much back," she said. "You tell me so little."

The words came quietly, barely whispered, yet sharp as a thorn.

"I don't know what you want to ..." I could not finish the lie.

"You don't have to tell me everything. And you don't have to tell me anything for my sake. Only for yours. Secrets kill the person who keeps them. Tell me your oldest secret. The one you can't leave behind."

I waited, trying to find the words, then trying to escape them, waited so long that I thought, hoped, she had fallen asleep again. But I felt her hand stir against my chest. She was waiting, and I knew I would have to begin.

"My father. He ..." I hadn't realized how difficult it could be to speak the truth. "He was always good to my mom and me. My mom had fought cancer and survived, and somehow, as a kid, I thought she'd lived because of how strong and good he was. He was a big guy, bigger than just his size. Had a big voice and this big determined way of moving, like he was leaning into something that he pushed back with every step he took. That's how I thought of him. Back then."

She looked at me, knowing there was more. I wanted a reprieve, wanted her to tell me that this was enough. But I knew it wasn't.

"I used to go fishing in the delta country, west of town. Me and a friend named T-Bone and a few other guys. We'd laze around half the day, talking, fishing. I wished my dad could come with us, but he was out driving, making a living for the family. One time we brought this guy Brad along. Smart-mouthed guy. Sat on the bank with his line in the water, talking the whole time, acting like he was some kind of comedian and we were his audience. After a while we stopped listening. We didn't care that he could see it. T-Bone said something about how we should have brought Pitchford with us. He was another friend. That's when Brad puts on this real sly grin. We weren't going to ask him what it was about, so he finally says he knows a lot about Pitchford—and his mom. Says he knows all about her, and someone's father. He looks right at me with that smirk on his face. And I understood exactly what he was trying to say. The next thing I know he's jumping to his feet, and that's when I realize I'm coming at him. T-Bone says something, trying to stop me, but he knew not to get in the way. I knock Brad on his ass with my first swing. He gets up and I knock him down again. He's trying to tell me that he didn't mean anything by what he said. I don't care. I just keep coming at him. T-Bone steps in this time, wraps his arms around me in a bear hug, tells me that the guy ain't worth it. For a moment I think he means my dad, and I'm ready to take him on too. But I realize he means Brad. And I know he's right, and I finally cool off. We just left him there to make his own way back to Stockton. I drove straight to Pitchford's house—this is in the middle of the day—with T-Bone trying to talk me out of it the whole way. But I ignored him like we'd ignored Brad earlier. When we pulled up, there was my dad's car in front of Pitchford's place. I can't tell you what that did to me. I got angry to keep from crying. I figured I was going to wait there until he came out and then I'd knock him down too. I told myself I'd punch him in the nose for my mom's sake, after all she's been through. But I knew it was mostly for letting Brad be right about him. And for breaking my heart."

I stopped then, as if the story were over. But, like that day by the river, I couldn't let it go yet. "I knew I shouldn't have gone there. I shouldn't have wanted to find out. But the sonofabitch ... And Mom still not really well. After a while, I let T-Bone talk me into leaving before my dad came out.

Because as much as I wanted to see him walking out of there, that's how much I didn't. From that day on, I could hardly stand the sight of him. We grew further and further apart. Every now and then he'd say something to me about how I shouldn't feel so bad about the distance between us, it was just part of being my age and we'd be all right one of these days. And I hated him all the worse for it. I didn't tell him it was because I knew what a phony he was. I wanted to tell Mom what kind of a guy she was married to. But I didn't. I kept it to myself. A secret.

"My dad had hoped I'd be a truck driver, too. I'd been talking about it since I was a little kid, how I wanted to be like him. Instead, when I got out of high school I went to college. With everything I did, I let him know that I wanted to put myself beyond him, do something entirely different. I couldn't tell anyone what it was really about. I figured that made me admirable. It was my secret, and I was proud to keep it.

"So I got a teaching degree from Sacramento State. Taught school for a couple of years. Then the foreign service. I liked that it hurt him, the apple falling so far from the tree. Dad figured a man should work at something that could be driven or cut or hammered or dug out with a backhoe. I wanted to show him I was nothing like him."

I tried to smile for Lilani, make like this didn't hurt anymore. "So here I am, a pinstriped cookie-pusher, and from this far away I never have to speak to my dad again."

I thought I would feel better, having told my story, vindicated, clean. And Lilani would understand the nobility of my suffering. Instead, I felt diminished. I had imagined many times sharing this with someone. Every time, when I saw the scene in my mind, I was with a woman who loved me and would understand that this terrible wound had festered within me for years, eating at my soul, and when I told it I would be free. Yet, at the moment of release, when I had finally found that woman, the one who could get me to share this deepest of my secrets, the secret from which all my other secrets grew, I could only think of how childish it all sounded. How could it not? I had still been a boy back then. And as long as I remembered the story and let it affect me, part of me remained a boy.

Lilani waited until she knew I had finished. Then she asked me, "Did you not even tell your wife?"

"No. I don't know why, but I couldn't."

I sighed as if it was the last breath I would ever take. "I can't get past it. I'm sorry, but I can't. After all these years. I still want him to make it up to me, to say he's sorry. But I've never told him what it was."

She ran her hand over my chest and looked up at me. "You think you want him to make it up to you, but maybe what you really want is to make it up to him. For not being the son he wanted. For turning your back on him. Maybe when you do that, it will be all right."

For a moment I wanted to argue, then realized that my only argument was with myself. Instead, I held her close and together we watched the warm evening sky grow slowly dark until we fell asleep in each other's arms.

32

I woke with a start in the middle of the night. Had someone spoken? Beside me, Lilani slept quietly. Moonlight filled the room. The only sound was the wind blowing over the ridgetop. I started to go back to sleep.

Voices came from the front room. Crazy voices.

"Where are they?" a male voice asked. The other man made an unintelligible reply.

Intruders. Thieves dangerous enough not to care that we knew they were there. A rush of adrenaline brought me fully awake. I slipped out of the covers and reached for the poker leaning against the fireplace.

Lilani stirred and whispered, "No, Philip." She rose from the bed, put on her robe and walked down the short hallway. A light came on in the front room.

"Do you know what time it is?" I heard her ask. "Don't you have any respect for anyone?" She sounded more exasperated than angry.

I put on my slacks and walked toward the main room, blinking against the light. Lilani stood in the doorway at the end of the hall, her back to me, arms crossed over her chest, shoulders stiff with resentment. Over her shoulder, I saw Bandula's fading grin. A look of confusion passed over his face. "I told you that I'd—"When he saw me, he spread his arms wide and put on a bad American accent. "Well, Phil, I just thought I'd stop by and say hello."

Kumar, as always, stood to one side of the door, his back against the wall.

"You really think that you can just walk in anywhere, anytime you want?" Lilani demanded.

Bandula stood unsteadily in the middle of the room, looking small and very young. He was drunk.

I shouldered past Lilani into the room. "What the hell are you doing here? How did you know we were here?

Bandula seemed surprised at the question. "I know everything," he said, his words eerily similar to his mother's. He forced a laugh and looked to Kumar to join it, but his companion only glowered back.

Bandula appeared puzzled. None of us were reacting as he wanted. After a moment of indecision he chose to brazen it out, and dropped onto the sofa in the middle of the room, flung a leg over its arm and looked at Lilani. "You didn't tell him why I wanted to talk to him?"

Lilani turned to me, her eyes pleading. "Philip, this isn't why I brought you up here."

Still half-asleep, I wondered if I had somehow missed some crucial part of this conversation. "What are you talking about?"

Bandula put on a disbelieving smile. "Talking about? We're talking about how ... " He looked at Lilani then back at me. "My mother! That's what we're talking about. We're going to play a joke on Chiran."

I blew out an oath and turned back down the hallway toward the bedroom. "I haven't got time for jokes."

"Philip."

The sudden gravity in Bandula's voice stopped me. "I know you. You want to do something important. We have always been alike this way. You and I need—" Before he could finish his thought, he threw up a hand to silence us and cocked his head to one side, rigid with tension. His eyes darted toward the door, then back to me, pleading with me to have heard whatever he had heard.

Without a word, Bandula jumped up and crossed to the window, looking into the darkness for a long time before flinging the door open and running out onto the lawn. Kumar, after a charged glance around the room—what thoughts hid behind those dark eyes?—followed him out. Their voices came through the open door, loud, agitated, though I couldn't make out what they were saying.

After a minute or two they returned, Bandula smiling broadly to cover his bizarre behavior.

"Do you think my mother wouldn't have me followed? Sometimes I wonder if …" He stopped himself, not wanting to divulge what he wondered.

With a strange laugh that chilled me to the bone, he retook his seat and stretched his arms along the back of the sofa. He again swung his leg over its arm, trying to recapture the insouciant pose of a moment earlier.

I'd had enough. "What do you want?"

The young man leaned forward, an intensity in his eyes that I had never seen before, an earnestness he had never shown. "What do I want? The question is, what do *you* want? Do you really want to do something while you're here in Sri Lanka, make a change in this country? From the moment I saw your picture in the paper, saving that woman, I thought to myself, 'Here's someone who can help me, someone who will understand what I want to do.'"

I felt my face redden. "I did nothing for her. She died in the ambulance."

"It doesn't matter." Bandula's eyes bore into mine. "You tried. You cared."

"It meant nothing."

"Did you mean it when you told me you wanted to do important things?" he asked, his voice barely a whisper. "Or maybe that meant nothing, too. I need to know. Now."

A deep stillness filled the room. I looked from Bandula to Kumar then to Lilani. Their eyes were charged with an anticipation I did not understand. I grabbed a straight-backed chair, turned it around and straddled it to hide the shaking in my legs. "All right, what do you want?"

Bandula smiled. He had his audience.

It had to do, he said, with Catton's visit, with the ceremony at the opening of the new power station. The government would summon every news outlet in the country and would compel the presence of the opposition leaders, turning them into props at an NRP photo-op, all of it on live TV.

"They'll get Tissa Sandanayake there?" I asked.

"If he doesn't come, Susan will make it look as if he doesn't care about the development of his own country. Believe me, Tissa will be there."

Struck by the casual way Bandula used the politician's surname, I asked, "You know him?"

Bandula looked at me, puzzled. "Of course I know him." He looked at me quizzically. "You still haven't any idea how this country works, do you?" The adolescent boy I knew so well had disappeared, replaced by a young man who had breathed the air of politics since his birth.

As quickly as he had shown this side of himself, he hid it away and a wicked, childish smile spread across his face.

"More than that—" With a quick gesture, he clapped his hand over his mouth, but the sound of a giggle escaped through his fingers. I saw the worry in Lilani's face and knew she wondered, as I did, how much control Bandula had over himself.

"More than that," he continued, "he knows all about it. We want him there. He wants to be there."

Slowly, it came to me. "J. R. Thilakaratne."

Bandula nodded, smiling, happy that his American friend wasn't as dense as he'd feared. "You figured it out."

"Not until now. I saw them together but didn't understand why. Now I do."

Bandula smiled. "J. R. is a valuable friend."

"That's how Tissa found out that I knew you, and that I'd been keeping it from the embassy."

"I didn't ask J. R. to tell that to Tissa."

"But J. R. knew, and he decided on his own to tell him." Only now could I see it clearly, like a fly who hasn't noticed the web woven around him until the moment he can no longer move.

The dinners, the nightclub, the long, wandering talks. Why could I see it so clearly now, when I had seen nothing before? I felt like a fool for flattering myself that Chiran had intended to use me in some way, wished to take advantage of me. The truth should have been obvious. While I thought I had been subtly cultivating Bandula, Bandula had been cultivating me. How like his mother he was. "What are friends for," she had asked me, "but to use?"

Taking my silence for agreement, Bandula began to explain his plan.

Everyone at the inauguration of the power station, he said, would give speeches, "pledging their cooperation and friendship and their blah-blah-blah." And there would be pageantry, a bit of ceremony to give the event the gravity of ritual. While Bandula wove his vision of that far-off hour, Kumar stood near the door as if he thought I might try to make a run for it. Lilani had slumped into an armchair, her head in her hands.

The request, when it came, seemed innocuous enough. Bandula wanted me to insist that a group from his orphanage perform at the ceremony. "Tamil children dancing and singing as a symbol of a happier future," he laughed. "You Americans will like the idea, and my family is addicted to empty gestures. But it has to come from you, not me."

I recalled the day we had stopped above the site of the power station on our way back from the orphanage, remembered Bandula talking about having the children dance at the event. It struck me now that even the visit to the orphanage, like so much else, had been a set-up. Our talk as we roamed the grounds had been nothing more than a chance for him to sound me out, see if I was the sort he could use. And I'd been callow enough, sufficiently self-regarding, that I'd blithely let myself be led wherever they wanted. I'd thought I was so clever, and I'd seen none of it.

I wanted to walk out of the room, not out of righteousness or even in protest, but because I couldn't bear to look at the people who had made such a fool of me. Yet I didn't move. My curiosity was too great. And I did not wish to have them see me run.

Oppressed by a sense of foreboding, but unable to see where this was going, I said to him, "I don't get it. So you get the kids to dance. So what?"

Bandula whisked his leg off the arm of the sofa and leaned forward like a salesman closing a deal. "Don't you see how Chiran does it?

He didn't call her "Mother," had in some way divorced himself from her. "How she keeps everything under control?" he continued. "It's all mystique. The name. *Jayatilaka*." He pronounced his own name as if summoning up the unholiest of demons, inviting the devil into our presence.

Bandula leaned closer, speaking rapidly, his words barely a whisper. "Don't you see? It's the name. My name. It carries weight. Nothing can touch any of us. Do you understand? Nothing can touch even me. That's the curse," he hissed. "It's like a bubble that surrounds her and Susan and all of us." He tried to smile to hide his growing agitation, but it looked more like the grimace of a man in pain. "If we can just prick that bubble, leave the Jayatilakas naked for even a moment ..." His eyes bored into mine like a man asking absolution for his favorite sin, the one he lives for. "We have to humble her," he said, his voice husky with desire. Once more he glanced toward the darkness beyond the windows, but managed to brush away his paranoia, the noises echoing in his head, and focus on me. "That's all I've ever wanted to do." He blinked, his eyes wet. "I want to see her humiliated. It would be worse than shooting her, worse for her than dying." With that he stopped, his eyes wide.

Out of the thick silence that filled the room, I asked, "What war are you trying to win?"

Bandula jumped to his feet. "It's all the same war. There *is* only one war." Whether from his drunkenness or the vertigo induced by his own vision, Bandula staggered then righted himself.

I took a breath and tried to think it through. My impulse was to stop this right now and throw Bandula out. Instead, I called his hand, had to see what he held. "All right, where are we going with this?"

Bandula's smile regained its warmth, though something desperate still resonated inside him.

The children would dance while the dignitaries took their seats, he said. Chiran would be among the last seated, coming onto the platform just before the Ambassador and Catton and President Susan. "And that's the moment!" Bandula's voice rang out in the small room. "While she's crossing the stage one of the students will take out a banner that he has wrapped around himself, under a sweater or something. He'll hand one end of it to one of the other children and they will unfurl it as she walks in front of it, the banner from the orphanage, saying 'Chiran, End the War!' And everyone will see it. 'Chiran, End the War!' The war she has waged against everyone." Bandula's eyes glowed, the vision of that moment clear in his mind. "You see." He nodded, frantic for us to see it too. "You see." It wasn't a question.

Bandula saw my skepticism, pressed harder to make me understand.

"It's all about power," he said, like a man trying to explain something to a child. "It has to do with power—and the power station," he said with a laugh bordering on manic. "It will all take place on television. Live. The picture will go around the world, with her standing in front of the banner, looking like a fool. After we play this joke everyone who switches on a light, turns on a radio, hears the refrigerator hum, will think of that ceremony and of that banner. And everyone, everyone in every country, will know that the Jayatilakas are no longer invulnerable."

I tried to speak, but the absurdity of his proposition stripped me of words. Bandula would never understand the difference between Sri Lanka and the world, between himself and the universe.

"You're nuts," I told him without heat.

Wagging his head in disbelief, Bandula said, "You don't understand," the playfulness gone from his voice. "Don't think of this as it would be in your country. Think of it as it is here. Symbols are everything. Saving face is everything. Everyone will see it. And they'll understand. People will see that the Jayatilaka's can't control everything, that even children can rise up and humiliate them."

"It'll go hard on the kids, hard on your orphanage."

Bandula shook his head, but I couldn't tell if he meant to say that Chiran wouldn't retaliate, or that he didn't want to think about it.

Lilani sat slumped in her chair, as Chiran Jayatilaka was supposed to look at the moment of her mortification. "This is it, isn't it?" I said to her, working to keep my voice even. "Why you turned up at the club that night when I hadn't seen you in weeks. You—he—were already thinking of bringing me here for this, to set up this prank. So he allowed me to see you again."

She started to shake her head to deny my accusation, but could not finish the gesture.

"Tell me," I said, fighting against a rising tide of anger, "were you already thinking of this when I found you at the library that day? Were you already setting this trap?"

She looked at Bandula as if for leave to speak then, her voice barely audible, said, "He never ordered me to see you. He only told me when I had to stay away. Except at the club that night. That time he said I had to come."

Feeling the blood rushing to my face—in anger or only shame?—I turned back to Bandula. "It won't work." I made it sound harsh, wanted to slap him in the face with it. "Okay, maybe you can wrap the banner around one of the kids, but even if he wears a sweater someone's going to notice. And even if no one notices, he's going to take too long unwrapping it. They'll stop him before he's halfway finished." I rose to my feet, too disturbed to sit. "And maybe you don't care about also embarrassing my ambassador and Catton, but I do. If I've been disloyal to the embassy—and I have—it's only had to do with me so far, with where I wanted to go with my career. I've thought that by serving myself I was also serving my country, doing the sort of thing a good officer does. But this is too much. I won't do it."

Bandula looked at me, puzzled, but willing to remain patient. "Yours is the most powerful country in the world." He spoke softly, the voice of reason. "A little embarrassment will do you good."

Wasn't that exactly what Richard Donovan had said about the Sri Lankan government?

"That day we saw J. R. at the university," I said, "you told me he had come to let you know that your father had been turned away at the airport. That's right, isn't it?" In my anger, I enjoyed the shock I saw in Lilani's face, and took some solace from the certainty that she had known nothing about it. "You wanted your father here, to embarrass your mother. But you had been afraid that, before he could do anything, someone would recognize him and he'd be turned around, and he—your father, not your mother—would end up looking bad. That's why you were upset as we drove away from the university. Because that's exactly what had happened, isn't it?"

Bandula's eyes went cold. "You don't get it at all. That day at the university, J. R. wasn't telling me that my plan had failed. He was telling me it had worked, that he had done what I had asked him to do, that he had informed the authorities at the airport that my father was on the plane. I wanted them to turn him back."

His words fell into a silence that deepened with every unsaid word, every pulse of bad faith. And in that silence, I came to a realization. No matter how strong the resentment, how deep the hurt, a man can't turn his father away without striking the most grievous of blows to his own soul.

I nearly laughed at our mutual folly, at our actions, our empty gestures, aimed at others, that in reality punished, first and most of all, ourselves.

It was Lilani who found her voice first. "My ... *Our* father wanted to come back? And you ... you..."

If she wanted an apology, or even a justification for what he had done, she got none. Bandula waved his hand, dismissing her words. "He thinks he can just come back when he pleases and everything will be fine. He thinks we'll all be so happy to see him. We'll be his little children again. Well, he can't. It's too late. Years too late."

Lilani blinked like a sleepwalker awakened. "Why did he want to come back?"

"It doesn't matter what he wants," Bandula shot back. "Something for himself, not for us. Not for me." He took a deep breath to steady himself. "Philip was right. He wanted to put his thumb in Chiran's eye. He was going to come out in favor of Tissa, help him defeat her."

Her face went blank. "But isn't that what you want too?"

For a moment I thought he was going to strike her. His face red, the veins standing out on his forehead, he leaned into her, spitting each word he spoke. "No. That's for me to do." A mirthless laugh escaped the black hole of his anger. "Our father expected me to help him. He sent the message through J. R. But he didn't understand. Bringing down Chiran is for me to do, not for him. Not for that coward. J. R. does what *I* tell him to do now. I told him to have our father turned away, and he did it. *I'm* going to do something for once. I don't need Chiran. I don't need J.R. I don't need our father. God, how I don't need him. For once I'm going to do something that makes a difference. Me."

Lilani's eyes were fixed, staring at the wreckage of her life. "You never told me he was coming," she said quietly, the barest hint of protest in her voice. "You should have told me. What would it have cost you?" She put out her hand to him. He looked away. "Since I was a girl, I've dreamed of him coming back. Coming back for us. There must have been nights when you dreamed the same thing."

"Yes, I've waited," Bandula said, "Waited all my life. Then I realized that the part of me that was waiting was just a child. And I was a man now. He said, years ago, to hell with me, to hell with both of us. Now I say to hell with him."

I felt the need to yank the conversation back. "You're still not leveling with me," I said to Bandula. "Let's start at the beginning. I want to know why you were going to help Potts head up north."

Bandula licked his lips, glanced at Lilani. "Potts? I barely knew him. And why would I… " His voice trailed off.

"You're not good at this," I shot back. "Stick to the truth. Why did you help—"

Before I could finish, Kumar shouted, "This American is not afraid for you, he only is afraid for his job!"

He sprang across the room like a leopard. I leaped from my chair and got my hands in front of my face, managed to block most of Kumar's punch, but its force threw me against the wall. All the time we were talking, ignoring him, he must have been growing increasingly angry that I would turn down Bandula's plan, that I would say no to anything Bandula wanted to do. While his rage built, none of us paid any attention to him until, finally, he could hold back no longer.

As I set myself for his next rush, Kumar suddenly stopped, his arms hanging at his sides, helpless, straining against invisible bonds that tied him as surely as the strongest ropes, ropes that now squeezed from him an anguished, incoherent cry. He stood in the middle of the room, tears of frustration streaming down his face, unable to move, unable to speak.

Slowly, Bandula crossed the room with the confidence of a lion tamer and the tenderness of a lover. He glanced at both Lilani and me. Then he put his arms around Kumar.

They rested their heads on each other's shoulders, like a couple of weary boxers in a clinch. Bandula whispered something into his friend's ear and slowly the wildness faded from the Tamil's eyes. Bandula spoke again, whispering, cooing. Kumar's body, stiff as stone, relaxed. To my astonishment, he began to sob, clinging to Bandula to keep from falling to the ground.

The thought flashed through my mind that Bandula's was the bravest act I'd ever seen, not so much for what it did as for what it revealed.

With Bandula whispering to him, Kumar, tears running down his cheeks, glared at us both—Lilani and me—but the rage had disappeared. It didn't occur to me until much later—until too late—to ask why Kumar had chosen that precise moment to attack me, to make us stop talking.

He blinked slowly, as if he might fall asleep. Then he threw off Bandula's hold. He turned toward Lilani. I braced myself to protect her. But Kumar had again hit some wall within himself and stopped. The momentum of his frustration made him fling his arms out, as if throwing off an attacker, when in fact, I could see now, his assailant lived within him.

"And you are no good. No good for anything!" he shouted. But at whom? Lilani? Me? Himself? "Stay away from him! Just stay away," the young Tamil cried. "Can anything change? How many people will die? Who can stop it? As long as I am alive it will never go right!" In his anguish, he doubled over as if struck by a blow.

"Enough!" In the bedlam, none of us had seen Lilani rise from her chair, but she stood now in the middle of the room, head down, eyes shut tight, fists clenched. "Enough!" she cried. And with that cry, her anger, as Kumar's, faded. In its place rose the sadness I had so often seen in her, a sadness that colored every word she spoke. "You're all crazy. All of you." She looked at us in turn. "You want to come up with something big. Some grand gesture that will make you feel like big shots, no matter how many other people get hurt." She pointed at Bandula and Kumar. "You want to use the children of the orphanage like stage props without considering what will happen to them." Like a child, she stamped her foot, then turned on me "How many times did I warn you that you didn't understand, didn't know what you were getting involved in? Oh, Philip ... "

She moved toward me, her arms opening like a flower.

"No!" I raised a hand to stop her. "You don't understand—none of you understands—when it's too late. You took me in good, Lilani. You really did. But you won't do it twice. You can tell everyone that you slept with a diplomat, some sucker from the American Embassy, got him to do anything you wanted." I knew the unfairness of what I said even as I spoke, but my words came from a frightened and angry place in my heart and I couldn't take them back.

"You know that's not true," she whispered, drawing herself closer to me. "You know that's not true, Philip."

We had all reached the point of exhaustion, when nothing we said could make any difference.

I put my fingertips against her lips. "All right," I said, uncertain whether I was conceding the truth of what she said or simply trying to stop her talking.

I looked at Bandula and Kumar. "Get out."

Bandula tried to smile. "Phil, you know I only want—"

"Yeah. You only want. Well, that's okay. But I'm tired of it. Now get out."

I turned back toward the bedroom. I heard the front door slam shut. Ignoring Lilani standing behind me in the doorway, I began to pack my bag.

"Philip—" she whispered.

I spoke without turning to look at her. "I hired one of the embassy drivers to come up here with my car tomorrow. Jayasinghe. You know him. You can go back to Colombo with him."

"Philip. It's late. Come back to bed."

I closed the bag, zipped it up. I wished I knew how to reach that part of me that wanted to stay but I couldn't find it. "I'll wake up a taxi driver in town."

"Philip … Phil."

She started to weep, but I didn't get the satisfaction from it I thought I would. And when, as I went out the door, she said she loved me, I knew she was only telling the truth.

33

The Christmas party at the residence of the British High Commissioner had fallen on a particularly warm night—this close to the equator the seasons delineated by the calendar make little difference—and the crowd had spilled out onto the lawn among the coconut oil lamps and palm trees. A lighted Christmas tree sprayed with artificial snow, stood at the edge of the veranda, looking as alien as a UFO in this tropical climate. "God Rest Ye, Merry Gentlemen" sounded faintly over the outdoor speakers scattered across the lawn.

Burt Steadman pulled at his collar as if fighting for air. "Anyway, they're both big ballroom dancers, this new political officer and his wife, and they're dancing up a storm, figuring they're making a big hit. First week at post and they're already stars. So, on the last dance, everyone backs off and lets them have the floor. They twirl around the dance floor alone, figuring it's just like a scene in the movies and they've made a big splash at their first event in Bangkok."

Burt took a sip from his drink, which seemed to strengthen the Oklahoma in his voice. "So, the next day the political officer's fishin' for compliments with the head of Econ, who'd been at the party, and he says, 'I guess they're not used to seein' such great ballroom dancing here.' And the Econ guy says, 'Probably not. But for sure they're not used to seein' people dancin' through the national anthem.'" Burt led the laughter to his story as he mopped his dripping forehead. "Let me know if I'm keeping you awake, Reid."

I forced a laugh.

Steadman blew out a breath, looked at the palm trees, mopped his brow. "Not much like Christmas, is it?"

"Not much."

"What's with you these days, Reid?"

"Nothing."

"Okay. But your nothin' is the heaviest damn thing I've ever seen."

I felt Steadman's eyes on me but said nothing. He stared into the gloom for a moment then suddenly brightened. "Hey, here comes your boyfriend."

Carefully guarding his drink as he pushed through the crowd, Nick Potts, grinning like a kid on Christmas morning, walked up and shook hands.

"I guess they've stopped checking for invitations at the door," Burt said.

"Be assured, gentlemen, that you will find the Associated Press wherever bullets are flying or free booze flowing." The scars around Potts' injured eye gleamed in the dim light.

Steadman nodded in greeting. "So, what's got you so happy?"

Potts tapped his highball glass against Steadman's. "Got my ticket out of paradise."

It had been easy to forget Potts was still in Colombo. Though the A.P. man had checked out of the hospital two weeks earlier and the Sri Lankan government said it had decided against prosecuting him, he had nevertheless been refused permission to leave the country. No one had given him a reason, but we understood it as the only form of punishment they could mete out for his transgressions. He had been forced to hang around the Hilton running up room service tabs until both A.P. and the embassy leaned on the Foreign Ministry.

Steadman shrugged. "When you leaving?"

"Tonight. One a.m. flight to London."

Burt looked at his watch. "Drink up, boy. You've still got five hours. But I guess you'll miss Catton's visit."

"Under Secretary for South Asia, right?" Potts asked, interested. "When's he coming?"

"Assistant Secretary. And don't push your luck. Get out before the Sri Lankans change their mind about nailin' you to a cross," Burt said. "The hearings Catton was supposed to attend got cancelled and he's comin' in a couple of weeks. Got the cable late this afternoon." He interrupted himself with a groan. "Look out, here comes McFee. Now we'll have to toast the Queen with bad champagne."

A toothy, likeable man, the British High Commissioner stood at the edge of the veranda next to his Christmas tree while a member of his household staff set up a microphone. After a few pops and some feedback he stepped up to the mic and thanked the guests for their attendance and wished them all "a Happy Christmas, especially those of you far from home," adding that a "special entertainment has been arranged for this evening, thanks to our Military Attaché, Captain Frank Clark."

The lights went out and the crowd watched half a dozen men, faintly discernible in the moonlight, advancing single-file across the slanting roofline of the High Commissioner's residence.

"Reindeer?" Steadman muttered as Clark, standing on the veranda, gave a thumbs up and a bank of spotlights lit the roof, revealing a row of Sri Lankans suited in a strange mix of military blouses and Scottish kilts standing at attention, bagpipes tucked under their arms.

At the first squeal of the pipes, the crowd reflexively stepped back in anticipatory horror. It took a moment to recognize "Deck the Halls" coming from a half dozen bagpipes played by men to whom it did not come naturally.

Burt Steadman sighed. "Am I on drugs, Reid? I sure as hell hope so, 'cause this can't be real."

Our small group retreated into the shadows of a palm grove set against the garden wall. It would all have seemed sufficiently bizarre even without the bats. But there were bats. Big four-foot wingspan bats, straight from a vampire movie, hundreds of them, shaken from their sleep by the high-pitched skirl that to a bat probably sounded like the voice of God. Into the air they swirled, like smoke rising from the surrounding trees, black shadows against the moonlit sky.

After the Sri Lankan pipers had played "Away in the Manger" and "White Christmas," I noticed a white-coated member of the household staff making his way toward us.

"You are enjoying the evening, gentlemen?" the servant asked with a deferential smile.

"Having a blast," Potts said.

The man waggled his head politely. "I am so glad. Still, I think you would enjoy it even more thoroughly if you were to come a few steps away from the trees."

Steadman grunted in a negative kind of way. "We like the view from here."

"Just so." The man nodded. "And yet," he added, "I'm sure you wouldn't want to disturb the cobra."

Potts' head snapped up. "Cobra?"

"Yes, many here consider them sacred. This is his lair, and he greatly dislikes—Sir, I would strongly recommend against any quick movement."

With agonizing deliberateness, we all tiptoed out of the palms. The brush with danger somehow reminding him of pressing duties elsewhere, Burt dived back into the crowd.

Potts eyed me. "You're awfully quiet. I thought you were supposed to hob-nob at these things."

"I'm the press flak. Talking to you is work."

"Hey, the feeling is mutual," Potts said. "So, what's this about Catton?"

I nodded toward Steadman, working his way through the crowd. "Until a moment ago, I thought we were still trying to keep his trip under wraps."

"But if the ambassador's deputy is talking openly about it …"

"Okay. He's coming to dedicate a power station—probably'll sign an agreement to help them build some kind of hydro project."

"Why?"

It was my turn to eye him. "You working?"

"Background. No attribution."

"A big boost for the economy without a big environmental downside. And the Sri Lankan government gets to show everyone that it can develop the economy without selling its soul to the Indians."

"What's in it for us?"

"Karma."

Potts snorted.

"Okay. Other side of the coin. We get to remind everyone of what we can do to help regional economies, that we're a serious player in the region."

Potts nodded, thinking it over. "And the Sri Lankan government will then find some opportunity to publicly kick you in the teeth so that they can show their independence. Tell me why we do it."

"It's one of the eternal mysteries," I replied. "Look, Potts, my turn now. Level with me. Why did Bandula Jayatilaka want to help you go up north? What's in it for him?"

Potts put on his blandest face. "Bandula who?"

"You're better at this than he is." I tried another tack. "Nick, it's not like I haven't helped you out a couple of times."

"I know him. We talked. That's all I can say." Potts swirled the glass in his hand, looking into its contents as if searching for answers. "You're trying to get to the bottom of something, Reid. I've been coming out here for years, and, believe me, there *is* no bottom." Potts interrupted himself to cock his chin at a figure coming across the lawn. "I think someone's looking for you."

The head of Diplomatic Security held out his hand to Potts. "Tony Spezza. Just wanted a minute with Philip."

Potts raised his eyebrows and made himself scarce. Tony nodded toward the reporter. "He looks like the face of guilty knowledge. We Catholics recognize that kind of thing."

I smiled to hide my discomfort.

"Nice evening they've organized," Tony said.

"But you didn't make a beeline over here to talk about what a swell time we're having."

"You doing all right these days, Philip?"

"I'm fine. You can tell everyone to stop asking."

"Philip ..."

"I know. I know. I just..." I blew out a breath. "Sorry. "

"You were up in Haputale last week."

"Yeah." I felt my collar growing tight. "I was going to leave a contact number with Post One, but it turned out there was no phone, and ..."

"It's okay. I'm not here to lecture you on security procedures. It's just that I heard you were staying at a house owned by the Jayatilakas."

"Yeah." I worked at sounding casual. "How'd you know?"

"Jayasinghe was talking about it."

Of course.

"Said he went up there over the weekend to pick you up, but you were already gone, and he drove back with some girl you'd left behind. He knew the house belonged to the family." He smiled at the unasked question. "It's a small island. Everyone knows everything. Everyone but us."

"I really have to find more discreet drivers."

Tony wagged his head ambiguously. Could he have guessed how far off the reservation I'd gone? Of all the betrayals I'd committed, this one against Tony was the hardest to live with.

"I didn't know whose place it was until after I got there. The girl has some connection with the family I guess." I shrugged as if all this were no big deal. "Am I supposed to tell you whether she was pretty?"

Tony made a smile. "I'm just trying to keep you out of trouble."

"And you figure I seem pretty determined to get into it."

"The Jayatilaka kid was there."

"Jayasinghe told you that?"

He smiled. "Just guessing this time."

I felt a flush of panic, repressed it. I reminded myself that I had turned Bandula down. Nothing had happened. Nothing would happen. "He came later," I said. "I didn't know he was coming." At least that part was true.

As on the day I'd stopped by his house, a compulsion for confession washed over me. I wanted to tell Tony everything—tell him about the scheme for a banner at the ceremony, tell him that Bandula was the one who had tried to help Potts get up north. I wanted to tell him about how crazy Chiran Jayatilaka was—and to confess how much I needed to get out of the middle of all this before I went crazy too. But it was too late. If I now told everyone how I had deceived them, I'd lose the confidence of the Ambassador, of Steadman, of everyone. It would look like hell on my evaluation, and my career would be wrecked.

I braced for the weight of another question, prepared myself to hand out another lie even while my earlier ones were unraveling around me.

At that moment a voice from behind me called, "Philip."

Mike Jarreau, the head of admin was walking across the lawn toward us, his face somber. He nodded to Tony. "I'm sorry, Philip, but Post One just called here. They got a phone call from your wife."

The once familiar term sounded utterly foreign to me. "My wife?"

"I've got bad news."

34

Exhaustion blunted my ability to think, or even feel as the plane touched down in Sacramento. I'd seen the dawn at Heathrow, then endured the long transatlantic flight, followed by customs in Chicago before this last leg home. I was still wearing the clothes from the reception at the High Commissioner's residence and felt the psychic disarray that comes with the most vivid nightmares or the longest plane flights.

I had driven home from the reception and thrown some clothes in a bag while Mike went into the embassy and made my plane reservations. Only when I had settled into a seat in the airport's business class lounge did I see Potts and realize we would be on the same flight.

"I'm sorry, Reid," Potts said when I explained what I was doing there. Then he smiled faintly. "I was afraid you'd come out here to just make sure I'd left."

"And I was thinking how you said in the hospital that you came here to get one story, but you ended up getting a different one."

"Did I?" Potts chewed on the olive from his cocktail. "Isn't that how it always is? You think you're following one story, then it turns out you were following another one all along."

I thought about my own story, the pattern of my life, what I thought it meant and where I wished it to go. I asked myself if in fact, as Potts said, I was heading somewhere else altogether, a place I couldn't yet see.

We sat several rows apart on the eleven-hour flight to London, but found ourselves standing next to each other as we shuffled off the plane at Heathrow.

I looked out at the gray and icy London dawn. "Well, Nick, you're home."

"Home?" Potts shook his head and peered through the scratched and cloudy windows of the airport ramp as if he had never seen the place before.

At the top of the ramp we shook hands and went our separate ways.

※

It was dark when I landed in Sacramento. Morning or night? I tried to remember. Peering through the plane's windows, I could barely make out the terminal through the fog. Walking up the ramp from the plane, I saw my mom standing at the gate. She looked older, diminished. She wore the same dark winter coat that she had worn for years, but it seemed to engulf her now, like a hand-me-down. I tried not to show the shock I felt. I had been gone for two and a half years.

She threw her arms around me and didn't let go for a long time. She felt fragile as a bird.

"How's Dad?"

She let out a long sigh. "Oh, not good, Buddy, not good."

A childhood nickname. She hadn't called me that in years.

※

I didn't know I'd dozed off until my mom stopped in the hospital parking lot. I had come adrift in time and thought for a moment that it was the middle of the night until I saw the dashboard clock saying it was six p.m.

I followed Mom down a corridor and into a hospital room as dimly lighted as a chapel. The hiss of a respirator, the tick of a heart monitor, the sinuous lines of breathing tubes and medicine drips made the small room seem less a place for a human being to get well and more like the interior of a machine—one that lived off the patient rather than the other way around. Amid these components of modern medicine lay my dad, his face like a deflated balloon, eyes closed, his body a shapeless lump under the thin hospital blanket.

At the sight of the old, sick man curled up on the bed, the world inside me turned upside down. The burden of resentment and anger I had carried towards my father over so many years—ever since the afternoon I'd sat in my car with T-Bone outside of Pitchford's house—evaporated, falling away so quickly that I saw them for the insubstantial shadows they had always been. Had I really spent my life trying to get even with the sad figure in the narrow bed? Why not try to get even with the wind, or a handful of dust? The old man evoked only sorrow and pity—and a dram of fear. This was me in a few decades. I was filled with an overwhelming sense of loss about wasted years

"Oh, it's all right, Buddy. Here, take my handkerchief." But rather than handing it to me, she held onto it and dabbed at my eyes, the bit of white linen smelling, as it always had, of the things she kept in her purse. "He had the heart attack on Tuesday evening and the stroke Wednesday morning here in the hospital."

"What day is it now? I can't quite …"

"It's Thursday evening. I had Jean call you because I just—" Her hands flew up nervously.

"It was fine, Mom."

We stood for a long time gazing at the man in the bed.

"The doctors say he'll pull through. He's a tough ol' bird." She chuckled fondly, giving herself courage.

I didn't want to ask what would be left of him.

"Does he know we're here?"

"Oh, sure he does. He may not be able to show it, but he knows."

I sat on the chair next to the bed and lifted my father's hand from the blanket. It rested limply in my own, like something dead. Repulsed and frightened, I started to set it back down. Then Dad's hand stirred in mine, clasped it with something of the old vise-like grip I'd known all my life. It eased up a moment, then came back, strong as a childhood memory.

※

I walked down the long corridor and knocked on the door of apartment 212. Jean opened it a few inches and for a moment looked as if she hadn't been expecting me, then undid the chain and let me in. She gave me a quick hug—an arm around my neck and her shoulder pressed for a moment against mine, nothing more.

We chatted over a cup of coffee at a little table next to the kitchenette, almost relaxed at first, then increasingly stiff as our painfully circumspect small talk etched ever more clearly the contours of the gulf between us. She said she had gone to work as a receptionist in a dentist's office. I nodded, letting my eyes ask, "Anything else?"

Her gaze dropped to her hands. "I'm filing for divorce next week."

I asked myself why I let it hit me so hard. I had told Lilani that it was over between me and Jean. But that had occurred on a different planet and seemed suddenly to have no relation to anything that happened here, at home.

Yes, she said, she'd be asking for alimony.

"Well, at least we don't have kids."

"Go to hell, Philip."

Somehow we pulled back from the edge, returned to safer topics. She had seen various friends a few times. She would say hello for me. Another awkward pause.

She asked me, "Have you got someone?"

"I don't know." I thought again of Lilani, a world away. I finally recognized Jean's question as a cue. "And you?" I asked.

"Yes."

"I'm happy for you."

"Now you don't have to feel so guilty, right?" She looked away a moment, frowned, looked back. "I knew you were always looking for something, but I thought when I left that you'd be willing to give it up and come back here to me."

"Then you never understood me at all."

We looked at each other for the span of a few heartbeats. Then we both let our eyes slide away to something, anything, else. Only gradually did we realize we had nothing more to say but neither of us knew how to end the conversation.

"How is Sri Lanka?"

"It's fine." I knew I needed to add something. "I have a good staff. The work is interesting. I think I'll get a good posting after I leave."

Something is Jean's expression stopped me. She tilted her head back like she wanted to laugh but couldn't. "Remember how we used to make fun of those guys in Paris? The ones who'd been in the service so long they'd become the Official Version of themselves. So careful. So reserved. You've become one of them, Philip."

When I left a few minutes later I said to Jean, "I hope we can still be friends."

She shook her head and said, "Philip" like she was going to tell me something important, but only added, "Just go."

She shut the door quietly behind me.

※

Dad improved a bit over the next couple of days. As Mom said, he really was a tough old bird. I spent most of the day at the hospital after I spoke to Jean. Late in the afternoon Dad managed to say something that sounded like it might be, "Philip." I wiped at my eyes and he squeezed my hand hard one more time.

※

Mom and I stayed the morning with Dad on Christmas day, then drove back home, where she had roasted a turkey and made enough dressing and potatoes and creamed onions for a dozen people. We laughed over some memories from when I had been a boy and worked desperately to make merry.

The next day we stopped by the hospital so I could say so long to Dad before Mom drove me to the airport for the flight back to Sri Lanka.

We arrived nearly an hour before I needed to go to the gate and neither of us knew how to fill the time. I looked a couple times toward security as if I needed to get going, but there was almost no one in line.

"Relax, Buddy. There's no rush."

I gave her an apologetic smile

"What's bothering you?" she asked, and tried to answer her own question "You don't want to leave?"

I shrugged. She waited me out.

"It's about Dad."

"Oh, he'll be all right You'll see"

"Yeah," I replied, thinking I'd stop there. But I couldn't. "I found out something about him. When I was a kid. And I couldn't get over it. Never have." I wanted her to ask what it was, so I'd be forced to say it, but she only looked at me. I'd have to do it on my own

"I found out that he and Mrs. Pitchford—"

She cut me off with a wave of her hand. "Oh, that."

For a moment I was too surprised to speak. "You knew?"

"Oh, yeah." She gave her head a tight-lipped shake. "Men. I was pretty upset. But I knew it would stop. And it did. Only lasted a couple of weeks. I wasn't happy about it, but I knew he loved me. And you. We got over it." She looked away, as if she was unable to talk about it and look at me at the same time. "It hurt a lot at the time. But, it was a long time ago and, like I say, we got over it. He told me how sorry he was and we never talked about it again." She took a quick glance at me. "I didn't know you knew."

"Yeah, I knew."

Maybe she heard something in my voice and finally turned back to me, with this stricken look on her face. "And you been holding onto it all this time? Oh, Buddy, let it go. It was all over years ago. He's a good man, your father." She saw the look on my face. "Let it go. 'Forgiving is giving up on having a better past.' I saw that on one of those plates you hang up in the kitchen."

Let it go? How could I let it go after holding onto it all these years? I had let my disappointment with Dad shape my life. I wanted to tell her you can't simply let go after nursing a grievance for so long. It was too big, too important. My anger, bitter as it was, had given my life meaning.

What I said was, "Okay, Mom." And that was it.

As at the hospital, when I first saw Dad, I was astonished at how the anger simply left me, not all of it, and not all at once, but most of it, and as if it had never existed—astonished, and ashamed. It had burned everything around me, this anger, this regret. This love.

Through all these wasted years, all I had ever really wanted to do was forgive him, for everything to be right again, as it had been when I was a boy. But I didn't know how. And I'd never said anything, never told Dad why I had turned against him, never given him the chance to say he was sorry.

It wouldn't be that easy, of course. Even now, I needed to hang onto some of it, just enough to hide from myself how big a fool I'd been. Yes, I'd hurt my dad, hurt my mom, but most of the damage I'd done was to myself. I thought of that night at the cottage near Haputale, and how I had understood that the punishment Kumar and Bandula and Lilani and I wished to dish out to others would in fact fall upon ourselves.

And I knew that, however often I might return, my parents' house, this city, would never again be home, that I would be forever a foreigner, an exile.

35

The eleven-hour trans-Pacific flight from San Francisco brought me into Tokyo just after dawn. Too tired to sit out the four-hour layover in one of the airport's plastic chairs, I wandered aimlessly around the shops and snack bars in the nearly empty concourse. Television monitors hovered over the ranks of seats around the departure gates, commentators chattering unheeded at the exhausted travelers who slumped in their seats, dozing or flipping through magazines, waiting for their flights to be called.

It was on one of these monitors that I saw the news footage of Tissa Sandanayake being murdered.

While a voice spoke excitedly in Japanese, the screen showed an election rally, a sea of white shirts, banners waving in the sun. Someone at a microphone introduced Tissa to the crowd, making a great sweep of his arm as the politician rose from his chair on the platform. As Tissa walked to the microphone, raising both arms to the crowd in greeting, a bright circle edited into the video image showed, rising from the first row of spectators, a hand holding a gun. Tissa gave a couple of little jumps, his shoulders hunching as if he felt a chill, then fell straight down, his legs collapsing under him. For a moment the crowd, or at least that part of it in the camera's frame, froze in shock. The killer still held his gun raised as if he, like everyone else, had frozen in shock. Finally, those nearest the assassin turned on him and he disappeared beneath their fists.

The Japanese anchorman reappeared on the screen, his face composed, authoritative. A photo of Susan Guneratne appeared on the screen as he spoke. Even if I'd known what the anchorman was saying, the words going through my head would still have been those Chiran Jayatilaka had spoken to me in her kitchen, telling me that Tissa's star had risen as far as it would rise. And I knew for a certainty that she'd had him killed.

A new image appeared on the screen. The news camera appeared to have been jostled by the knot of people crowded around a man standing in front of a white house. Then it righted itself, and a slump-shouldered, desolate figure that I did not immediately recognize as Ranjith Sandanayake appeared on the screen, Nili behind him. The politician's father stood before the crowd holding a piece of paper over his head for all to see.

None of those in the airport looked up from their crossword puzzles or their troubled sleep as I caught my breath. I didn't need to see it any more closely to know it was the letter I had delivered.

The news broadcast moved on to other stories and I found the strength to walk away, my mind whirling with disordered thoughts. Yet I could see one thing clearly through it all—Ranjith and Nili Sandanayake in their house near Badulla. I could not rid myself of the thought that they had nothing to fear anymore. For them the worst had already happened.

36

After an endless hour and a half in the basement conference room, Richard Donovan's voice had gone flat under the weight of tedium and frustration. "Burt?"

Steadman pulled at the knot of his tie. "I don't know. It doesn't seem ..." His thought trailed away.

"Robert?"

McWhirter looked first at me, then at the Ambassador. "With this total lack of evidence, I just can't see how ..." He paused held out his hands, palms up, to show that further words were unnecessary.

Peering through his reading glasses at some notes in his hand, Donovan sighed. "There's this mysterious letter his parents say came from their son. Something to the effect that he was aware of a plot by the government to have him killed."

"A letter delivered by some Western embassy, they're saying," McWhirter interjected. "I don't buy it. Too convenient. I've asked around. No one claims to have heard anything about a letter. And this isn't a city that keeps its secrets. Carl"— he nodded at the defense attaché—"says Sandanayake's parents gave no indication they had received any such letter when he and Nancy and Philip visited them. The way I see it, his parents are hurt and angry and want to blame their son's death on the people they hate the most. Lacking any evidence, they invent the letter to give credence to their accusation." Like a chess expert anticipating one more clumsy move from his opponent, he looked at me, then back at the ambassador. "Besides, even if they did receive such a letter from an unnamed outside source, it doesn't prove anything."

Richard Donovan took off his glasses, frowned and looked over his shoulder at Gwen, who was taking notes of the meeting. "Can't anyone get some air into this room?" The relentless buzz of fluorescent lights, the ceaseless whoosh of fans, and the dreary, drifting debate had sucked the life out of the room, putting everyone on edge. The ambassador looked toward the end of the table. "Carl."

The defense attaché took a long time answering. "Colonel Abeysekera over at Army intelligence tells me it doesn't have the hallmarks of a Tiger operation." He frowned, shrugged. "That's not to say it's impossible."

Donovan absently massaged his left eye, as if trying to coax from it some crucial thought that had lodged there. "Tony, help us out here. What do you know?"

Alone among us, the head of Diplomatic Security appeared crisp and professional, the creases on the short sleeves of his white shirt as sharp as when we had come into the room and started this conversation of averted glances and unfinished sentences. He looked down at some notes in front of him then said to the Ambassador, "I'm not getting much from my contacts. The suspect was twenty-seven years old. Had no known political affiliations. No job. Few friends. Wife recently left him." He glanced at his notes once more. "And he's dead."

"That thing about having a wife wasn't in the papers," McWhirter said, sitting up a little straighter to clutch at the straw.

"He was a drinker," Tony continued, "but apparently not drunk on the day of the shooting. No one had ever heard him talk about politics. Police can't figure a clear motive, can't trace the gun. They can't trace his movements on the day of the shooting. He was as anonymous as a man could be and still exist. A ghost."

"A ghost," I muttered.

Burt turned to me, his face a mix of disdain and weariness. "Say what?"

I looked at him for a long time then slowly at the others around the table. They were all foreigners. Everyone had become a foreigner to me. I had no connection to them. "Nothing. Didn't say anything," I told him even while thinking that Ajith Sandanayake had been right about that, too, that even the living had become ghosts. Only in Sri Lanka could a man be gunned down by a ghost.

The Ambassador cocked his head. "I read he's a Tamil. Maybe ..."

Tony Spezza nodded. "Yes. Everyone comes back to that as if it explains everything." He shook his head. "It's too easy."

The room once again lapsed into silence. Donovan looked around the handful of faces at the table. His gaze lighted on me for a moment, then slid away. "So, where does that leave us?" He unclasped his hands to show he had nothing. "Philip, I appreciate the sincerity of your position. And I compliment you on your willingness to come in here almost straight from the airport."

I could hear the implied message that my proposal had come from an unstable mix of self-righteousness and jetlag.

"But," Donovan continued, "we have no evidence of any involvement by the NRP or the government. Canceling the Catton visit would be seen as an accusation for which we have no grounds." He sighed. "We all want to do something. But I'm just not ready ..."

McWhirter assumed his oratorical voice. "If we cancel the visit we'll become a lightning rod for every political faction on the island. Half of them will conclude that we must be sitting on evidence of the government's culpability. The other half will march on the embassy for slandering the country's good name. Either way, we'll have become the story—and we'll look bad."

I didn't care anymore. I knew I was losing, had in fact already lost, but added, "Tell them we cancelled it due to the unsettled security conditions in the country."

"No one will buy it," McWhirter replied, looking at the Ambassador, not me.

With the direction of the wind clear now, Burt Steadman joined in, grunting with impatience. "What makes you think the NRP did this, Reid? What do you know that no one else knows?"

"What do I know?" I repeated and let my pain escape in the form of a chuckle that I knew must look and sound bizarre, nudging me another step further from the others around the table.

When no one wants to deal with the matter at hand, meetings obsess on secondary issues. And I had become the issue. I tried not to laugh at the thought that Tissa had asked me to deliver the letter, had wanted it to come from a foreign embassy, from an outsider, in order to give it credibility in a society that had lost faith in itself. And now the same embassy was dismissing it as fake. "I'm not saying the party leadership sat down and made a show of hands to shoot—"

Burt Steadman broke in. "Okay, but you're saying the Jayatilakas did it. Same thing. Tony's already told us that no one has any reason to believe they're behind it."

Tony only had to raise his pencil to take the floor. "That's not what I'm saying. I'm saying that I haven't seen any evidence. You asked me what I know, and I told you. But—" Burt Steadman raised a warning eyebrow at Tony, but the head of security continued. "But I can't dismiss this letter as easily as Robert does. My gut tells me it's Chiran Jayatilaka or someone close to her, no matter how much we don't want to think about it."

A bleak sigh rose from the others in the room.

Throughout the meeting I'd felt Tony's eyes on me. Alone among those in the room, he had seemed willing to consider my proposal to cancel the Catton visit, had kept a door open for me to walk through, and let the others know of anything I was holding back.

Meanwhile, I inspected the wreckage of my hopes of bureaucratic glory, my daydream of using my connections with the Jayatilakas to inspire awe in the Ambassador and admiration from Steadman and McWhirter—the more grudging, the better—was as childish in its own way as Bandula's. From the ruins of these ambitions, I could retrieve only the fact that I had decided to live outside the grace of the embassy and now did not know how to come back in.

Finally, what did I have to tell anyone? Could I say to the others in the room that a woman who could treat her son so cruelly was capable of murder? That someone who married for power, married without love, could commit any conceivable enormity? Even the one thing I knew—her remark that Tissa Sandanayake had risen as far as he could—could be dismissed as a political judgment, or wishful thinking about a rival. Worse, they might think I'd invented it to justify myself.

And the letter. If I dared to tell them it was me who had, without authority, passed this political bombshell to the Sandanayakes at their home in Badulla, I'd likely be on the next plane back to Washington, where I'd walk the halls of the Department for a few months before being quietly fired.

So I could give no reason for my proposal to kill the Catton visit other than the gut feeling of a relatively junior officer who hadn't slept in twenty-seven hours. My bitterness over my impotence drove me toward anger—and recklessness. "I'm sure that the Jayatilakas had him killed," I said. "And we should cancel this visit to let them know we know."

Steadman and McWhirter, the ones on whose political judgment the Ambassador relied, snapped back with bitter dismissiveness, enumerating all the assumptions that I had made and why they were misguided and unsubstantiated, insisting once more that the embassy should do nothing.

Finally, Richard Donovan waved a hand to end the debate. He pursed his lips before saying slowly, "Every embassy ends up reflecting the characteristics of its host culture. People in this country see conspiracies behind everything from politics to the weather. We can't fall to the temptation to do the same."

I wanted to say that people who constantly see conspiracies were also more apt to hatch them.

Donovan continued. "The simplest explanation, the most likely explanation, is that this was done by a lone gunman with who-knows-what grievances, real or imagined."

"Yeah," Carl Bogdanovich made a crooked grin. "Lee Harvey Dharmapaula."

Donovan gave his defense attaché a warning look and Carl's gaze dropped to the table top.

The Ambassador looked at me. "Philip, I appreciate your suggestion. If there were any real evidence against the NRP or the Jayatilakas, or if we find something before Catton comes, we might need to reconsider. I'm not rejecting it out of hand." He looked at Robert McWhirter and his deputy to make sure they understood they were not to put their fingers near their temples and make little whirling motions whenever my name was mentioned, then continued. "But in the absence of such evidence, we can't take actions based on hunches—or mysterious letters." He nodded over his shoulder to Gwen, who folded up her notebook. The meeting was over.

As everyone rose to go, Robert McWhirter, with a winner's magnanimity, leaned over the table toward me. "Sorry about your father, Philip. We all hope he gets well soon."

I threw my pen on the table, watched it skitter across the polished surface. I knew how childish it made me look but was beyond caring. "This isn't about my father. It's time to stop meeting and talking, meeting and talking. We should do something."

Burt Steadman, red with anger, stepped in front of McWhirter. "Go home, Philip. Get some sleep. Now."

I felt my face flush, sensed my anger kicking the props out from under my self-control. But as I rose to my feet, not caring what my next words were, Tony Spezza, who had stayed seated, put his hand on the table and almost imperceptibly wagged a finger in warning. I slumped back into my chair.

I watched the others file out and felt my resolve grow as the room emptied.

I knew what I was going to do now, what I had decided I had to do. If I had managed to persuade them to cancel the Catton visit I wouldn't need to do anything. But now I felt certain I had no choice. It was J. R. Thilakaratne who had said it best: "What appears as betrayal often proves to be the height of fidelity."

Maybe Tony sensed something in me was about to explode. "It's okay, Philip. Just take it easy," he said as he rose. "See you tomorrow."

"Yeah." I watched him walk away. "Tony."

The head of security turned in the doorway.

"Tony, he was the best thing this country had. And we know who did it. We should have done something. We needed to *do* something."

Tony nodded. "Yeah. We probably did."

37

I wandered barefoot through the high-vaulted temple, tasted again the perfumed air, looked in wonder at the soaring vault, walked past the men in sarongs murmuring prayers near the altar, past the women in their saris, their bright colors richer and warmer in the shaded light.

The great reclining Buddha greeted me as before and I again felt drawn by its faint smile, the blush of playfulness at the corners of its mouth, hinting that even the weightiest of human affairs were only illusion. I looked at the others in the temple, the people among whom I lived but with whom I had so little real contact Had they ever seemed so foreign to me, so far away? I watched them as they finished their reverences and departed the temple, their step a little lighter, their burdens eased, walking back into the sunlight.

I thought of the church I had known, not well, back home, the occasional visits on warm summer Sundays or on rainy mornings in winter, the hard pews, my father uncomfortable in his sport coat and his one tie, Mom sitting with her hands folded in her lap while the preacher's words lulled us like one of those white noise machines. Had time and distance reduced the carpenter's passionate imperatives to a tight collar and quiet comportment? And here, in Colombo, would the Buddha recognize what his adherents had made of his teachings?

I turned and gazed again at the illustrations from the five hundred and fifty lives of the Buddha painted on the towering wall of the temple, I felt once more disarmed by the bright colors and clear truths of their shadowless world.

Turn as I would in every direction, no one looked at me, though I knew they were aware of my presence, the foreigner in their midst. And the priest, with his smooth, untroubled features reflecting the calmness of a soul at peace, did not appear, did not come to ask me again how many lives I had led. I was sure I would give him a different answer this time.

Would he think to ask me how many lives I was leading right now?

I left the temple as troubled in spirit as when I'd gone in.

※

Bandula sat in the overstuffed chair in his study, one leg dangling over its arm, looking up at the ceiling, contented as a man planning a party for his closest friends.

"How long will your mother be gone?" I asked mechanically, not really caring about the answer. I had driven straight from the temple to the Jayatilaka's place outside the city and, like a diver who has come too fast to the surface, was suffering a case of the spiritual bends.

"Four, five days. Maybe a week. I don't know. She likes London—even in February."

"A week?" I said, "But that would be after the ceremony."

Bandula shifted his gaze from the ceiling and looked closely at me.

Had the others also heard the note in my voice, the faint pleading of someone who, now that I had decided upon a course of action, was looking for a way out of it? Kumar stood in a corner, watching everything closely, saying nothing. Lilani sat on a leather stool near Bandula, her head down.

Persuading the rest of the country team to invite dancers from a nearby orphanage had proven easy. After the tension of our previous meeting in the basement conference room, the others had been happy to grant me a request, bring me back into the fold. I didn't bother to speak to Bandula of my struggle to persuade myself that I was only doing what the others in the embassy should have done, that I was acting for all of them.

"You've picked the ones to carry the banner?" I asked.

Bandula smiled, shook his head.

I didn't kid myself. For all his talk of, ending the war, of making a new nation, Bandula's wish to bring his mother low spoke above all to his thirst for revenge and had little to do with Tissa Sandanayake.

Why had the others decided to take part? Lilani perhaps because, as was true of so much of her life, she felt she had no choice. And Kumar. Kumar did it for love, and for hate.

I tried not to consider how many things could go wrong with an act driven by such tangled motives.

"I decided you were right, Phil," Bandula said lightly. "The person carrying the banner will walk in with the children from the orphanage. But it will be someone who is not really one of them."

I waved my hand to stop him. "Look, if it isn't someone from the orphanage carrying the banner, who—" I started, but before I could say more, Bandula cut me off and continued his increasingly agitated monologue.

"It will be easy," Bandula said, springing from his chair into the middle of the room. "They'll come marching up onto the platform." Wearing a childish grin, he marched in place, knees high, elbows swinging. "The minor dignitaries—" Bandula scrunched down, parodying his mother's minions. "—will begin to take their seats as the dancers perform. The children will be dancing as far back on the platform as possible. That way all the bigwigs will have to walk in front of them rather than behind them." He walked stiffly, like a statue come to life.

I thought, yes, this was what he had always wanted, to be a one-man show.

"Then," Bandula stopped and glanced dramatically at us, his audience of three, "just as they bring on Chiran—with your ambassador and your secretary coming right behind her onto the platform—that's when he'll come running up from the back, the banner in his arms."

Kumar had not moved or changed expression, but appeared somehow transformed, as if he were a planet into whose orbit everyone must finally fall.

Into the angst-filled silence, I said, "No. The banner's too big for one person to hold up. There would have to be a second person to hold up the other end." I was still groping for a way out of carrying through on a plan that looked both dangerous and ridiculous. If I'd hoped this was it, I was kidding myself.

Bandula thought it over and said, "Yes, we'll have to let one of the orphans in on the plan. Only one." He looked at Kumar. "Maybe Fareed. You know Fareed. He'll be the one to step out front with you and open the banner." The spark returned to his eyes. "And there it will be." Playing now the part of the unfurled banner, he spread his arms wide. "'Chiran, End the War!' The photographers will all snap her picture, the TV cameras will be turning. And there will be my mother, looking confused because she hasn't yet seen the banner behind her—looking foolish, for everyone to see."

"You don't see what's going to happen?" Lilani hadn't moved, had barely raised her voice, and we listened all the more carefully for it. "You don't see?" She barely nodded at Kumar. "If he comes running up like that they'll think he has a bomb. Susan's bodyguards will shoot him before he gets halfway there."

Bandula looked at her, seeming to ask why she would disdain the plan into which he had invested so much care, so much venom.

Still grasping for an insurmountable problem that would doom the plan, I cut in. "She's right. Look, Bandula, you say that this could make a difference, be the first step in bringing your family down. Well, that's exactly how dangerous it is. You may think it's a joke, but it's not."

Bandula looked at me, at Lilani, licked his lips, tried to continue, but the lightness in his tone was counterfeit now, the brightness in his eyes clouded with unease. He turned again toward Kumar, who alone betrayed no sign of fear.

"Everyone will think it's part of the program until we get the banner unrolled," Bandula said, "so there's no need to rush." He told Kumar, "Walk. Don't run." He smiled at Lilani and me. "It will be a non-violent act. I wish to be like Gandhi."

Lilani laughed mirthlessly. "Just because you want things to happen this way doesn't mean they—"

"No!" The word came like a pin bursting a balloon.

"No!" Kumar repeated. "Fareed will talk. It must be someone else." He lifted his chin, his eyes on Bandula. "No. It will be you."

Bandula took an awkward step back and tried to smile, tried to persuade Kumar he was joking. "It can't be me," he said, embarrassed that he would have to state what he thought obvious. "I can't march up there in front of everyone pretending I'm an orphan. No. You know I can't," he said softly. "You know I won't be there."

It took me like a slap to the face. "You won't be there?"

Bandula shrugged, trying not to appear apologetic. "I never come to this kind of thing. If I'm there, she'll know something's up."

Lilani laughed. "You want to use your family's connections to make this happen, but you also want to remain anonymous. Bandula, you can't have it both ways. You can think of getting away with this only because you're a Jayatilaka. If your name was Gunawardena or Abeynaike you couldn't dream of doing this."

Bandula smiled weakly. "If my name was Gunawardena I wouldn't need to."

I brought the conversation back, trying now to sound lighthearted to hide my desperation. "But, think of it, Mr. Gunawardena, your mother will recognize Kumar. She'll know something's wrong."

"No. People like Kumar don't exist for her. She won't recognize him because she has never really seen him. Besides, before she notices him, he'll have the banner in place."

We all looked at Kumar, as if to consider the hypothesis that he didn't exist. He stood, immovable, undeniable, in the middle of the room, his eyes smoldering with some deep and unfathomable emotion, and looked at each of us in turn before saying, with a quiet finality, "Then it will be you."

Lilani looked up at Kumar with a gaze as steady as his own, a look saying that whatever sleight of hand he had been using to deceive the others, she had known all along that it would come down to this.

Kumar glared at me, then at Bandula, daring either of us to contradict him. But I looked only at Lilani, who hardly bothered to nod her head in acquiescence. Then she stood and ran from the room.

38

Paul Catton, Assistant Secretary of State for South Asia, came in on the two-thirty flight from Delhi. A tall, vinegary man in his sixties, with a fringe of white hair, he sat at the microphones in the airport VIP lounge and, in a flat tone read most of the arrival statement I'd drafted for him. He responded to a few of the journalists' questions, saying the right things, but clearly resenting the need to answer to a bunch of locals. The journalists responded by refusing to ask more questions—an odd, but somehow effective kind of protest.

Sensing the tension, Ambassador Donovan made some remarks to end the event, his affability lifting the mood a little.

Afterwards, a small circle of reporters gathered around me to ask about Catton's schedule and the following day's signing ceremony. As I made a few brief responses and started to leave, I stopped and stared at a figure at the back of the crowd. Nick Potts.

While the others drifted away, Potts came up to me, trying to hide the pleasure he took from my surprise. "I have to be in Bangkok for the IMF meetings Thursday," he said with a shrug. "Thought I'd come through here on the way, just to see if the Sri Lankan government would let me back in. Apparently, all is forgiven. Or they just forgot who I was." He glanced at his copy of the embassy press release. "Big doings tomorrow, right?"

"Yeah, I guess so."

"Should I show up for it?"

For most of the day I had managed to concentrate on Catton's arrival and the press conference, driving the next day's ceremony from my thoughts. Potts' reminder came like a glimpse of the hangman waiting.

"Something wrong?" Potts asked.

"No." I forced a smile. "Everything's fine. Glad you're here for this. I'll see you tomorrow." My words sounded right, but in my mind, I still stood in Bandula's study in the Jayatilaka's mansion the week before, and Lilani had just run from of the room with tears in her eyes.

※

I had been unwilling, that day, to follow Lilani out the door of Bandula's study or, more truthfully, been unwilling to be seen following her out the door. But Kumar and Bandula had lapsed into an argument in a mix of Tamil and Sinhala that I couldn't begin to follow, and I slipped unnoticed out of the room and down the long hallway outside the study that led to a large dining room. I crossed the room and pushed through the double doors at its far end.

Empty of guests and with daylight streaming through the windows, the great salon hardly looked like the room in which the welcoming reception for Ambassador Donovan had been held on that hot and humid night only five months earlier. It seemed like as many years.

In my imagination, I dimmed the morning sun, and the room became as it had been that night, dark and close, the heavy shadows softened by flickering oil lamps, the women in their gowns, the men speaking in confident undertones the language of money and power, couples walking out into the moonlight, where I too, had wandered in those last moments before I met Bandula and Kumar and had first seen Lilani sitting in the shadows, before I started down that path that had somehow led to this moment. Or had this moment always existed, like that door at the end of the long hall, waiting for me to walk through it?

Caught by this disorienting eddy in time, I missed the sound of footsteps on the wooden floor until they stopped behind me. I felt my heart lift. I turned and opened my arms.

And my mouth dropped open as I found before me a short, swarthy maid of perhaps fifty years, dressed in an ill-fitting white uniform. Shrieking oaths, the woman leaped back in horror from my embrace.

"I ..." Flushing with embarrassment, I gestured awkwardly at the empty room. "I was looking for ..."

The woman pointed toward the veranda and said something in Sinhala, either throwing me out or telling me where to find the person she somehow knew I was seeking.

※

"Oh, it's *you*." Catton said with a sour smile as I came into the Ambassador's office. He seemed to think his remark was funny.

Nancy Kawabata and Robert McWhirter, sitting on the other side of the large coffee table, manila folders open to Catton's schedule, each managed a sickly smile.

A few minutes earlier Catton had spoken to the full country team, telling us how important our work was and how highly we were regarded by all the right people back in Washington, the effect of the little speech undercut by its flat, preoccupied delivery.

I made a smile that I hoped appeared as insincere as Catton's. "The reporter from *Business Monthly* is here. We can use my office downstairs for the interview."

Catton snorted. "Why don't we just do it right here?" He indicated the ambassador's office with a negligent wave. "No, don't go looking at him," Catton said to me while cocking his head at Richard Donovan, "I'm sure my authority is sufficient. Isn't that right, Ambassador Donovan?"

"Fine," I said, "I asked him to submit his questions ahead of time. You'll find them and your talking points in your—"

"You figured I wouldn't know what to say?" Laughing harshly, he looked to Donovan to share his hilarity. Donovan didn't smile.

Caught between embarrassment and anger, I glanced at Robert and Nancy, who were giving me a "better you than me" look, and started to open my mouth, not much caring what came out.

"Just kidding, just kidding," Catton said with a dismissive laugh. "Bring your reporter up."

To my surprise the interview went well. Catton read the traps behind the reporter's questions and turned them into opportunities. Robert and Nancy watched it like a tennis match. It hurt to admit to myself that this guy had chops. Afterwards, the others accompanied Catton downstairs where a car waited to take him back to his hotel for some down time before a reception that evening.

The office seemed unnaturally quiet after they left. I

suppose I should have gone down with them, or headed back to my office, or checked with Steadman about which journalists had confirmed for the reception. Instead, I was seized by an irresolution veering toward panic as I thought of the ceremony, and felt my gut twist with the creeping fear that our plan—Bandula's plan, I insisted to myself—would slip out of control at the moment of its execution. And I remained haunted by that day at the Jayatilaka's when we had made our plans final, and the memory of Lilani running from the room with tears in her eyes.

※

I walked through the French doors of the Jayatilaka's mansion, crossed the lawn, and headed toward a rutted dirt road the maid had indicated. I soon came to a small cement-block house set among the trees. I entered without knocking. I knew Lilani wouldn't have let me in.

She lay in a back room, curled up on her bed, facing the wall. I pulled a straight-backed chair to the side of the bed and sat down. Gently, I set my hand on her hip. To my relief, she didn't knock it aside. For a long time I watched the rise and fall of her quiet breathing, each breath like a suture in the rift between us.

Her bedroom had all the anonymity of a waiting room—a minimum of furniture, no flowers, no books, not even a radio. Maybe she did this deliberately, to remind herself that none of this was hers, and that her presence depended wholly on the sufferance of a woman who hated her. Only in the solitude of the mountain cottage did she know a place she could call home.

After a long time, she rolled over and looked at me.

"I died." She whispered, as if pain had stolen her voice. "I died when you left me at Haputale. It was easier to die than to hope." She searched my face. "Why have you come back here, to this house?"

It took me a moment to find any words. "You know why."

"Tissa Sandanayake is dead. This won't bring him back."

I whispered in her ear. "I know."

"No, you don't know," she insisted, her voice more urgent than any shout. "Do you really think Chiran will be so embarrassed by this prank that she'll just crawl away? Is that what you think will happen?"

"I don't know. But, maybe it will make a difference, even a small one. I'm willing to risk my career for it."

"Your career. Do you think anyone but you cares about your damned career?" She half rose from the bed, her face inches from mine. "You think everyone is like you. Like Bandula. Like Chiran. Living for politics. Everyone in this country has gone mad with politics. All politics means to me is that I have no father. Politics means I have no home." She shuddered as if politics were a fever she couldn't throw off. "Do you know why Kumar wants me on the platform with him? Why do you think he picked me?"

I hesitated. "Because he wants someone he can ..." My answer died on my lips.

Her laugh sounded like death. "Because he hates me even more than he hates you. And neither you nor Bandula step in to tell him no. Bandula's right. Chiran will look right through Kumar. He doesn't exist for her. But I do. When she sees me, Bandula won't be able to protect me. You won't be able to protect me. And when it's over, she'll do what she's always wanted to do. She'll send me back to that tea village, the one where you put your hand over your nose to keep from smelling the filth. Where you were afraid to sit on the chair because you thought you'd catch some disease. That's where I will spend the rest of my life."

"Then why are you doing this?"

"Tell me what choice I have! I have no one to protect me but a foolish boy who insists we play this game." She turned away and her sigh sounded like her soul fleeing from her body. When she looked at me again her eyes had gone dull. "I will lose everything. I knew I had already lost you when I brought you to Haputale, because I knew he would come and that would be the end of us."

I remembered the sadness I had seen in her eyes that day, lying on the bed in her cottage near Haputale, and finally understood it.

"No," I said. "I'm still here." I slid from the chair onto the edge of her bed and leaned over her until my mouth nearly touched her ear. I felt her warmth on my lips and breathed the familiar scents of her body. I had come home. "Marry me," I whispered. "Marry me and I'll take you with me when I leave, put you where they can't touch you anymore." She didn't move. "Marry me, Lilani." She didn't reply, but I knew we didn't need any words between us now. I wanted to tell her that, whatever deceptions I had practiced in the past, the bad faith I had shown toward others and, more truly, toward myself, those days were over, that I had found something true.

Later, I would wish that I had told her all this, told her what was in my heart, just to be sure she understood. Told her before it was too late.

She looked at me and shook her head slowly, not in refusal, but fearing to believe. And I felt her eyes searching my face for her future.

39

The day started long before dawn with the ringing of the telephone.

"I didn't wake you up, did I?" The void of ten thousand miles hissed in the receiver like the sound of the ocean in a seashell.

I looked at the clock. Three-thirty. "It's okay, Mom."

"I can never remember whether to add the hours or subtract them."

We talked for a moment of the weather and family, but I could feel the emotion from something else spilling over into her words. I let the conversation pause and she leaped into the gap. "Your father said he wanted to talk to you. He's so much better." She sounded like a proud parent announcing that her baby could walk. "Here he is. Just a few words. It tires him out so, but he wanted to talk to you."

I heard the receiver changing hands, then after a long pause. "Hey, pal, whatcha doin' out there?" He tried to put on the amiable gruffness I had known forever, the relaxed, manly tone that had once assured me the world in which I lived held to a stern but humane order. Yet, after that afternoon when I had sat in the car in front of the Pitchford's, it was also the tone that carried to me the poison of mendacity, even while I still wanted to love it. Now illness and the immeasurable distances of space and time had made his voice slack, like something recalled, not created. I had, that last evening in Stockton, forgiven all that without even thinking about the fact that I had forgiven him. The world had fallen into disorder, and I feared it was too late to recover, not because of what he had done. No, I feared that the world I had once known would soon lie forever beyond my reach because of what I was about to do.

"Whatcha doing out there, huh?"

※

Within a few hours I could have honestly answered, "Not much."

Inside the dusty grounds of the still-unfinished power station, the ministry had roped off an area for the print journalists and put up short risers for the television crews. Left to wait in the sun, the journalists read the press release I'd handed out and the texts of the anodyne speeches. TV reporters busied themselves underlining the good bits so they could cue their cameramen when to roll. In the tedium of waiting for something to happen, they talked among themselves, occasionally laughing at some joke.

Neither the journalists nor any of the other bureaucrats on hand approached J. R. Thilakaratne, the melancholy official censor, who sat by himself, surrounded by a ring of empty seats. Did he know about Bandula's prank? I felt sure he did. What was he doing here? That was easy. He was doing whatever it might take to retain his position. In spite of all the faith Bandula put in him, I felt sure he was in business for no one but himself and intended to outlast all his benefactors.

Columns of official cars kicked up dust as they dropped off scores of middle-ranking officials and businessmen, who took their seats within the expanse of folding chairs set in the sun. After them, two busloads of low-ranking government employees came from town to swell the crowd.

The signing would take place at a table in the middle of a large raised platform. A set of metal steps led up to the platform from the left. To the right, well back from its edge, stood a couple of rows of chairs for the various dignitaries who would form an impressive human backdrop for the ceremony.

A techie placed a microphone on the table in the middle of the platform and wired next to it two electric buttons to a sort of wooden pedestal, only a few inches tall. Catton and President Guneratne would together push the buttons to activate the power station.

With the site separated from the outside world by an eight-foot high cyclone fence, the presidential security guards, looking like overstuffed chairs in their bulging coats, looked almost relaxed. Only a large bullet-headed man in a dark suit, who appeared to be in charge of security, took things seriously, scowling and pacing around, barking at the soldiers near the gate as well as at two other plainclothesmen who, when he turned his back, would smile and roll their eyes.

The lightness of their mood lifted my own. I began to think that this might, after all, pass off as the big joke Bandula had always described. The fact that the complacent-seeming security detail was about to let in the one thing that everyone thought had been squeezed out of the event—a moment of spontaneity—brightened my mood further.

I heard them before I could see them, the fifteen or so kids from the orphanage, singing as they marched up to the gate after the long walk along the dirt road. The younger ones were dressed in T-shirts and blue shorts, the older ones, the teenagers, in slacks or skirts, all of them wearing the clothes Bandula had brought to the orphanage that day, now covered in dust. The soldiers at the gate smiled as the children entered. No one seemed to remark that Kumar and Lilani, coming up in the last rank, looked a little older than the teens in the group.

Standing on the TV risers, I feared that I would somehow give things away if I looked at them too closely. So I barely glanced at the kids as they entered, catching only a glimpse of Lilani. Next to her, Kumar held to his chest a rolled-up cloth bundle. They had decided that carrying the banner in the open posed less risk than trying to hide it. After all, why shouldn't they have a banner?

A plump woman with a large smile met the orphans as they came through the gate and began to lead them toward a large tent in back of the platform where they would wait for the program to begin.

They had not got halfway there, though, before the bullet-headed chief of security came jogging up from the direction of the portable toilets, waving his arms and shouting for the group to halt, gesturing for the soldiers at the gate to hustle over. No one was getting in until he had asserted his authority over them.

The children stopped, the youngest ones blinking at the large man who blocked their way, the older ones looking around with a mixture of resignation and resentment. I hoped that no one but me saw that Kumar and Lilani had turned rigid as statues.

With the security man prodding them, the two soldiers half-heartedly poked at the children and asked a couple of them to turn their pockets out, making clear that their diligence had more to do with the big man's ego than with any real suspicion of the dancers. Exasperated with their sloppy work, the security chief waded into the children, grabbing several of them by an arm or a shoulder, making a show of glaring at each of them in turn, sizing them up, judging them harmless and releasing his grip, working his way ever nearer the back row, where Kumar and Lilani stood.

Like a small fish swimming in the wake of a whale, the plump woman followed the security man, waving her hands in protest.

Wiping a film of sweat from my hands, I jumped off the risers and began to edge my way toward the clamor.

By now the security chief had reached the back row. He looked Lilani up and down in a way that made me want to bust his chops. He asked her a question. She said something in reply. His next words made her eyes go hard. She stared straight ahead and said nothing. The man made a face and shrugged. He glanced at Kumar without interest and started to make his way out of the throng of orphans.

I let out a breath I didn't know I'd taken.

But the big man had no sooner turned away than he turned back again, eyeing Kumar once more, poking at the banner the young Tamil held tightly against his chest. Kumar coiled within himself, like a spring wound to the edge of its limits.

An instant before he snapped, Lilani insinuated herself between Kumar and the security agent, smiling up at the big man. What I saw next made me catch my breath. Lilani had taken the nearest edge of the banner and was beginning to roll it out for the security man to read. I asked myself why I hadn't seen it coming, hadn't understood that Lilani would find the first opportunity to betray not so much the plot, about which she was probably indifferent, but Kumar.

Assuming a nonchalance I didn't feel, I sauntered up to the group as Lilani struggled to unfurl the banner, most of it still caught in Kumar's arms. "What seems to be the problem here?" I asked, trying to hit just the right tone, relaxed but firm—a diplomat who wanted no problems on such an important day.

The plump woman who had been protesting the security man's treatment of the children smiled distractedly. "I'm just trying to get these children over to the tent." She made a vague gesture toward the area in back of the platform.

"I'm with the American Embassy," I said to the security chief. Almost casually, I put my hand on Lilani's to keep her from rolling the banner out further. But she pulled away from me and continued to tug on the canvas. Kumar appeared unwilling to hold the banner tight enough to stop her. If I hadn't already been sweating, I would have started.

"These dancers," I continued, "are here at the embassy's invitation."

The bullet-headed man glared at me.

Lilani gave me a ferocious smile that couldn't mask the desperation in her eyes and said to the security man. "Sir, just let me show you—" She tugged loose more of the banner.

"Lilani," I said between clenched teeth.

She didn't look at me, but held out a portion of the banner as if offering a fine fabric for inspection. "You see, sir? It's just a friendly message." In fact, the portion of the banner she held out read, "Welcome, Presi—"

I nearly laughed with relief.

Though vibrating with tension, Kumar did nothing, had done nothing, as no doubt he had promised if they were challenged. Lilani smiled at the security man to cover the care with which she was rolling up the banner, being sure not to show its other side where, I realized now, the real message had been written.

How could I not love a woman who could stay cool through a moment like this?

With a huff of impatience, the big man waved them on before shouting at the soldiers to get back to their positions.

While the two soldiers strolled back toward their posts, Ambassador Donovan's dark blue Lincoln came through the gate and rolled up to a low cinderblock building which served as the reception point for the dignitaries who would sit on the dais. Tony Spezza got out of the front seat of the car and gave a quick look around to make sure everything looked secure, then opened the door for the Ambassador.

I was grateful Tony hadn't witnessed the little scene with the incoming dancers and wondered why I had put myself in the middle of it.

The Ambassador's car took its assigned spot in the makeshift parking lot. Only Chiran had not yet arrived.

※

Eleven o'clock, the hour for the ceremony, came and went. The journalists and the members of the audience, still sitting in their folding chairs under the sun, began to wilt, fanning themselves with copies of the event's program or holding them over their heads for their meager shade. The security officer looked increasingly hot and impatient. The soldiers guarding the perimeter twitched nervously. I looked toward the gate and the empty road beyond.

"She coming?"

I somehow managed not to jump out of my skin.

"Tony. I thought you'd gone into the… " I nodded toward the cinderblock office.

"No, I decided to— You all right?"

"Yeah, fine. The sun." I made a vague gesture, hoping to explain away my anxiousness as the effect of the heat. "She's been in London, but I think she's back."

"Mrs. Jayatilaka?"

"Yeah."

Tony made a face. "I hope she is—or that they decide to go ahead without her pretty soon. It's four degrees hotter than hell."

I feigned a relaxed smile. "Everything under control?"

"Yeah. Presidential security seems to have it all sewn up." He clapped me on the shoulder. "I'm just a tourist this time. Talk to you later."

Nick Potts had barely nodded at me when he arrived on the bus with the other journalists, but now walked over, grouchy from the heat and the delay. "That's your security man, right? He know when this thing's going to start?"

"We're waiting for Chiran Jayatilaka."

"Beats the hell out of me why I came out for this story. Could have written it from the bar in the Hilton. How much longer we going to—"

"Say, Philip …"

Tony had come back, smiling quizzically. "I was just wondering. How did you know she was in London?"

A wave of cold heat rolled up my back. "What?"

"Chiran Jayatilaka. How did you know she was in London?" Tony glanced at Potts as if hoping he would go away.

"Don't know." I tried to sound casual. "Must have read it in the papers or something."

Tony cocked his head. "Funny. I thought I would have caught that."

"Maybe that's her now," Potts said, cocking his chin toward the gate.

Grateful for his interruption, I noticed a couple members of the security detail—the bullet-headed man and another in an open collared shirt—trotting beside a long black Mercedes as it made its way through the gate and up to the offices where the VIPs had gathered.

Like a machine set into motion, the site began to stir. The two guards who had trotted alongside the President's car took their positions on the platform. Bullet-head planted himself at one end of the platform, a few feet from the steps where the dignitaries would walk up. The other stood at the platform's far end.

A man in a suit ran out of the office building and shouted to a small military band that had been resting in the shade of a banana tree. The musicians got to their feet and lumbered toward the platform.

Onstage, the techie stepped up to the microphone to make one more sound check and take a last look at the wiring of the electric buttons on the small pedestal. As he did, the security chief walked over to observe the technician's work. Frowning, he reached down and picked up a strand of wiring that came out from under the table, following it with his eyes to where it snaked down through a hole in the floor of the platform. The techie gestured at him to put it down, indicating that the wiring simply led to a generator at the side of the platform. The security man stared at the wiring a moment longer and wagged his head unhappily, but returned to his place at the front of the platform.

Tony shrugged. "Well, I guess I'd better get back to the boss."

The members of the audience sat up a bit straighter, fanning themselves more discreetly.

After a short pause, the plump woman who had taken charge of the children began leading them out of the tent, up the steps on the left and onto the platform in a long, uneven line. The woman glanced nervously at the security officer as she passed behind him, but his eyes never left the crowd.

The journalists pressed up to the rope that kept them a few feet back from the platform. Standing behind the television cameras, I felt my heart pounding as the dancers came onstage.

Most of the younger children marched with precocious gravity, faces solemn, eyes front. A few stared out at the audience open-mouthed, like kids back home in a Christmas pageant. I tried not to look at Kumar or Lilani coming up at the rear of the column.

I was looking toward the cinder block building to see if Catton and the Ambassador were on their way when a vague commotion caused me to glance again at the center of the stage. And my mind refused to take in what I saw.

It seemed hardly believable that Bandula's plan could have unravelled the moment the kids walked onstage. Yet, up on the platform, the line of dancers and singers had stopped moving forward and were curling into a couple of overlapping coils.

I nearly laughed at the absurdity of it. Why hadn't it occurred to any of us during Bandula's easy-as-pie walk-through that there would be a large table in the middle of the platform for the signing ceremony? And why hadn't we seen until now that it would ruin everything?

If the dancers lined up in the narrow space behind the table, it would mask their dance—and the banner. No one would be able to see them. But if they lined up in front of the table, Chiran would have to walk behind them to get to her seat. Kumar and Lilani would end up holding the banner in front of her, screening her rather than posing her against it, and the gesture would be lost.

With a giddy flash of shame, I realized that, rather than disappointment, I felt an enormous wave of relief.

Onstage, Lilani and Kumar hesitated, Kumar still hugging the banner to his chest like a life-ring. Hoping, I suppose, that they could still somehow hold it up behind Chiran as she crossed in front of them, they tried to lead the children toward the back of the stage, but some of the youngest ones had already lined up in front of it. Others, confused about where they should stand, bumped into each other like windup toys let loose in a box. With a sheepish laugh, a couple of the older boys made as if to jump up and dance on the table, but the plump lady waved them away while trying to corral the little ones.

Drawn by the sounds of disorder behind him, the big security man, who had taken his place in front of the steps, turned and waved his arms at the dancers behind him, shooing the confused orphans from their place at the center of the stage toward its far end, beyond the table and the chairs set out for the dignitaries. Here, they would find enough room to perform, but would be so far toward the end of the platform that Chiran would not walk in front of them at all.

Reluctantly, most of the dancers drifted down the platform. Kumar, though, stood his ground in the middle of the platform, looking around uncertainly, as if hoping that Chiran might cooperate by dashing up onto the platform right then. Quicker to admit defeat—and no doubt happier—Lilani took Kumar by the arm. Kumar refused to move, unable to accept how quickly the plot had fallen apart.

He might have stood there forever, but the security chief came over and shoved him in the chest, sending him stumbling backwards. Kumar puffed up like a cobra and looked ready to square off with the man. But Lilani plucked at his sleeve, coaxing him back. Slowly, he retreated with the other children, his eyes burning with animosity.

Directing a thin-lipped smile of triumph at Kumar, the security man strolled back to his position in front of the steps.

The audience took all this in with an air of idle amusement, like fans watching the undercard of a title bout.

I wondered if Kumar still intended to go through with the gesture of unfurling the banner. I hoped not. With the banner at one end of the platform and Chiran walking up the steps at the other, the act would carry no impact. The television cameras, the key to Bandula's dreams of broadcasting Chiran's humiliation to the world, would manage to keep the banner out of the frame. I felt sure that Lilani, at this point, would refuse to help Kumar carry out an empty gesture.

I found myself smiling. It wouldn't work now. The plotting and dreaming, the drives of hate and love and sex and politics and loathing, all the varied impulses from which the plan took its life, were overthrown by the presence of a wooden table. I recalled Rohan Jayawardene telling me at his office in Kandy of Sri Lanka's ancient name, Serendip, the land of serendipity. Could serendipity have a negative sense, describing something that by chance did not occur? On this unhappy island could it have any other meaning?

I saw my future clear before me. And Lilani's, too. I could keep her safe now from Chiran's cruelties, Bandula's fecklessness, Kumar's hatred.

"What's so funny?"

Potts was looking at me, puzzled.

"Nothing, just the ..." I nodded toward the platform, catching the eye of the security chief standing only a few feet in front of us. The big man glowered at me. I smiled back.

The kids from the orphanage had finally sorted themselves out and begun, on their distant corner of the stage, to perform a folk dance, with the youngest ones playing cymbals and bells they had brought with them. The older ones danced and sang a strange, dreamy melody—all but Kumar, who stood close-mouthed, his eyes stony with rage.

The line of dignitaries, mostly men in suits with a couple of women among them, began to make its way down from the cinder block offices toward the platform, where they would sit between the table and the area occupied by the dancers. The sight of the orphans dancing in their honor brought smiles to their faces as they mounted the steps.

The photographers split into two groups to cover the scene, a couple of them snapping pictures of the kids while others stood at the other end of the platform taking photos of the high-ranking arrivals. Even bringing the country's highest dignitaries together on the same platform with the young Tamils could not force them to live in the same world.

As conspirators, Bandula, Lilani, Kumar and I were worse than incompetent. Why had we ever thought we could, with a paint-smeared banner, bridge the gap between the orphans and the elites, between war-makers and war victims? The only ones humiliated, I thought, would be us. At least our humiliations would be private. No one else would know of our failure. Security seemed redundant when the dice were so heavily loaded.

As Bandula had predicted, Chiran waited for everyone to find a seat before she made her entrance. She would walk on as a diva, not a spear carrier. Behind her, Richard Donovan and Catton, the latter wearing his sour smile, waited their turn.

"Look out, here comes the Dragon Lady," Potts muttered. "She really knows how to—Christ!"

Something in Potts' voice, not so much of urgency but of astonishment, made me look at him then follow his gaze toward the far end of the platform. He was looking at Kumar.

As little as we had imagined that a table would wreck our plans, none us anticipated that someone in the audience would recognize the young Tamil.

I struggled to put on my calmest manner. "What?"

Potts pointed. "The kid from Kandy. The Tamil."

I could hardly speak for the lump of panic that had formed in my chest. "Oh, yeah. I guess I didn't mention it, but he's Bandula Jayatilaka's friend. I saw you and Bandula at the Hilton one evening, and I figured that was how you got connected to the Tamil kid."

"Him? Jayatilaka's friend?" Potts said, shaking his head. "No way in the world. Does security know he's there?"

"Security? What are you talking about?"

"That night in Kandy wasn't the first time I'd talked to him." Potts spoke rapidly, not taking his eyes off Kumar. "I'd already met him here in Colombo. He's the one who was going to lead me up north. A couple of other Tamils introduced me to him. He's got some big connection to the Tigers. Some sort of deep cover thing."

I looked at Kumar as if seeing him for the first time.

And in that moment, Kumar saw Potts. Whatever the young Tamil's English skills, he had the outsider's ability to read faces and knew that Potts and I could be talking about only one thing—the thing he, Kumar, had hidden from all of us, even from Bandula.

For a delusional moment I tried to laugh at the absurdity of it. "A Tiger? No, he can't—" Then it all became clear. "My god."

A young protocol functionary standing at the foot of the steps nodded at Chiran, who began to mount the platform. She had taken no more than a few steps when she stopped, staring at something in front of her. As Bandula had predicted, she appeared to have missed Kumar entirely. But, with the banner not yet raised, she had seen Lilani.

Alone in the middle of the stage, Chiran Jayatilaka cocked her head quizzically, then turned back toward the young protocol assistant, looking for an explanation. The troubled expressions of the audience, reflecting Chiran's puzzlement, probably gave the big security agent his first hint of something gone wrong. He turned away from the crowd toward Chiran, who stood frozen behind him. Then he looked down the platform and saw Lilani, stunned, step out from the group of dancers, like a boat drifting from its moorings.

Lilani looked in horror at Chiran—the horror of the trap into which she and Chiran had both fallen—just as Kumar began to run toward the center of the stage.

At the sight of the Tamil running toward Chiran, the security man deftly stepped in front of her and with a flick of his wrist pulled back his coat to draw his pistol.

"No," I muttered, then shouted, "No!" as vainly as a man trying to shout a rock slide back into place, doomed even as the first pebbles began to fall. I leaped from the risers as Kumar broke through the line of dancers at the far end of the platform.

It all happened in slow motion: Kumar letting the banner fall onto the platform, no longer caring who saw the bulge under his sweater. The security chief stepping into the middle of the platform to shield Chiran, pistol aimed at Kumar. The crowd groaning in dread and awe. The guard at the far end of the platform drawing his gun too, not on Kumar, whom he hadn't yet seen moving behind him, but on the American—me—who had jumped off the press risers and was running toward the edge of the platform.

With a few long strides, I crossed the distance between the risers and the only point near the platform I could reach in time. The crack of the pistol made me turn my head toward the stage. I saw Kumar stop as if he had run into a wall, saw his head thrown back, would remember forever the smile on his face as he began to fall.

Catton gaped in astonishment as I reached the steps and caught him full in the chest with my shoulder. At the same instant I clothes-lined Ambassador Donovan with an open arm, knocking them both off the steps.

As we fell, I heard Lilani's voice pleading, "Mother?" as the blast tore the air to shreds.

40

The monsoon arrived a few days later, bringing to the parched land the balm of plentiful rains, the promise of life. In the city, children ran into the streets, their faces upturned, catching the downpour in their mouths, dancing with happiness at the smiles they saw on the faces of their parents after a long season of anxiety.

The joy did not touch everyone. Sleepless, dumb with exhaustion, I wandered the nighttime streets of Colombo, soaked to the skin by the life-giving downpour that mocked the death I held inside me.

Like a thief, I shunned the light of the streetlamps and the sight of anyone I might chance upon, as if they, not me, were the ghosts haunting the night.

Once, crossing from one side of the street to the other to avoid even a fleeting encounter with a passerby, I stumbled into the path of an oncoming car. The scream of brakes and the screeching of tires on the rain-slick pavement jarred me awake, while an unbidden impulse toward self-preservation drove me back to the curb. The startled driver shouted something unintelligible at me, though the words surely meant, "You trying to get yourself killed?" If I could have answered, would I have said, "Yes?"

※

Tony Spezza waited nearly a week to come by my office, until everyone's most visible bruises had healed. Among the Americans, only Catton had suffered anything like a real injury—a couple of cracked ribs where I had caught him with my shoulder—though he had popped up like a jack-in-the-box when he landed, asking me what in the hell I thought I was doing, even as the dead and dying lay scattered on the stage.

"You probably saved his life, and the Ambassador's," Tony told me.

I shrugged, sick of asking how it was that only the privileged were saved, with me the means of their salvation.

Outside, the monsoon flooded the streets. The faint sounds of cars horns honking their joy at the return of the rains penetrated the Mylar-covered windows of my office.

Catton had flown out of Colombo that same night after stopping by the military hospital for a quick check-up, even as surgeons a floor above struggled to save Chiran Jayatilaka's life.

I wondered whether I could have chosen duty over my own life, as the big security agent had done. The modest size of the bomb, the open nature of the stage, the distance of most of the audience from the explosion had limited the deadliness of the attack. A number of people had been injured, some of them badly, but only a few, those closest to the bomber had died—Kumar, the security chief, a military officer in the front row of the audience, a nine year-old dancer. Lilani.

※

The Department's regional psych came down from Delhi. He told me that my depression was "not an atypical response to this category of trauma." I mentioned that I had known a young woman killed that day, but told him no more than that. The psych nodded and held out his hands in a palms-up "there-you-have-it" gesture

I never told the doctor, nor anyone else, that I had promised the young woman I would take care of her, would put her "where they can't touch you anymore." I had been as good as my word.

"You feeling better?" Tony asked.

"Sure."

"You knew this guy—the bomber."

"Yeah."

"The Jayatilaka kid's friend."

"Yeah."

"But Jayatilaka wasn't there."

"No."

"Why?"

"You'll have to ask him."

Tony let his head drop. "You know I'll never be allowed near him." A beat. "You had no idea about ..."

"None."

I could see how the task ate at Tony, his difficulty compounded by our friendship and his sense of culpability for not seeing something coming that in fact he could not have seen.

I wanted to care, but couldn't.

Tony nodded to himself. "Funny. This kid had a banner of some kind. 'End the War.' Something like that. Sri Lankan police think maybe he'd planned to open it out—who knows how—then blow himself up. Or maybe he was supposed to open it with someone. Maybe the girl who was killed."

Tony waited for me to add something, to help him out. After a while he looked at some notes in his hand. "I can't get any fix on her. When I ask who she was, the police tell me they have no idea—and that I'd better stop asking."

I said nothing.

Tony started over. "Nick Potts said he knew the bomber. Named Kiran or something."

"Kumar."

"Kumar. Potts said he'd been introduced to him as a Tiger. Funny thing, if he was Jayatilaka's friend."

"Bandula never knew he was with the Tigers."

"You're sure."

"I'm sure," I said, but asked myself how I could really know that, any more than I knew at the time that Kumar had attacked me in the cottage that night because I had asked Bandula why he had helped Potts. Kumar had known that Bandula would make clear that he hadn't helped him, and then his role as a Tiger agent would have come clear. So he jumped me rather than let us ccontinue.

Tony shrugged to change the subject. " Another odd thing. You jumped off that riser and made for the Ambassador before this Kumar guy even moved."

"No. I didn't."

"A couple journalists swear to it. Even this Potts guy—"

"I didn't." The rain beat against the window. The telephone buzzed on my desk. I didn't answer. "Or maybe Potts said something that made me realize …" I left the thought unfinished.

"Yeah, I guess he told me something about that." He snapped his notebook closed. "Philip, this wouldn't look so bad if you hadn't been the one insisting that the group be invited to perform. And if the bomber hadn't been a guy both you and the Jayatilaka kid knew." He blew out a breath. "This is the damnedest investigation I've ever seen. The police tell me that no one at the orphanage knows how these two—this Kumar guy and the girl—got in with their kids." He blew out a disbelieving breath. "They don't know?" Tony put his pencil in his pocket. "And that's the end of it. The orphanage has been closed down—by who? why?—and no one can find the administrators."

"I didn't know anything about it."

"Philip, I'm not saying you …" Tony sighed, clasped his hands together. "Okay. Maybe you knew about the banner."

I tried to smile. "Y'know, I had a friend here who was always telling me I never understood anything about what was going on in this place. She was right."

We both knew my story would hold up, that anyone else who knew anything about it was dead—except one, and he had been placed off limits by his family.

On his way out, Tony stopped in the doorway. "That letter. The one from Sandanayake. It was you who delivered it, right?"

Even while the question hung in the air, we both knew Tony wouldn't be able to explain to anyone why he had suspected me of delivering the letter but said nothing. Like me, he was a prisoner of what he had not done, of the secrets he had kept.

I tried to smile but feared I would start weeping. "We started with one bomb, you and me. That first day I was in country. So we had to end with another. Maybe we should have seen it coming."

Tony stood in the doorway for a moment, waiting for more, for an answer to his question, but I had nothing more to say. I let my head settle against the back of my chair and closed my eyes.

41

The story of the bombing disappeared from the newspapers as quickly as the public's curiosity allowed. News accounts never mentioned the attackers' names. Both were simply described as Tiger terrorists. In a press release from their office in London, the Tigers denied any connection with the attack. Even in death, Kumar and Lilani were orphans.

Chiran Jayatilaka lived. She had been badly cut up and lost a great deal of blood, but she survived. Susan Guneratne, who had still been in the cinderblock office talking on the telephone at the moment of the explosion, saw election gold in the attack. She whipped up nationalist fervor by promising a new military offensive to "wipe the nation's enemies off the face of the earth."

※

Chamalie took the call and passed the message to me, something about meeting a Mr. Gunawardena at the Hindu temple near the port.

"I don't have *any* such meeting on your calendar, Mr. Reid, and have never known any Gunawardena who was a Hindu."

"Gunawardena?" It took a moment for me to put it together. Up at the mountain cottage, Lilani had told Bandula he couldn't have even dreamed of carrying out his ridiculous plot if his name were Gunawardena.

"Yes," I said. "I've been waiting for his call. I'll be back in a couple of hours."

※

Vents in the low ceiling of the stone temple allowed just enough fresh air to keep worshipers from choking on the clouds of incense. The glow of scattered candles and the thin shafts of light from the vents barely penetrated the thick blanket of smoke and darkness, making the worshipers appear no more than fleeting shadows, chanting their prayers of supplication in the temple's many small recesses—sanctuaries devoted to eerie demi-pythons, serene elephant gods and many-armed goddesses.

I trod barefoot through the dim and smoky passages, repressing a vague dread of the unseen presences—exalted and damned, veiled and transparent, creative and destructive—that inhabited the temple's dark precincts.

I found Bandula sitting in the shadows of an isolated sanctuary. I had half-expected to find him in some sort of disguise, but he was once more dressed in a polo shirt and slacks, as if the fallen prince had failed to understand how much everything had changed, how he himself had been transformed.

He gave no sign of greeting as I sat down beside him.

Eventually, he had to say something. Looking at the floor as he spoke, he told me, "I wanted to say goodbye. To express my … regrets."

I didn't want to hear what his regrets were, for fear of finding out what they were not.

"Who would have imagined that we ...?" I started, but couldn't finish.

"Of course we imagined it," Bandula said. "We willed this. At least I did, even if I never admitted it to myself. Kumar knew what I meant, what I wanted, even if I didn't. Yet she lived."

He made no mention of Lilani, and I hated him for it.

"Can't you explain to your—"

"Explain? What? To whom?" Bandula shot back. He lowered his voice and continued. "Do you think I need to protect myself? Defend myself?" He blew out a bitter breath. "No. I'm still not allowed to be responsible for what I do. I do nothing, right or wrong. I make no mark. I pay no price. The family closes around me like wolves protecting one of the pack. You were right that day, at the university. That's what we are. Wolves."

"They know?"

"Of course, they know. They know everything. And they do nothing to me. I'm not even worth killing." He shook his head, a thin, bewildered smile on his face. "That's the part I can't forgive. That's why I must leave."

"Leave. Where will you go?"

"Somewhere I can't be found. Where they can't help me when I fail. Where I can be free of them. Somewhere I can rise on my own merit." His smile flashed like a dead man's grin. "I tried to free the country of the Jayatilakas, and ended up only freeing myself of them."

We spoke in the dark corner of the temple for a little longer, though it felt increasingly like one of those forced conversations at a funeral, the funeral Kumar and Lilani had been denied. Finally, inevitably, J. R. Thilakaratne, looking serenely out of place in a suit and tie, appeared out of the gloom, standing at the edge of our corner sanctuary, hands clasped in front of him. He nodded to me, his sad smile more than ever like that of a modestly successful funeral director. No explanation was necessary. The Official Censor had come to bundle Bandula into the back of a car and, without the knowledge of the family—or perhaps with it—whisk him to the airport and into exile, like Charon ferrying a soul to hell.

The similarity in the names of the two specters of death reverberated in my mind.

※

In the end, Bandula's little joke was on him. His plot only intensified the war. And his failure drove him forever out of the favored circle from which he had hoped to transform his country. The spring elections went off as scheduled. Stirring up nationalist sentiment and boosted by the karma gained by the return of the monsoon, the NRP swept the leaderless opposition.

Once back in Washington and over his anger, Catton reflected on the value of his own survival and put me up for the Department's award for heroism. I was thankful when I didn't get it. But everyone in the Department knew I was the one who had saved an ambassador's life. It cast a glow over every word in my evaluations, turned my corridor reputation to gold. Promotion came quickly.

42

On the street outside Frank Schaeffer's apartment the rain has stopped and the wind picked up. I draw a deep breath, and try to clear my head, dissipate the shock of seeing Bandula again, of recollecting a past I had tried to forget. "History is a nightmare from which I cannot awake." Rohan Jayawardene's words, spoken in the office of the *Kandy Herald* the morning after the temple bombing, bite me to the quick.

I glance back toward the fifth story windows. The last light goes out, and I start the long walk home.

The kids playing soccer near the Champs du Mars have all gone home and the brightly lighted fields lie empty. I look into the tops of the trees, swirling in the gusting wind. The rain has washed the sky clean and, like living things, the stars wink at the earth through the darkness.

Once, as a boy—I couldn't have been more than twelve—I rode with my dad in the chill of a short autumn afternoon to a large farm near the slopes of the Coast Range. After a long day of driving, we'd come to pick up the last of the season's tomatoes. The sun had already set by the time we got there, and the guys on the loading dock worked quickly to get the pallets onto Dad's truck so they could all go home.

While the crew stacked the tomatoes on the flatbed trailers, I silently followed after my dad as he walked across the dusty field to where a line of plane trees screened the intruding lights of the loading area. As we stood in the shadow of the trees, our eyes adjusting to the darkness, I followed Dad's gaze, looking up into the sky. At first I saw nothing but the infinite blackness of the heavens. Then I watched the Milky Way emerge like secret writing from the night sky.

We said nothing to each other—what could words have added to the ineffable sight of eternity?—but my father, his hands shoved into his back pockets, looked up at the infinite sky and sighed with wonder and satisfaction.

As I watched him, back in those days when Dad still strode the earth like a giant, I felt I had learned something about him, caught a glimpse of a larger spirit than I would have imagined in my old man. In the memory of that sublime moment, as my father looked up at the stars and sighed, I found more than enough to forgive him. Maybe I could still find in it enough to forgive myself.

Cancer, not a stroke, finally took him, seven years later. I flew home from my post in Nairobi to sit by his bed in the nursing home those last few days. One evening, an attendant, tired and bored, had thrown back the covers to turn Dad over, negligently twisting the hospital gown nearly up to his chest, revealing the flesh-covered skeleton—the withered buttocks, the gray and flaccid genitals—all that remained of him. I'll never forgive her for that last glimpse. My father appeared to take no notice of the indignity and smiled weakly as he asked her to give him a sip of water from a glass with a plastic straw.

A little later my father asked, "So, you ever going to explain to me what you do for a living?"

"I'm not sure I have it figured out myself."

Dad nodded, working up the energy to say, "I tell people you're a spy. Hell of a lot easier to explain." He wheezed out a laugh that held no hint of the old full-belly guffaw that used to put the world in order.

I started, "So—"

Before I could say more, he cut me off.

"So, it's like this. The first half of your life, you go ever' which way at once, stirrin' things up, just to show you got the balls to do it. The second half of your life, you try to put it all back together again, make some kind of sense out of it. Figure out what your life's been about. That's the hard work. That's the part a lot of fellas can't do." He made a humming noise in the back of his throat, as if searching there for the right words. "For me, it was always about you and your mom. Always."

As he panted with the exertion of his little speech, he looked at me with an intensity that I didn't know he could still muster. Maybe it came from a long-held remnant of that evening when he looked up at the stars. And in his eyes I saw that he knew, had always known, how angry I had been at him and why. And he had accepted my judgment, lived with it all those years without trying to beguile me out of it, without pleading for my forgiveness which, I suppose he knew, would only have made things worse.

In that instant, I loved him more than I could say.

I worked around the stone in my throat and managed a smile. "That's all there is to it?"

My dad smiled back at me. "Pretty much."

Soon after, he slipped the short distance back into sleep. I stayed for a long time, until well after dark, before returning to my mother's house.

※

The wind blows at my back as I walk back to my apartment along the rue de Varenne, past the darkened government buildings and shuttered shop windows. Wasn't this the corner where the wind had blown Jean's umbrella inside out while we tried to wave down a taxi one day? No. That was somewhere else.

Pages from a newspaper swirl in the eddies along the deserted sidewalk, coming to rest directly in my path. With reflexive foreboding, I look at the headlines, wondering if they hold some story I'll have to deal with in the morning. It's only the sports page. Maybe it will be a quiet day at work tomorrow. That's as far as my ambition goes anymore, quiet days in which no one bothers me.

Lights from a late-night bar throw their warm glow across the pavement as its door swings open and a young couple walks out laughing, arm in arm, a snatch of music spilling out with them. Before the door can swing shut, I slip inside, the bar's warm, heavy, almost tropical air pleasant after the cold outside. Not wanting to be bothered by anyone from the embassy calling me, I'd left my phone at home for the evening, so I ask the man behind the bar if the place might still have an old pay phone. With a Gallic shrug, he reaches into his pocket and hands me his own phone and I walk a few feet away into a quiet corner.

"Hello?" Frank Schaeffer's sleepy voice wobbles between irritation and anxiety.

"Frank? Phil. I was wondering if you had the number of that man who served at your dinner tonight."

"Jesus, Reid. What time—? Can't it wait until tomorrow?"

"Wanted to do it while I was still thinking about it."

In the silence we each wait for the other to give in.

"All right," Frank mutters irritably, "but I got to tell you I didn't like the son of a bitch—putting on airs like he thought he was some kind of king."

"He was," I say quietly. But Frank has already put the phone down to look for Bandula's number.

I imagine the scene, the one after I had left. With the last guest finally departed, Frank stuffs a couple of bills in Bandula's coat pocket, like a man giving bread to a beggar, then claps him on the shoulder with unearned familiarity and pushes him toward the door. Bandula bridles but says nothing and walks with stiff-necked dignity out of the cold apartment near the Eiffel Tower, making his way back home. Frank comes back on the line. I take down the number.

I return the phone to the man behind the bar and go back out into the night and the wind.

※

When I get home, I stand for a while in the living room of my empty apartment, looking out at the Pantheon, big as a cathedral beyond my living room windows. How many of France's immortals are interred there, their tombs a monument to their mostly forgotten achievements? I once read the number but have forgotten it now.

I throw my raincoat on the couch, go over to the alcove in the hallway and pick up the receiver of the old land line that came with the place and fumble for the scrap of paper with Bandula's number on it. As I do, I picture him walking into his own empty apartment, cold and dark, in this most beautiful of cities, the City of Lights.

I look at my watch. Past midnight. What time is it back in Washington? My wife will be home from work, our daughter home from school. In Stockton, Jean will still be at the office. I'm sure I have the number somewhere.

A lot of calls to make, but there's plenty of time. I have all night. Time enough to begin the long task of repairing the past, exorcising its ghosts, finally banishing the secrets slowly killing me, so that I can once again, after many years, live in the present.

For a long time, I listen to the hum of the dial tone and hear, beyond its void, the faint hiss of immense possibilities calling to me.

※

Acknowledgements

First of all, I would like to thank my dear friends Richard and Jane Ross for relating to me a story that set this work in motion. No book is written alone. Even writing is a team effort. My thanks to the short story master Mark Jacobs for his helpful comments on an earlier draft. My gratitude to Tissa Jayatilaka for his help on a number of points regarding Sri Lankan culture. I can only hope I got it right. As always, my love and thanks to my wife, Felicia, for the many corrections she made to the several drafts of this story. Also, thanks to my agent, Kimberley Cameron for her hard work and kind advice. And a big shout-out to Kristy Makansi of Blank Slate Press and Lisa Miller of Amphorae Publishing for their support—and their patience.

About the Author

With his critically acclaimed novels, *Tangier* and *Madagascar*, author Stephen Holgate's work has been compared to that of masters such as Graham Greene, John le Carré, and Alan Furst. *Tangier* gained the Independent Booksellers Silver Medal in fiction. *Madagascar* has gained similar acclaim, receiving a coveted starred review from *Publisher's Weekly* and being named as a finalist for the *Forward Reviews* Book of the Year in general fiction. Bookreader.com listed both novels among its top ten mystery/suspense books of the year. Characterized by intrigue, romance and danger, his books have quickly gained an appreciative audience among readers and critics alike. *Sri Lanka* is his third novel.